Pasha
and the
Lost Mountain

T.C.C
Gary Webster

Fullproof Publishing Inc.
Arizona USA

Pasha and the Lost Mountain All Rights Reserved. Copyright © 2009 T.C.C V2.2

Cover Image owned by Fullproof Publishing Inc

Fullproof Publishing Inc PO Box 1213, Sahuarita, AZ 85629

http://www.Fullproofpublishing.com
http://www.pashabooks.com

ISBN: HB 978-0-9822326-0-6
ISBN: PB 978-0-9822326-1-3

Library of Congress Control Number: 2008943220

Fullproof Publishing Inc and the "PB" logo are trademarks belonging to Fullproof Publishing Inc.

PRINTED IN THE UNITED STATES OF AMERICA

Acknowledgments

I would like to thank Justin Duncan and the amazing Kaela Manger (Alias KK) for all of their hard work and imaginary input.

I am also most grateful to my wife for her unconditional support and patience throughout the five years it has taken to get this first installment of the Pasha series to print.

Last but certainly not least my beautiful Pasha, who never ceases to amaze!

Prologue

The Keeper's Succession

The Great Hall of the castle was supercharged with an energy only present when the four Master Wizards gathered in the same place at the same time. They and their attendants had traveled from the four corners of the Earth, each from his or her domain, to witness the end of an era. Tonight, they would bear witness to the passing of the great charter from the old Keeper to the new.

There was restlessness in the air. The very walls of the white marbled room could not settle. The gleaming walls and columns suddenly looked like the sun-washed grasslands of the South, and then changed to the lush woodlands from the East. Finally, the walls appeared as the blue endless oceans of the West.

The Master Wizards each sat at the head of a table, boasting of their successful adventures and the greatness of their realms. One table remained empty, awaiting the arrival of The Wizard of the North and his party. An almost empty, grand mahogany chair stood at the head of the masses. A large book bound in black dragon scales lay closed on the seat, patiently waiting for its master.

After much anticipation, a boisterous voice from the far end of the hall halted the festivities.

"There had better be food, and a lot of it. I'm so hungry I could eat a dragon," remarked the Wizard of the North, who was also known as the Jolly Wizard. He was a large man, jolly and loud. The Wizard and his servants made their way from the hall's towering entrance to the remaining table. The hall responded by transforming into images of snow-capped mountains and whistled with the sound of icy wind.

"And not one of those pansy forest dragons," he continued. "A mere morsel they are. I mean one of the great ones, an ice dragon, fearsome and oh so juicy." The Jolly Wizard's accompanying chuckles literally shook the hall, rattling plates and utensils, even making one poor attendant fall off his stool with a crash. The Jolly Wizard's wishes were immediately answered as the four tables filled with delicious food. The Wizard of the North took his seat, plopping down so hard the same attendant once again fell off his stool, landing on the mosaic floor with a thud.

"I will miss this Keeper," blurted the Jolly Wizard. "He has style, no show-off with his magic and he knows what I like." He tore the leg from what once had been a freakishly large bird and tucked into the meal with lips smacking.

"Another grand entrance," remarked the Wizard of the South. "Has it only been a thousand years, Jolly?" The ebony skin of her face never cracked with emotion as she stared at her fellow wizard.

"It has," interjected the Eastern Wizard. "That is, far too long indeed. We were discussing the new Keeper. I hope that this one is no mere human; I want something a little more... mystical. What say you, Jolly One?"

"Not a good time for conversation with so much food in that great mouth," excused the Wizard of the West. She sampled the roast pork in front of her, eyes closed at the flavor in the jerk spices. The Northern Wizard nodded in agreement and drank deep from a large iron tankard of mead, then cleared his mouth with a belch.

The Keeper shuffled into the hall, his once tall frame hunched over from centuries of faithful service. His once jet black hair was now heavily peppered with grey but his piercing blue eyes were still as sharp as ever. The diamond-encrusted slippers on his feet never seemed to touch the floor, while his long, white embroidered robe swayed about his ankles. The black book in the chair sprang from its place and hovered clear of the Keeper's approach.

A mysterious cloaked figure followed into the hall behind the Keeper. A large hood hid the figure's head and identity from the inquisitive stares of the hordes. The ground to the right of the grand chair bulged upwards, shaping into a smaller but identical piece of furniture. The marble patterns faded to an aged brown, looking more like wood. The hall was silent; even the Jolly Wizard put down the leg bone in reverence of the Keeper's Presence.

The Keeper reached his chair and the hall ceased its shifting. Once again, gleaming white marble decorated the beautiful open space. The Keeper sat majestically, while the cloaked figure silently glided to its place on the smaller chair. The dragon-scale clad book opened and tilted to allow the Keeper access in which to read.

"Be it known that all mankind makes a choice between good and evil. In both life and death, we journey on our chosen paths. Though the virtuous road has seen many travelers, a few always trudge the path of wickedness. With my reign as the Keeper nearing its end, I am duly bound to deliver this record of my reign to both you and my successor. I hope that all of you will have found my reign to have been an honorable one and that evil found no great success on my watch. Open your minds, my friends, and receive the sum total of my life.

This was what all the wizards had been waiting so eagerly to see. Every being in the hall relaxed, forgetting all worry, hunger, and all doubts, as the will of the Keeper reached out to bind with them. A tiny pinpoint of light shone before their eyes. It grew in size until finally blotting out all visions of the hall. Beneath the black cowl of the Keeper's mysterious guest, two bright suns bloomed where eyes would be. Every creature in the hall began to see a forest, thick with a fresh snowfall. The view was flying through the pine trees, over running wild animals, and into a clearing where there stood a tiny cottage.

Chapter One

The light faded through the thick Bavarian forest, casting shadows like witches' spells over the mossy uneven ground. Towering trees commanded a darkness to embrace the crisp winter evening, their finger-like branches outstretched, waiting to welcome any that dared disturb such an ominous peace. Stillness suffocated the bitter air as a deep mist rose gently from the frosted ground below.

The eerie silence was violated by the shrill cry of an old woman's voice from a modest cottage in the midst of the trees:

"Hans! Hans! Come quickly; it's time!"

Almost instantly, the sound of breaking branches drew rapidly nearer the source of the cries. The stocky man moved quickly in spite of his large frame, his heavy snow boots splintering the forest carpet of brittle twigs and pine needles.

Hans, though a giant in size, was a peaceful man who lived just outside the Bavarian village of Freiheit—a German word meaning "freedom." As with all the residents, he and his beloved wife Greta had lived there for as long as they could remember.

Hans rushed into the clearing where his brightly lit cottage stood. Smoke rose lazily from the tarnished stone chimney. Opening the creaky wooden door, Hans gazed down to see Greta, a petite woman with long thinning silver hair. Silently, he watched his wife kneel beside their German shepherd Sasha, like a mother hovering over a sick child. Sasha lay, softly whimpering, her pristine black coat glistening in the firelight.

Hans had found her over twenty years ago, wandering through the forest with her mate Spot. Spot and Sasha would have been impossible to tell apart if not for the thick white ring around his left eye. After all these years, the two of them remained inseparable.

Spot stood beside his mate, keeping a vigil over the impending birth. Sasha released another series of whimpers, which Spot immediately echoed sympathetically.

"Shhhh, my lady," Greta whispered, as she lovingly stroked Sasha's head. "It will not be much longer now."

"How is she doing?" asked a concerned Hans, as he shut out the bitter cold with the closing of the door. He dropped his load of wood, save for the couple of pieces that went straight into the fireplace.

"This old girl is really something," Greta declared. "A dog of her age really should not be giving birth."

As far as Greta and Hans knew, these puppies were Sasha's first litter. Hans had gathered long ago that Sasha was special, but he could never quite put his finger on exactly what made her so different. They both were amazingly intelligent dogs, at times with an almost human understanding of their masters.

He remembered the countless times Sasha and Spot had saved him from injury and even death. To caution him, they would bark or pull him away with their teeth. Sometimes, Hans got the feeling Sasha was actually trying to talk to him.

Regardless of what his imagination might do at times, one real oddity was the way he had found them, though, to be truthful, he wasn't entirely sure who had found whom. Either way, it was as though the two humans and both dogs were destined to be together.

Hans had first seen them over the mountain, not far from old Freiheit Castle. It had been presumed empty and nearly a ruin for as long as he could remember. Hidden in the forest, it had a strange presence about it. The local villagers thought it an evil place, but Hans had yet to experience anything that suggested it was more than an eroding pile of stones. He always tried to avoid it for Greta's sake, since she became frightened at the mere mention of it.

That fateful day, Hans had been looking for a rare purple flower that only grew around the castle. Though Greta feared the place, she loved the sweet smell of the fragrant blossoms. As Hans knelt down to pick the flowers, he thought he caught a glimpse of something in the bushes; looking around, all he saw was the natural beauty of the tall trees, branches majestically displaying their deep green leaves.

Yet, something was missing. Usually, the forest bustled with the cheerful chirping of birds going about their daily business. That day, only silence filled the air.

After Hans had picked an adequate bouquet, he noticed the setting sun and falling darkness. On the way back to the cottage, though, he could not see or hear anything; a feeling of uneasiness gripped him.

He sensed that something was following him, and although never one to frighten easily, Hans quickened his pace and moved skillfully through the forest. It was not long before he entered the clearing lit by an old oil lamp hanging next to the cottage door. With only the door separating him from the certain safety of the cottage, his eye caught a flash of movement. He turned instinctively, and the silhouettes of two animals became apparent. Wolves were his first thought, a notion he quickly dismissed as two German Shepherds emerged from the brush and calmly approached him.

Hans could not help but be stunned by the blackness of their coats. Curiously, the two large dogs had each carried a small golden ball in its mouth. At least, that is what Hans remembered. Once he had got them both inside the warm cottage, the orbs had vanished. That was only the start of the unexplainable things that always seemed to occur around these dogs.

Sasha interrupted Hans's memories with a loud whimper as the first puppy entered the world.

"Well, this one takes after Spot! A boy," Hans informed, while inspecting the pup. It had a jet-black coat, except for its completely white left ear. Sasha's maternal instincts kicked into gear, and she quickly turned to groom her newborn. Her long moist tongue wrapped completely around the pup, lovingly cleansing it until it was immaculate.

Once Sasha had cleaned the pup, she picked it up by the back of its neck and placed it next to her belly. Even with eyes still tightly closed, the little mite honed in on one of Sasha's nipples, immediately beginning to suckle. Spot approvingly barked loudly. Was Spot trying to form a smile?

Sasha let out a loud cry, alerting Greta. "Here we go... There are two coming out!" Within a few seconds, two more pups had indeed entered the world. "Good girl, Sasha. You are doing so well." Greta beamed her beautiful smile to Hans.

Sasha repeated what she had done with the first, and nestled them against her warm belly. As the two new pups began to suckle, Greta noticed they were also boys with white markings much like the first, though in different places: one had a white ring around its left eye, much like its father, and the other, a beautiful, pure white tail.

"They look so cute with their white markings!" exclaimed Greta.

"At least we'll be able to tell them apart," Hans replied, chuckling.

Though time had seemed to pass quickly, it had been over two hours since the first pup was born. Sasha's pain had not ceased, signaling another eventual birth. Hans realized it was going to be a long night. He placed another log on the fire. "Why don't you go to bed?" he suggested to his wife.

She shook her head to wake herself up. "Sasha is like a daughter to me, and I will be here for her, however long it takes."

Hans smiled and dropped the notion. "Well, I suppose you could say we are at last grandparents!" They had tried for years to have children, but it was not to be. It was true, though, that Sasha and Spot had made excellent replacements. Spot barked loudly. Something else was happening.

Sasha lifted her head and let out a strange noise—a cross between a howl and a cry as another puppy entered the world. This one was pure black, with no white markings at all.

"I bet that one's a girl," remarked Hans. Before Greta could check, Sasha jumped up on all fours, then onto her hind legs. Now standing over five feet tall, she let out an enormous howl that was so loud, it shook the cottage windows. Almost simultaneously, two large flashes of lightning and an enormous clap of thunder rattled the cottage through to its foundations. The humans were dumb-struck. They had long grown accustomed to the strange phenomenon that occurred around their pets, but this was something new.

Greta stood and moved toward Hans, who, in turn, put his arms around her. Sasha swayed uneasily on her feet, lovingly supported by Spot. A golden glow began to brighten the room. Hans and Greta gripped each other tighter as a bright golden orb appeared above each of the adult dogs. As Greta shielded her eyes from the luminance, Hans just stared in recognition.

The orbs floated down toward the four puppies and stopped. They hovered just above the newborns for an instant, before slowly coming together and fusing as one. The single orb immediately began to shake, emitting pulsing rays of light. Greta took another step backward, pulling Hans with her. The orb flashed so bright that neither human could see for several seconds. When everything came back into focus, Sasha was once again lying down, cleaning the last puppy. Spot sat vigilantly behind her. Above the heads of all six canines hovered a separate golden orb. The dogs seemed to pay them no attention. Hans could not resist stepping forward and squinting to get a better look.

"What's happening? Stay back!" Greta pleaded with him.

"It's okay. I think I have seen these before, many years ago."

Hans peered into the orb above Spot's head. He could clearly make out the image of a dog deep inside the golden sphere, a tiny model encased in a crystal ball.

"It's all right, Greta. Come closer. Look at this," he assured, as he turned and beckoned her forward.

Hesitantly joining her husband, she looked over each of the golden balls in turn. There was a tiny effigy of a dog in each. They were so beautiful to behold, Greta could not resist attempting to touch one. The instant before her finger made contact, the orbs were gone, leaving the flickering firelight as the only illumination. Hans and Greta looked to their pets as if expecting an explanation. Both Sasha and Spot were just staring blankly back at them with expressions of calm.

"Oh my, you never cease to amaze me," Greta rejoiced, kneeling again and caressing Sasha. "Four beautiful children. You should be proud, Sasha. Hans, these puppies are miracles."

Hans had silently retreated to their ratty old couch, trying to make sense of what he had just witnessed. All of the dogs' quirks and amazing abilities marked them as special. They were, in fact, seemingly so much more than that. There was also a sadder possibility upon this discovery.

"Greta, my love," he began. "I don't think we will be able to keep them."

She turned to her husband, a solitary tear running from her eye, and reluctantly nodded in agreement. They had already discussed their lack of space and money to keep so many dogs. Adoption had been the best recourse, and whatever powers these dogs possessed could not change that.

Sasha and Spot released long, softly lilting howls into the last hours of the morning.

Chapter Two

Eight weeks later and six thousand miles away, in what could just as well have been a completely different world, the blazing Arizona sun powered through the windows of a trendy house in suburban Tucson. Fay Baer swept her long blonde hair behind her ears as she stretched to reach her ringing cell phone. She perked up with excitement when she realized it was her husband calling.

Much like his wife, Steve Baer was also tall and thin, but his British heritage set him apart. He had met Fay while on a holiday in the States, and their marriage of fifteen years was nothing less than a marriage of two countries. Although their family home was in Arizona, Steve would always be English in his heart. He owned a successful business in London, and they traveled there often.

"Hello, Darling! How was the flight to London?" asked Fay, smiling as she listened to her husband's usual complaints. "How's Tiff? Did she say anything to you about...?"

"Tiff is fine, Fay. She kept to herself on the flight, but... "

"I can hear you, Dad," interrupted Tiffany, then louder, "I'm fine, Mom."

Steve sighed, positioning himself against the wall, while keeping an eye on his daughter as he spoke. She moved off to the baggage claim, eyeing the moving belts filled with a mess of luggage. Because of her family's bi-continental existence, she was quite familiar with the routine and, therefore, paid little attention to the throngs of Heathrow travelers or her father's absence from her side. Tiffany, nearly eleven years old, had been extremely withdrawn since losing her best friend Jasmine in a tragic car accident about a month back. Her parents had been patiently waiting on her to come to them with her feelings.

"So tomorrow," Fay continued, "you pick up the, you-know-what?"

"Oh yes. Off to Germany to take care of a little business."

"I know about the dog, Dad." Tiffany walked up, pulling her pink Prada suitcase, putting it beside Steve's ratty old bags. "You guys are terrible at secrets. Why else would you take me on a business trip instead of leaving me with boring Peter?"

"At least she is speaking," said Fay. "Tell her I love her." A little louder: "I love you, honey."

"I love you too, Mom."

"No love for me, Princess?" Steve asked, grinning.

Tiffany answered his grin with a slight turn at the corner of her mouth. It was a start.

"I love you, Dad, but please don't call me Princess."

"OK, Steve. I am glad you made it safely," interrupted Fay. "You tell Tiffany to be nice to Henry's son."

"I am not a miracle worker, Darling. We have to run. I love you, and Tiffany loves you too. We will talk to you soon. Bye, Love." Steve hung up the phone. "How long have you known about the dog?"

"About a week," Tiffany answered. "You guys talk loudly at night... when you think I am sleeping. It's all right, Dad. I am feeling better. It is just... I miss my friend."

Steve gave his daughter a warm hug.

"Of course, princes," he caught his slip. "Tiff."

"I still want the dog, okay?"

"Well, that, as they say, is a done deal."

Almost an hour later, their taxi pulled into a very foggy northwest London suburb. They soon stopped in front of a large old house, partially hidden by massive trees and foliage shrouding the entire yard with shadows. The pebbled driveway wound around toward the front of the stone house, covered largely with unruly fingers of thick ivy. The curtains were drawn and the shutters tatty. In the slowly setting sun, the house seemed almost sinister.

"Don't they ever fix this place up?" Tiffany asked. "It looks like a house from a horror film."

"Don't be disrespectful. This house has been in Henry's family for generations. This is fine English craftsmanship."

"Whatever."

Henry was the manager of Steve's business and had been his friend for over twenty years. He was a typical English gentleman, from his tweed suits to the moustache he waxed to two points every morning.

"It's just; I don't mind Henry as much as Peter. He's weird, Dad, and he smells like the house," Tiffany grumbled.

"That will be £8.75 please, Governor," the taxi driver demanded in a strong, cockney accent.

"Now I know I'm home," Steve chuckled, grinning as he paid the driver.

The pebbles on the drive crinkled under their feet as they approached the medieval looking arch. Inside it were two large wooden doors, each with a tarnished brass knob so big, only a giant would be able to grip them. Steve used the more modern doorbell to announce their arrival.

"What do you think the house smells like?" asked Steve.

"It's bad. Kind of like an old sock stuffed with used kitty litter." Steve shook his head and stifled a laugh. "Don't be so silly," he scolded.

A short, tubby boy opened the door, and before anyone could say hello, Tiffany went straight for the jugular.

"Peter, you have put on so much weight!" she pronounced, walking, uninvited, past him and into the house. Steve handed out some swift justice with a quick tap on the back of her head and a look sharp enough to kill anyone at twenty paces. Tiffany knew she had stepped over the line and quickly tried to make amends. "But it looks so good on you, and I do believe you get more handsome every time I see you." She looked back to her dad for approval.

The boy's face flushed a bright shade of crimson; at age twelve, Peter Teague was still very shy. Steve had known the boy his entire life, long enough to know Peter had a crush on his daughter. He tried to diffuse the boy's hurt.

13

"You're looking great, Peter. How is everything?"

Looking back at Tiffany, who was now poking and prodding things in the house foyer, Peter sighed. "They were okay, until now."

Steve gripped his shoulder gently. "She'll behave. I promise."

Henry entered from the family room and announced in a loud, refined voice, "Steve, it's good to see you, old chap! And Tiffany, you certainly have grown into a beautiful young lady!"

"I always liked you, Uncle Henry!" Henry was not really Tiffany's uncle, but he was her godfather, so she always called him Uncle—or Unks for short.

"Welcome, my friends. Peter, please help Steve with the luggage. Your rooms are just as you left them." Henry turned to Steve. "Everything all set for your German trip," he said, adding a ridiculously not-so-stealthy wink.

Steve chuckled to himself.

"She already knows about the dog, but it was a valiant effort, Henry."

"What dog?" questioned Peter, while tugging at a large black suitcase.

"Well then, you must be absolutely famished!" Henry exclaimed, putting his arm around Steve's shoulders.

"Who's getting a dog?" Peter persisted, plopping down the suitcase.

"I am! I am getting a dog. I am also very hungry, Unks. What have you got?"

"Peter, will you assist Tiffany in the kitchen? I need to speak with her father for a moment." The children disappeared into the kitchen, with Tiffany's smug banter still wafting in from time to time.

"Come into the family room, Steve. I have a few papers for you to sign." As they moved into the next room, Steve became aware of a musty odor. Henry pulled some folded papers out of his desk and spread them across for his friend to look over. The room was in a terrible state, shrouded with random stacks of paperwork, tea mugs, and general dust. It was a similar theme throughout the old house. Henry, though nearly 50, was looking closer to 60. His eyes looked strained, which substantially increased the wrinkling around them.

"The house is really looking shabby these days, Henry. No offense, my friend, but so are you. Jenny?"

Henry hung his head at the mention of his late wife. Her sudden death had been difficult on both him and Peter, an event made even grimmer by the knowledge that no doctor could explain exactly what had happened to her. In the eighteen months since, he had neglected his home for the comfort of busying himself with work. Steve gave his signature to a couple of papers and turned back to his friend.

"You need a new presence around here. I would like to take Peter with us to Bavaria. He should have a puppy as well."

"I don't know."

"A new presence around the house would be good for both of you. Think about it as a hobby. A hobby that eats, barks, and, well, you know."

Henry smiled weakly. "I have no argument really. I thought it would get easier... with time. I miss her Steve, and Peter... he could use a friend. He does not have any as far as I can tell.

"He is having a tough time of it, bullied endlessly at school; he then comes home and comfort-eats, which makes things even worse. I really am getting worried bout him. I do not know how to snap him out of it. I can't remember the last time I saw him really happy."

"Then it's settled. Peter is to come with us to Bavaria and get a puppy."

Tiffany and Peter appeared at the doorway to the family room. "What time is our flight in the morning, Dad?" Tiffany inquired as they entered.

"We take off at 9 a.m., which means we need to leave here by 6 a.m." Steve looked at his watch. "Wow, time is getting away from me. It is almost 8. You had better get off to bed now or you won't want to get up."

15

"I hope I can sleep. I get bad jet lag." She made sure to let Peter know this useless fact about her.

"Oh, and that goes for you as well, Peter," added Steve. "You're coming with us. Your dad has decided you may have a puppy."

Tiffany grumbled, "Oh, great," and rolled her eyes as she headed toward the stairs. "Well, I'm having first pick!"

The boy's eyes grew twice their normal size. "Really, Dad? I can have a dog?"

"Yes, Peter, you may, but you are going to have to take care of it…" Peter ran to his father and gave him a big hug. Henry's eyes lit up as he warmly embraced his son.

"Oh, please!" Tiffany turned dramatically away and headed for the stairs, pausing only to get her luggage before trudging up with a final "Night, everyone."

"The Queen has left the building," Steve announced with a chuckle.

"All right, my boy," said Henry. "Get upstairs and pack. Do it quickly and get some sleep." Without a word, Peter ran up the old winding staircase to his room, brushing past Tiffany near the top of the stairs. She screamed at him to watch it.

"Expect him to get nothing resembling sleep tonight," Henry muttered, as he sat down in his tatty old chair. "Thank you, Steven."

"We're family, Henry—well, sort of, and you are welcome."

The men sat quietly for a while, enjoying the first silence of the evening. The silence was short-lived as Peter bounded loudly back down the stairs, vaulting over the last four steps as if jumping a hurdle.

"I've found it!" he shouted with a big grin on his face.

"What have you found, son?" Henry asked, still somewhat bewildered with the boy's boisterous reappearance.

"My passport, Dad, my passport! I can really go now!" The two men burst out laughing, both extremely relieved they were seated for such an entertaining incident. Tiffany peered down from the top of the stairs.

"What's going on down there?" she demanded.

"Come on, off to bed with you." Henry pressed his son to retreat upstairs.

"That means you as well, young lady. I have a few more papers to sign, and then I'll be going to bed as well," Steve said, still chuckling to himself. Tiffany huffed her way back to her room as Peter ascended the stairs once more.

Steve finished signing the business papers for Henry and trudged up the stairs with heavy feet. "Am I in my usual room, Henry?" he asked.

"Yes, my good friend, it's all ready for you. Good night, old chap."

"Good night, Henry."

Chapter Three

Greta sat on the floor before a crackling fire, gently petting Sasha. Spot was on puppy patrol, barking loudly as he herded the four growing puppies back to their mother. Rarely did any of the young dogs sit still or fail to end up somewhere they did not belong.

"Come on, Spot, can't you get a handle on your children?" Hans asked, bringing Greta a hot cup of coffee from the kitchen. After handing her the cup, he flopped down on the couch with a grunt. "These little terrors never seem to know a moment's peace."

"Hush, you. They're only young." Greta smiled warmly at her exasperated husband. "I remember a handsome man who would cross streams, hills, and forests just to tell me goodnight. He never sat still either."

"Touché, my love," Hans replied with a wink.

Four black and white streaks of fur came from out of nowhere and pounced on Greta and their mother. Spot followed closely on their heels and barked again. As quickly as they came, the four puppies were off again, bumping into one another at every turn. The pure black pup knocked the little one with the white tail flat onto his back. Sasha had had enough; she climbed to her feet and let out one short yelp. The four puppies stopped in their tracks and slowly came trudging back to Mom. They all sat down at her feet obediently, barely contained coils of energy ready to spring again.

"It is almost 4," Hans observed. "They'll be here soon."

Sasha looked at Spot and released a faint cry of her own, in acknowledgement of what was about to happen. Hans caught a glimpse of glistening tears from edges of both dogs' eyes.

"Hans. Look."

"I see. They know the puppies are going," whispered Hans.

"In all my years, that is the saddest thing I have ever seen," Hans confessed, as he and Greta both wiped tears from their eyes. Greta stood and turned away from the scene, unable to bear the sight of her dogs' pain any longer. She joined her husband and buried her face in his shirtfront, her shoulders shaking slightly as she wept.

"That first night, those glowing balls," she asked, pulling back. "Did we imagine that?"

"It seems like a dream now," Hans replied, then shook his head. "No, we did not imagine it. There is something peculiar about these dogs. You look into their eyes, and you see them watch you as well. It is as if they are in full control and we, well, we are just here as their companions. One thing is for sure. They are smart, smarter than any dog I have ever seen."

"They are quite special," confirmed a smiling Greta. "Whatever happened that night, I know it was a good thing. I felt safe and relaxed. Should we tell the new owners? Would they believe us? Maybe they would not want to take them if they knew the strange things that happen around them."

Sensing the direction Greta was taking the conversation, Hans immediately put an end to her notion of maybe keeping the pups.

"I regret we cannot keep them together, but you and I, we are too old to have such a large family. The people I have found for them are a good family. In time, they may discover the secret of these dogs, but not today. I don't think we are supposed to do any more than we already have."

Hans heard the sound of a car struggling up the snowy path from the village. "Come now, my love, let's put on a fresh pot of coffee and meet the new masters."

*****

As Greta opened the door, she was surprised to see Frederick from the village standing on the porch, his clenched fist poised to knock. "Hello, Greta." Frederick gestured over Greta's shoulder to Hans, who held back an anxious Sasha and Spot. "How is everything?"

"We are fine, thank you, Frederick," she answered with half a smile as she moved aside to allow him, along with the snow-covered group of travelers, to enter.

Frederick introduced them as they stepped over the threshold into the cottage. "This is Steve Baer, his daughter Tiffany—"

"Hi," Tiffany interrupted, her eyes searching around the room for puppies.

"And her friend Peter," finished Frederick.

"It's nice to meet you, Steve." Hans moved forward and extended a hand, which Steve willingly accepted with a "Thank you; it is nice to meet you too." Both Sasha and Spot moved forward, sniffing the newcomers rigorously. Tiffany and Peter responded with enthusiastic petting. The four inquisitive puppies ran toward the visitors, tumbling, looking more like a furry wave. The puppy with the white tail ignored the children and went straight for the open door.

"Whoa," Steve yelled, catching the little thing before it made its escape. "I think this one has a bit of adventurer in it." He held the puppy up as if inspecting and then went to petting him. Tiffany did not hesitate.

"Let me see it, Dad," she demanded, as she tried to snatch the dog from her father's arms.

"Tiffany?" he said in a raised sharp tone, with a look to match.

"Please, please, let me hold it," she pleaded, almost painfully.

Peter fell to the floor, swarmed by the other three. Sasha also joined in, licking his face in approval. He laughed and beamed a smile that had not been possible since the loss of his mother.

"Any trouble finding the cottage?" Hans asked, directing everyone inside and shutting the door.

"Not at all. I asked for directions in Frederick's butcher shop, and as you can see, he was kind enough to give us a lift."

"Let's all sit." Greta gestured to the couch and chairs near the fireplace. "We have coffee and tea. Frederick, could you go outside and bring in a few more logs for the fire?" They talked for the next half-hour or so over warm drinks in front of the crackling fire. Tiffany and Peter jumped about the room, alternating puppies as if they were trying on shoes. Sasha and Spot at first joined in, testing the potential new companions for their children. For no apparent reason, Sasha suddenly began to whimper, which caused the entire room to fall silent and look at her, even the three puppies. Spot ran about the room at his love's urgency, sniffing and probing, before running to the front door, where he barked continuously.

"Oh my, what is this about?" asked Greta.

"Hey," Tiffany alerted. "There's a puppy missing, the one with the white tail."

"What?" Hans was up and surveying the room quickly. He glanced at Spot by the front door. The large dog turned to Hans and barked directly at him. "Frederick. When you went out, would—?"

"I saw nothing. I think I would have noticed a nearly all black pup in white snow."

Peter, tense, held one of the tiny puppies a little too tight as it squirmed to get out of his grasp. "We have to go find it."

"I will find him, young man," Hans assured as he grabbed for his coat. Frederick quickly joined him, suiting up in his woolen coat against the cold. Spot scratched at the door frantically. As Hans opened it, the dog was out in a flash. The snow had begun to come down, prematurely darkening the skies in the afternoon. "Hopefully, we will be back very soon." With that, they were gone.

Sasha sat down near the fire and yelped. The other three puppies came at her call, all nuzzling against her, with no thoughts of play, as the fate of their brother unfolded outside.

"Hans and Spot will find her," assured Greta. Her smile was strained but genuine. "I have put a stew on. Let us eat something warm while we wait."

*****

Spot was alone in the snowy forest. Above him, the ground sloped up into the mountains. He had lost any trace of a scent for his son, but he did have other options. He looked back in the direction of the cottage and confirmed no humans were in sight. A golden glow enveloped him. His golden orb appeared in front of his nose, pulsing. Spot willed the orb to find its companion, the orb of his son, somewhere ahead of them. The orb vibrated for a moment, as if planning its action, then disappeared from sight as it sped off into the distance. Spot could still feel it, now hundreds of feet further along the forest. In his mind, he could see a tiny puff of black fur. Spot barked loudly a few times before he too disappeared with a loud "pop" sound. The forest at that place was suddenly empty and only a set of dog tracks remained.

Somewhere behind Spot, Hans and Frederick hurried through the forest, following the dog's prints in the snow.

"How could such a small puppy get this far?" Frederick, though much younger, was already huffing and puffing with the effort of keeping up with Hans.

"Good question. Spot seems to be following something," Hans replied, stopping for a quick breath. "Peculiar dogs," he muttered to himself.

"What?"

"Nothing," replied Hans. There was a series of barks ahead. "That's Spot; maybe he has found the little one. Let's go."

*****

Spot stood above the forest top on a narrow path that wound its way along the mountain. The little puppy was just ahead on the path, struggling through the snow. It would occasionally jump up and fall back in a heap. Spot advanced slowly, barking continually to mark his direction for the following humans.

For one so small, the little one was moving quickly through the snow. It continued up the path, eventually making its way onto a narrow ledge. Spot followed slowly along behind. The path was treacherous and one false move could bring disaster.

*****

"Time is short for the little mite," stated Hans as he started to climb the steep ridge, leaving the shelter of the forest. Frederick was not too far behind, breathing hard and struggling. Their feet occasionally slipped on the snow-covered rocks. Another series of barks came from somewhere just ahead and above them.

"Tell me we are close, Hans. I do not think I can go much further."

"Close enough, my friend, almost there."

It took Frederick and Hans only a few minutes to get just below Spot, who was standing on a flat ledge about one hundred feet up. The light was fading fast in the late afternoon. Hans leaned against the rock and reached for his torch to help him choose his footings. Frederick did not have the luxury of a flash-light every step he took seemed more uneasy.

"Up there," Hans shouted, turning the torch to the ledge.

"How did he get up there?" asked Frederick, defeated.

"That is a good question, my friend."

The thick snow blotted out most of the torch beam. Spot's black coat was the only marker of his presence. The dog continued to bark as he watched the humans approach but did not want to teleport. It was his power, as all warriors of the orb had their special abilities. He also knew it could be dangerous for others to travel with him and his exhausted, freezing little pup was especially vulnerable. He alternated barking and picking up the puppy in his mouth to keep him warm. He had to make a choice. The night of the birth had exposed too much to the human couple, though they were kind and trustworthy. The other one, now that was a completely different story. Frederick may not react very well at all.

"I'll try and reach Spot. You should stay here and rest, my friend."

"I think that would be best," agreed a now exhausted Frederick.

A deep rumbling began from the ridges above them, cutting off the man's words. Hans knew it signaled an avalanche and constantly jerked his attention between his friend and Spot. "We have to get down from here now. Turn around, Frederick, run!"

Frederick wasted no time and spun on his heels. He almost fell off the path several times as he made his way quickly down the mountain to the relative safety of the ground. Spot also heard the rumbling and made his choice.

Hans looked once more to the ledge and saw nothing. Feeling a nudge on his leg, he looked down to see Spot standing right before him, holding the puppy in his mouth. The golden orb hovered just over the dog's back and then slowly faded away.

"Well, you are just full of surprises," Hans gasped. The rumbling grew in intensity from above. Instinctively, Hans reached for the cold little pup and placed him within the warm confines of his fur coat.

"Quick, Spot, let's get out of here." Hans turned down the path and the world went white.

*****

There was a nervous energy inside the cottage. The children sat beside Sasha and her other puppies while Greta and Steve attempted small talk. The snowstorm outside continued to build as dusk set in.

"It appears that you all may need to stay the night with us," informed Greta as she picked up some of the empty mugs and took them into the kitchen, anything to stay busy. "No offense to the young man, but I wouldn't trust Frederick's car going back to the village in these conditions."

"Greta," asked Peter. "Is everything going to be all right?"

"Hans and Spot have walked these mountains for many, many years, so yes. I am sure, they will be okay."

"What about the puppy?" Tiffany questioned.

"All we can do is hope," the woman answered, then turned toward the sink while shedding a tear.

"I think staying here is a good idea," agreed Steve. "But all of our stuff is down in the village."

"Not a problem, Mr. Baer." Greta dabbed her eyes.

"Steve; please call me Steve."

"We have all you will need here for just the one night."

"Thank you, Greta. I want to pay you something for your hospitality."

"No pay. You just give these puppies a good home."

Sasha jumped to her feet and started whimpering. She frantically moved to the front door scratching at it with the same intensity as Spot had earlier. The remaining puppies also began to whine, burying themselves in fear around the two children. Greta hurried to the door.

"What has happened, Sasha?" she asked. For one instant, Steve swore the dog opened its mouth to answer her but all that came forth was another series of barks and scratching. Greta did not hesitate and obliged the dog's wishes by opening the door. Sasha quickly disappeared into the coming night.

*****

Hans first poked a hand out of the thick mound of snow above him, following slowly with the rest of his body. Spot was gone, as was the mountain path. Hans looked up and noted the jutting section of rock that had, undoubtedly, saved his life. It had created enough of a shelter to take away some of the force of the crushing snow. Sadly, Spot had not been under it.

He began to dig more and more frantically along where he thought the path extended. If he stepped too far, he could tumble off the side. He dreaded the thought that Spot may have been swept down the mountain. Whatever luck or magic that dog possessed would be the only thing that could have saved him.

There was a series of barks approaching from the distance. They soon came from just above. Hans looked skyward and nearly fell down. Sasha was flying out of the storm, barking for her mate. A glowing orb trailed behind her. She hit the snow and began alternately sniffing and barking. Hans just watched her, dumbstruck. Had he just seen Sasha flying? The little puppy inside of his jacket began to squirm. It let loose a muffled yip. Sasha stopped searching at once and approached Hans. She gave one short, sharp bark, then turned back to the snow and continued searching.

Hans understood... somehow, he realized that he had just been given an order from Sasha, and he knew he would follow it. He immediately turned and began his descent, staying close to the wall of the mountainside. Sasha would be okay, but the puppy needed to get back to the cottage. He turned all of his attention to do just that. On reaching the ground, Hans was reunited with his friend. The pair immediately set off for the warmth of the cottage.

*****

Frederick and Hans burst into the cottage, a howling wind at their heels. Everyone inside jumped to his or her feet. Outside, it was now almost dark and no one was going outside again tonight.

"Hans," asked Greta with urgency. "Where is Spot? Sasha? She went wild, wanting to go outside."

"Sasha?" Frederick was puzzled. He had not seen the dog anywhere along the trail back to the cottage.

"She must have run by us in the dark." Hans gave Frederick a look, but the young man was already near the fire, warming up. "I do have something special here though." He slowly undid his coat buttons to reveal a tiny head.

"The puppy!" Greta shouted with glee, as she plucked the tiny mite from his jacket. "The poor thing is freezing."

"It's already had a long, cold night." Hans took a deep breath while he removed his coat slowly. "There was an avalanche up on the pass."

"No," she screamed. "Spot!"

Hans shook his head and put his arms around her. Greta, looking grave, carried the puppy to the fireplace and laid him next to the other pups. The three remaining ones huddled close to their white-tailed brother, adding body warmth to the crackling fire.

"You must be freezing, my love." Greta led Hans to sit on the couch. "Sit by the fire and I'll get some hot soup for you. If Spot is still alive, Sasha will find him."

They sat close to each other, talking in low tones for almost an hour. Steve tried to make small talk, but failed utterly. Tiffany and Peter continued to hover around the puppies. Tiffany lavished most of her attention on the only girl, the all-black one. Peter continually went back to the adventurous pup with the white tail, even when it answered his affections with bites. The other two did not go neglected. Frederick and Hans each kept one, petting the soft fur and waiting for any sign of their parents.

Finally, Hans proclaimed, "I am so tired; we should all get some sleep. Tomorrow is going to be a tough day. Steve, you and the children take Greta's and my room. Greta and I will stay down here in case Sasha returns."

Steve was about to object to them giving up their bedroom, but Greta stopped him, whispering, "Don't say anything; he won't change his mind." Steve smiled warmly at Greta and thanked Hans. He gathered the children, nearly having to pry the puppies from their hands. Tiffany and Peter had been nodding off from the cozy surroundings and a bit of jet lag. Both children willingly followed Greta wearily up the stairs.

As Greta closed the bedroom door, Tiffany pointed at Peter and complained to her father, "Do I have to sleep with him in the same room?"

"Don't be so spoiled. We can all sleep on the bed; I'll sleep in the middle." Steve glared at his daughter.

Tiffany, still fully dressed, laid her head on the pillow and tensed her body. "Just don't take up the whole bed or cause an earthquake from your snoring, Peter," she commanded.

Steve quickly apologized to Peter for Tiffany's rudeness. "That's OK, Uncle Steve," he replied, as if it was no big deal. "I think I am used to it by now. Besides, Dad says she can be a spoiled brat at times."

Steve laughed aloud. Not amused, Tiffany turned and scowled at Peter. Steve lay down between them on the great oak bed. "Things will get better, Peter. I promise you."

By the time Greta returned downstairs, Frederick had already fallen asleep in the arm-chair. Hans patted the sofa, inviting Greta to sit with him. They agreed to take turns sleeping, so at least one of them would be awake if Sasha returned. Hans closed his tired eyes to take the first nap. The puppies were all facing the fire, silently sleeping. Greta laid her head wearily on her husband's chest and wondered what would happen if the dogs never returned. The flickering shadows of the fire dancing on the walls became hypnotic to her. She shook her head gently several times, trying to keep herself awake, and thought repeatedly; I must not go to sleep. However, between Hans's comfortable chest and the warmth of the fire, it was too much for her, and she drifted off.

Chapter Four

Frederick was woken in the early morning by strange sounds coming from outside. He jumped to his feet and raced to the door. On opening it, he was shocked to find Sasha dragging Spot through the thick snow toward the cottage!

"Hans! Greta! Come quickly! It's Sasha!"

Greta, woken by Frederick's shouting, raced to the door with Hans close behind. They all stood there in amazement; Sasha had found Spot. It appeared she had dragged him all the way from the mountain's edge, but Hans thought otherwise. He imagined her out there all night, digging through several feet of snow to find her mate. The question he had to ask himself was, had she possessed the strength to fly back with the larger dog, or did she actually drag him the full two miles from the mountain's edge? Spot looked lifeless, lying on his side with his paws and back legs just flailing in the snow.

"Quick, put some more logs on the fire!" Hans yelled as he raced into the snow. On seeing her master, Sasha simply collapsed, exhausted. Hans gently scooped up the 100-pound Spot in his arms. His head hung lifeless. Hans was struggling to control his emotions as he staggered back inside the cottage; all he could think was, "No, God! Please, no!"

Frederick tugged at Sasha's collar, urging the exhausted dog to her feet, explaining, "I am not as strong as your master; you will have to make your own way inside." Sasha dug deep, summoned her last reserves of energy, and slowly made her way to the safety of the cottage. Her bloodied paws left patchy, crimson imprints in the snowy blanket that still covered the ground.

Hans made his way toward the fireside with tears streaming from his now puffy reddened eyes. Greta kept his way clear by shooing the inquisitive puppies away.

"Not too close to the fire," she warned. "He must not warm up too quickly."

"I'm not even sure if he is alive," blurted a tearful Hans.

Greta rubbed Spot's ice-cold body with a soft, clean towel, whispering to him constantly, "You'll be OK, Spotty. You'll be OK."

Hans gingerly bent down and laid his head on Spot's chest. His anxiety evaporated as he shouted with excitement, "I can hear his heart faintly; he's still alive!"

Steve's feet hurriedly descended the stairs. "What's all the excitement about?" he asked as he walked into the living room, then looking across the scene could manage only, "Spot."

"Oh, yes," exclaimed Hans with a big grin on his face. "He's extremely cold, but still alive."

Tiffany and Peter had followed Steve down the stairs. "Good morning!" Tiffany announced as she swayed into the room. "Spot, oh my God. Is he okay?" Both children ran to the dog's side.

"Sasha's hurt as well," Peter whined as he pointed to her paws, which were still raw and bloody from the night's digging.

"She found him. In all that snow, Sasha brought him home," Greta announced proudly as she shook her head in disbelief. The puppies did not really understand how close to death their parents were, except for the little black one. She sat quietly, gently licking the face of her father. The other three all seemed to feed from the excitement and ran about, nipping at heels and getting in the way. Spot actually raised his head slightly and licked his precious daughter in return. Peter could not contain his excitement and clapped loudly, only stopping when he caught sight of Tiffany giving him a vacant stare. His clapping was then replaced by the red flushing of his cheeks.

There was far more mirth throughout the morning. The next couple of hours passed in making Sasha and Spot as comfortable as possible. Greta made a big breakfast for everyone and the kids continued to play with the puppies. Both Spot and Sasha lay still, safe for now, but both remained very weak.

Time grew short, and soon it was time to leave. The trio of guests had to catch a plane in a few hours. Steve, although reluctant to leave while Sasha and Spot were in such a state, made the announcement.

"Oh, good. I really need a shower," stated Tiffany. "And so do you." This came at Peter's expense, whose face once again flushed a bright red.

Hans moved toward Steve and took his hand in friendship. "Are you going to take a puppy, my friend?"

"I think so, but I will leave the choice to Tiffany, if that's OK?"

Tiffany did not wait for an answer. Kneeling down, she looked over each puppy in turn. Her eyes took in their peculiar markings, a white ring around one's eye, and a white tail on another. The one with the white leg was just plain lopsided. It came down to a simple factor: Tiffany did not particularly care for boys and only one of the puppies was a girl.

"I want the all-black one, the girl," she stated in a loud voice as if buying it from an ordinary pet store, then adding in a softer voice, "and I would like to name her Pasha, sort of taking after her mother, if that's OK? I promise I will love her forever."

"That is a very nice name," Hans said approvingly. "See, you really are a nice girl under that hard exterior." Everyone in the room burst into laughter. It was now Tiffany's turn to go bright red, embarrassed by the thought of her showing her feelings. Hans looked at Peter, who was eagerly waiting for his turn to choose. "And you, young man?" Hans asked in his deep voice.

Peter quickly replied in his squeaky cockney accent, "Could I have the white-tail one, please, Mister?"

Hans looked at the puppy, which was currently chasing said tail. "Yes, Peter, I would be very happy for you to look after him. Do you have a name for him yet?"

"I'm not sure, sir," Peter meekly answered.

"That's fine, young man. You take your time and pick a nice name for him."

"Are you sure you do not want to take the other two as well, Steve?" Greta asked with a sly grin.

"Yes, Daddy, please, can we have the rest?" Tiffany pleaded, beaming her enthusiasm at the idea.

"Oh no you don't, young lady. I am not springing that surprise on your mother. The one will be enough," Steve assured Hans. "Have you not found a home for the others yet?"

"There has been interest, but... these are special dogs." Hans continued, "I would not feel right just giving them to anyone. In time, I hope to find good homes for the others."

"Take care of your new friends, children," said Greta, warmly hugging both Peter and Tiffany in one wide embrace.

Steve put on his heavy coat. Still concerned about Spot, he asked, "Should I send a vet out here for Spot once I get back to the village?"

"No," shouted Hans. "The nearest vet is twenty miles away and, to be honest, we can't afford him."

Steve eagerly offered a solution. "Then I will pay for him. You won't take any money for the puppies, so at least let me pay for his vet bills and your superb hospitality."

"I cannot accept your money for our hospitality, Steve," insisted Hans. "I will, however, accept your offer to help with Spot. If you can get him to a doctor, we would be eternally grateful."

"I will do better than that. I will arrange the vet to come here. It's the least I can do." Steve accepted Hans's firm handshake.

Greta handed Tiffany and Peter a small blanket each. "That's for keeping the pups warm on your trip." As the children accepted the blankets, they both thanked Greta and carefully placed their new pets into them, gently wrapping each one, so only their little heads peeped out.

Everyone moved toward the cottage door. The puppies seemed to get more and more agitated with every step. As Hans finally opened the door, they started yapping continuously as if trying to say something.

"Shush, puppies, you'll wake your mother up, and I was hoping we could spare her this goodbye," Hans snapped.

"Too late, Hans," Greta informed him with a frown, as she pointed to Sasha. "Oh, well. Sneaking them out is not an option now. Come on, girl, come and say goodbye."

Sasha struggled to her swollen feet and hobbled toward her pups. Spot lay with his eyes open, but was far too weak to move. All he could manage was a whimper of goodbye. Sasha approached her two children leaving for distant shores. She gave a motherly lick to each, and let out one soft bark. "My God," Steve murmured "She's crying!"

"Oh, Sasha, now don't get me started," Greta whispered, while letting loose with tears of her own.

Peter knelt down to Sasha. "I promise I will take care of your baby." He reached out and gave Sasha a hug, which wobbled her a bit on her weakened legs. Strangely, Sasha then turned to Tiffany, holding Pasha.

"What?" Tiffany asked, looking around at the expectant group of people. "You want me to promise to a dog? Oh, whatever." She knelt and faced the expectant dog. The look in Sasha's eyes changed her demeanor; she could really see a sense of loss in the dog's eyes. "I promise that nothing bad will ever happen to Pasha. She will always be safe with me. This I promise you with all of my heart."

Sasha realized that the human had been sincere in her promise. She lowered her head and turned back toward her wounded companion. The remaining puppies darted about her legs. With an enormous effort, Sasha lay down beside Spot and was soon asleep.

Frederick dug the car out of the snow, and they were off. Hans and Greta waved good-bye to their new friends. Just as they pulled out of sight, the old couple closed the cottage door and retreated to the warmth of the fire. Pasha was off to America.

Chapter Five

A Year Later

Tiffany had an eager look on her face as she told Pasha, "I can't wait until next week!" She was just about to feed the now quite large German shepherd when the dog began to get antsy. "What's the matter, Pash? You seem excited and I haven't even fed you yet." Pasha turned to look at the door before Tiffany even heard the knock. "Ugh! Hold on, girl." Tiffany opened the door to discover a petite girl with honey-colored eyes and long wavy brunette hair.

"Hi. You're Tiffany, right?" the stranger asked.

"Maybe," Tiffany nonchalantly answered. "You live next door. Your family drives that crappy looking truck."

"Nice to meet you too. I'm Chloe, and you're right, the truck is crappy. I have seen your dog in the yard, she's beautiful. What's her name?"

Tiffany replied proudly, "That's my beautiful Pasha," just as Pasha barked loudly, drowning out the end of the answer.

"Weird," Chloe stated. "I think I heard Pasha. Hi, Pasha, how are you doing?" Pasha answered by barking several times.

"She just wants some food. Come in." Tiffany cleared the path for Chloe who strolled in and began to pet Pasha. That only lasted a few moments before Pasha was away to her now full food dish.

"I've seen you around," said Chloe, taking a seat at the kitchen table. "I thought it was time I finally said hi."

Tiffany joined her. "You haven't lived here long, have you?"

"I did as a baby, just up the street actually. My dad passed away not long after I was born, so my mom moved out of state. We've only been back for a couple of months."

"I guess I am a terrible neighbor," Tiffany huffed. "Want something to drink?"

"No, thanks. I also stopped by to offer some help. I work after school at the local animal shelter. I was wondering if you'd like some help with Pasha."

"I don't need any help with Pasha. Do I, girl?" Pasha ignored Tiffany to the further exploration of the food dish.

"I've seen you out in the yard with her. Pasha doesn't seem to obey you at all. I give the dogs at the shelter a little training since most people want an obedient dog to take home. I also take care of all the animals: feeding, grooming, as well as cleaning the cages."

"That's because Pasha is a strong-willed dog," explained Tiffany. "I like her that way. Anyway, she listens to me. Watch this."

Tiffany kneeled next to Pasha, commanding, "Pasha, give me your paw." The dog looked at her master directly in the eyes and just burped. Embarrassed, Tiffany sighed and repeated the command a few times. Although knowing exactly what her master wanted, Pasha sensed that for some reason, it was crucial that Chloe was included in their future. She just stared blankly as if she did not understand. "Maybe that's actually a good idea," Tiffany relented. "I don't know what it is. I've practiced with her, and she's a super-smart dog."

"You need to use a firm voice. Not angry or innocent, but firm."

"Right, I knew that. Pasha, give me your paw!" Pasha ensured Chloe would be around as she eagerly did as Tiffany asked. "Wow, that was easy!"

"This is just the beginning," stated an enthused Chloe. "Soon you will be able to get Pasha to do anything you want."

At that, Pasha let out a sharp bark, as if to tell Chloe that total obedience may be asking just a little too much, before she sauntered out of the room.

Tiffany and Chloe giggled as though they had known each other for years.

The girls talked for hours, and Pasha, as ever, was happy to have company over. She was thinking that maybe this could be Tiffany's new best friend.

*****

The next week passed quickly, with Chloe and Tiffany spending most of their free time together. Chloe was to be the guest of honor at Tiffany's birthday party and had agreed to spend the night at her house while her parents were out for the evening.

The light from twelve candles danced against the wall and the sound of singing filled the room: "Happy birthday to you, happy birthday, dear Tiffany, happy birthday to you!" Taking a deep breath, she made short work of blowing out the candles all at once.

"Yes!" she cried, rubbing her hands together at the thought of her wish coming true.

As the lights switched back on in the crowded room, Tiffany looked around. So many people, she thought. All of my family and friends have come. This really is the best day of my life! Absolutely everyone at school will be talking about my party for months!

A deep bark announced Pasha was back from a visit to the vet. She immediately jumped up and rested her paws on Tiffany's shoulders, licking her face with long sweeping motions.

"Hi, Pash, I missed you, too," said Tiffany, acknowledging Pasha's undoubted love for her. "I suppose it's sort of your birthday as well."

"Yes, it is," agreed Tiffany's mother, Fay. "She should have a cake as well!" she said, rushing to the kitchen, then reappearing a few moments later with a small cupcake with one solitary burning candle in it. As everyone began to sing "Happy Birthday" again, Pasha sensed this one was for her and sat upright, her ears pricked high.

"Blow the candle out, Pasha!" Fay whispered, placing the small cake right in front of the dog. The room went silent as everyone waited expectantly to see what Pasha would do.

"I know she's a special dog, but blowing out candles may just be a little too much to ask," Steve added, chuckling. As he reached for the cake, Pasha jumped up on all fours. Her tail wagging furiously, she started barking at the candle, as if demanding it extinguish itself.

Everyone watched in amazement as she realized the breaths from her barks were actually moving the flame. Pasha edged toward the candle. With each step, she let out another bark, and each time the flame flickered a little more.

A shout of encouragement from the back of the room became contagious as everyone started shouting, "Go on, girl! You can do it!" Pasha did not want to let anyone down and, relishing the attention, took another step forward. Now so close her nose was nearly touching the flame, she opened her mouth and let out the loudest bark she could. With a single stream of smoke rising from the extinguished candle, everyone burst into applause.

"Well done, Pash!" Tiffany congratulated her pet by stroking the proud dog's head, while she whispered in her ear, "I hope you made a good wish, because it will come true."

Answering with a lick, she immediately bounded off to the garden to see if her wish had come true. Looking around the large tidy yard and checking all her secret hiding places, she began to think despairingly that the "wishing thing" only worked for humans. Finding nothing in the last possible place, her head dropped so much, her cold black nose nearly dragged on the ground. Tail motionless between her legs, she shuffled slowly back toward the house.

When Pasha reached the door, two legs dressed in white cotton trousers blocked her entrance. Stopping without looking up, she just stood there, waiting for them to move. A deep, husky voice declared, "Now, now! Don't you go sulking on me."

Pasha knew that voice and lifted her disappointed head slowly to confirm her hunch. Standing there was Tiffany's grandpa,

Joe, a tall man with light medium-length hair that looked so much lighter against his dark Arizona-tanned face. His short beard completed the picture of the wise old cowboy so typical of any decent Western. Pasha's face lit up as she saw Joe was holding a bowl containing the biggest bone she had ever seen.

"I bet this is what you wished for," Joe stated, placing the bowl on the patio floor. Pasha let out a double-yap in agreement and wasted no time getting right down to the business of the bone.

Joe was a wily character in the afternoon of his very adventurous life, most of which he had spent working for the government. Those long, hard years had taken a toll on his health, and though he was retired, he always kept himself busy, mostly collecting various interesting things.

As the party started to wind down, Tiffany still glowed at the thought of her party being the talk of her school for weeks. With the last of her school guests gone, Louise, Joe's wife, was on the prowl for volunteers to help clean up. Tiffany was one step ahead of her as usual, jumping to her feet and announcing, "I really would love to help you, Gran, but me and Chloe really do have to go to the candy store."

Louise laughed before saying, "Oh, go on then. After all, it is your birthday. Be sure to take Pasha with you."

With Tiffany, Chloe, and Pasha gone, the rest of the adults (except Joe, who was in his back room as usual) tackled the messy house. "How could so few people make so much mess?" questioned Steve.

"Well, that's one of life's little mysteries," answered Louise, whisking past him with the vacuum.

Within an hour, Louise's house was back to its usual immaculate condition. Just as the three of them sat down to relax, Tiffany burst through the door.

"Good timing, Tiff. All the work's done," stated an exhausted Steve.

"Never mind all that," she shrieked as she and Chloe ran into the family room.

"What have you got there?" asked her mother.

Holding her arms out, she excitedly answered, "It's a kitten!"

"You're not bringing that cat home!" Fay snapped back at her.

"Did you just buy that?" Steve questioned.

"No, no!" Chloe jumped in.

Tiffany was still so excited she was having trouble getting the words out fast enough. "Pasha found it in a bush. It was as if she knew exactly where it was. I would do anything to keep it! Oh please, please, please, Mommy!"

"OK, now slow down, take a deep breath, and tell me exactly what happened," asked Steve, the voice of calm. Tiffany let the kitten loose on the carpet, sat by her father's feet, took a deep breath, and began her story again.

"We were walking down Pewter Hill; Pasha was being really good, walking right next to me. We got about halfway down when she just stopped, pricked up her ears, barked once, and then took off at full speed down the hill. We chased after her but she was so fast we couldn't catch her. She ran off the road into the desert until I could just barely see her. She stopped by a big bush and started barking. I shouted at her to get away from the bush, in case there was a snake in there, but she started clawing away dead branches and buried her head deep into the bush. When I finally reached her, I started tugging at her collar, telling her to get away from the bush. She finally brought her head out, and she had this oh-so-cute little kitten in her mouth. She was so gentle with it! I took the kitten from her, and we started to look around for its owner or mother. We looked for ages but couldn't find anyone, so I thought the best thing to do would be to bring it straight back here."

By the time Tiffany had finished her story, Fay already had the kitten in her arms. She stroked it and questioned, "It's so tiny! How could anyone leave something so cute in the desert? You're very lucky to be alive, little kitty."

"Maybe we should keep it," suggested Steve. "After all, Pasha seemed to know exactly where it was, and it's so small and vulnerable."

Fay looked at the kitten long and hard. Pasha was sitting right in front of her, waiting for Fay's decision. "I just don't know if you can take care of another animal, Tiff."

"Well, I could always help. Cats are my favorite animals, and I know everything about them. I see them everyday at the shelter," Chloe offered in a persuasive tone.

"Would you like a little friend to play with, Pasha?" asked Fay. Pasha continually barked loudly. "OK, OK! You can keep it on one condition."

"Anything!" Tiffany blurted with excitement.

"You have to clean up after it," Fay told her. "One more thing: I get to name it."

Tiffany quickly agreed, asking, "What are you going to call it?"

"Let's see..." Fay said, looking deep into the kitten's eyes. "I know. You found him on Pewter Hill, and he's so little. We'll call him Little Pewter."

"Well, whatever you're calling it," Steve said impatiently, as if not liking the name she had picked, "we have to go now. It's getting dark already."

"My goodness!" Fay blurted urgently. "It's already eight o'clock! You know I don't like to drive down the mountain in the dark."

Tiffany thanked her granny for letting her have her party at their house, while Fay and Steve said their goodbyes to Joe. With everyone loaded into the car, they set off toward home.

Little Pewter seemed to like the safety of Fay's lap. He purred endlessly while Steve drove down the mountain road toward Sahuarita. Tiffany and Chloe were singing in the back, trying in vain to teach Pasha Tiffany's latest favorite song. They had barely made it halfway down the mountain when Pasha started growling and barking so furiously, Steve had to pull the car over to the side of a level clearing.

"What's wrong with her now?" Steve shouted from the front. "Don't tell me she's seen another cat! That dog can be really weird at times."

"You'd better let her out; she may want to pee or something," Fay countered.

Steve opened his door and got out. It was so dark, looking out into the desert, he could not tell where the land ended and the sky began.

He started to open the back door for Pasha, who was still barking furiously. As soon as the door was open enough, Pasha leapt from the far seat, across Tiffany and Chloe's laps, out of the car, and sped off past Steve into the desert. "Don't come back with anything!" he shouted at her.

"Will she be OK?" asked Fay.

"Yes, I'm sure she'll just do her thing and come straight back," Steve reassured.

Pasha had seen something in the darkness. She ran deep into the desert where the ghostly figure of a Native American chief in full ceremonial costume sat proudly on a pure white stallion. As she cautiously approached, the chief turned and beckoned her to follow him. Pasha looked back toward the car, which was by then out of sight, not knowing whether to return to her loved ones or follow the ghostly chief. As he motioned again for Pasha to follow, her inquisitive nature made the decision for her; she began to run directly behind the big white horse. The trail was steep and rugged, but the horse seemed to glide effortlessly over it.

By this time, everyone was standing outside the car, waiting for Pasha's return. Steve had tried to follow her, but his efforts were futile without a flashlight in the pure darkness. On returning to the car, he tried to calm frantic Tiffany by putting his arm around her. Although he was not certain himself, he assured her, "Pasha will be OK. Call your Grandpa Joe. If anyone can find her, he can. He knows these mountains like the back of his hand."

By this time, Pasha and the chief had reached the top of a mountain. Looking around, she saw a great valley below and, beyond that, a large stream running along the side of a small village consisting of skin-covered tepees. Continuing, they headed toward the center of the village where a large bonfire crackled. As Pasha and the chief drew nearer, the whole tribe came out of the tepees to follow them.

The chief stopped just short of the fire and dismounted from his horse, which an Indian squaw immediately took from him and led away.

The chief summoned Pasha to sit next to him by patting his hand on the ground beside the fire. Pasha's eyes scanned the whole tribe, who were all silently staring at her. Their eyes filled with a sadness Pasha had never seen before.

A wrinkled, bent-over man carrying a long stick joined them. He shook the stick violently from side to side and a rattling sound carried across the valley. The chief spoke for the first time, looking directly into Pasha's eyes.

"We are the Katoka tribe. We fled from the plains to this, 'the Lost Mountain,' during the war of the long knives." He then introduced the strange man shaking the stick as Shuno, their medicine man. "He has spoken to the Great Spirits, and they have confirmed that the gods have sent you to save the White Buffalo." Raising his hand and pointing directly at Pasha's face, he stated, "You are the special one, the one who can free us. We have been waiting for you for many moons."

The chief continued, "When the moon is full, our spirits return to the place of our ancestors. We are then tortured by the sound of the suffering buffalo. This will continue until the Great White Buffalo's spirit is rested."

Although Pasha did not fully understand how she could help, she could see the pain in the chief's eyes. She let out a faint cry, as if she too were sharing their pain. The medicine man's instrument fell silent; the only sound was the crackling of the burning wood on the fire.

A tremor shook the ground and a thunderous noise filled the air. Pasha stood and looked around. She could not see anything that would make such a noise, but barked furiously, jumping around in circles.

The medicine man started to walk away from the fire, waving at Pasha to follow him. She obliged, barking with every step.

The farther they got from the fire, the darker it became until they were in total blackness. With the noise now almost unbearable, the medicine man stopped on the edge of a deep canyon.

"Look! Look!" he shouted, pointing down into the canyon. Pasha peered over the side. Although she could tell this was the source of the noise, it was too dark to see anything. Straining her eyes, it looked to her like the whole ground was moving.

Pasha turned and started to head back to the fire, but stopped as a bright light surrounded her. Looking up at the sky, the dark clouds were now moving faster, revealing a brilliant full moon. Pasha raced back to the canyon's edge and peered down. The cause of the noise was then apparent. A herd of buffalo seemed to be coming out of one side of the mountain and disappearing into the other.

As fast as the noise had started, it stopped. The medicine man turned to Pasha and told her, "This will happen every hour as long as the moon is full." Pasha licked his hand sympathetically as they both returned to the fire.

*****

Joe had received a call from Steve and caught up to his family at their car. This is where the search would begin. He planned to go straight for the base of "Isandlakara," which translated to "The Mountain of the Clenched Hand." This was the mountain's name because the peaks looked like the knuckles of a clenched fist, but there were other legends about the mountain. It had been a mythical place as long as anyone could remember. People had long since stopped camping near the mountain, and he had heard many stories of the eerie feelings people got whenever they went near it. Joe had never experienced anything strange near the mountain, but he did not exactly go there often. There were stories of ghosts, phantom herds of buffalo, and many stories about disappearances near the mountain. This had earned the mountain another name: "The Lost Mountain." Joe prayed that Pasha had not become a part of that legend.

Once he reached the base of Isandlakara, he looked around. The night was bright and clear with a full moon. The beam of his flashlight shone onto a set of paw prints going right up to the steep side of the mountain. It was a hard climb of about two hundred feet to a ridge which gave a great view of the canyon on the other side. Joe had climbed to its top once before and swore he would never do it again. It was treacherous even in daylight, and the whole mountain just gave him a bad vibe. He paced a bit, deciding what to do. Finally, his impatience got the better of him. He gave a shout of "That dang puppy!" and started to climb.

As the going got tougher, Joe questioned himself for the first time, realizing he was not so young anymore. This pile of rock is not going to beat me, he thought. As he reached his goal, panting heavily, he confirmed to himself, Ha! There is still life in this old dog yet! Lying down on the narrow peak, he peered over the other side. "Well, would you look at that," he whispered to himself, as his eyes looked disbelievingly down at... none other than Pasha.

She appeared to be sitting all alone beside a withering fire. For an instant, Joe thought he saw crowds of people around the ghostly fire and, beyond them, a small village. His attention drawn to the scene below, he lost his footing and slipped. Rocks tumbled down, making a large racket. His flashlight fell out of his hand and bounced downwards, going out along the way. The sound carried all the way to Pasha, who immediately looked upward.

The fire, the village, and all of its inhabitants disappeared at the sudden noise. Pasha looked again to the rock face and saw movement way up high in the bright moonlight. She turned and ran away from the intruder. The moonlight gave her a good view, but the path was running out. The edge of the canyon loomed ahead.

Joe caught himself, but now had lost all sight of Pasha. Had he imagined the village? It remained on his mind as he began to descend after the dog. In all his years living in the area, he had never seen anything like that. He stopped for a moment and looked ahead to the Lost Mountain. It stood out in the moonlight against the starry background. He had heard all manner of legend about the mountain; he had even told a few second-hand. This was the first time he had started to believe them.

Pasha reached the canyon's edge and stopped. She could still hear something far behind her, coming down the cliff. The ground began to shake once again. The hour had passed quickly in the village, and it was time for the buffalo to run.

Joe reached the flat area where the fire had been. There was no trace of the village, and he was entertaining thoughts that he had imagined the entire thing.

"Pasha!" Joe called out. "Pasha, come here, girl!" He looked out across the expanse and thought he saw a black blob against the moonlight, a dog-shaped blob. The shaking had now reached Joe. He was unsure of what was happening, and just froze on the spot.

Pasha heard the human voice call her name and wheeled around. It was Grandpa Joe's voice. Pasha really liked him and always felt at ease when he was around. He must have been coming to find her. The ground almost bounced beneath her feet as the herd of buffalo exploded from the side of the Lost Mountain. The great White Buffalo raced at the head of the others. Pasha gave one sharp bark to let Joe know where she was, and the ground was no longer under her feet.

Joe heard the bark come from the canyon's edge and his paralysis broke. Disregarding the noise, he focused back on finding Pasha. He had just caught sight of the dog near the canyon's edge when she disappeared from view.

Pasha's world was spinning as she tumbled down the steep canyon wall and ended up in a heap at the bottom. She quickly got to her feet, feeling sore all over, and turned to face a giant white buffalo bearing down on her. Pasha ran for it, barely getting out of the way before finding herself directly in the path of a hundred more buffalo, all of which seemed to be following the white one. She dodged first left, then right, almost getting squashed on several occasions. Even in the moonlight, Pasha could see the fear in the rushing buffalo's eyes. They were running from something that utterly terrified them.

As the moonlight began to dim and everything went dark, Pasha was scooped up by a whirling vortex of wind and golden sand. The whirlwind lifted the helpless dog from her feet, bumping her into kicking and snorting buffalo. Pasha felt herself being pulled along, toward the Lost Mountain and could only bark in fear for her life.

There were two flashes of lightning, followed by a rolling crack of thunder, as a voice echoed through the canyon, "Paw Power!" The sky cleared and Pasha found herself lying on the canyon floor. All around her, the howling wind and swirling golden cloud continued toward the mountain. She could see the terrified buffalo inside as it pulled them along. The last thing that passed her was a large white shape, held firmly by a great fist of gleaming dust.

Pasha felt a tightening on her collar, and she left the ground completely, pulled into the air. As she ascended higher and higher, Pasha watched the buffalo taken back to their mountain prison, and all was silent in the night once more. Pasha looked up to discover that what was lifting her was another large, black German shepherd. The two of them passed through the light of the moon before Pasha recognized her savior as her mother, Sasha. Sasha gripped her child's collar tightly as they disappeared into the starry night sky.

*****

Pasha's journey was short, but strange. She looked down, failing to recognize any of the landscape. The trees were plentiful, tall, and so much greener than those in the desert. She heard a voice that told her to close her eyes as their journey was about to end. With her eyes closed, it was not long before she felt the safety of the ground once again. Eyes still shut tight, she sniffed at the cold, smooth floor beneath her.

"Open your eyes, darling," commanded the same voice that had shouted "Paw Power." Pasha once again obeyed the voice. Her eyes blinked several times in amazement as she found herself in a large hall. Dust filled the air, and the tall, dirty, stained-glass windows allowed only a few beams of sunlight to pass through. She looked up at the vaulted ceilings filled with cobwebs. She then fixed her eyes on a single beam of sunlight that came from a small hole in the middle, the beam cutting through the dusty air to the floor where it split into many rays. They, in turn, filled the hall with enough light for Pasha to observe all around. How can it be daytime already?, she thought. Where am I?

Sasha sat directly in front of Pasha, looked her in the eyes, and opened her mouth as though to bark, but it was not a bark that followed. It was a human voice—the same voice Pasha had heard both in the canyon and on their journey.

"I know you are confused right now. Take heart, daughter, you are safe now, though I cannot tell you where you are."

Pasha not only wondered how her mother could talk human, she was also surprised that Sasha knew exactly what she was thinking.

Pasha let out a bark, testing whether she could also speak human. "You cannot speak in human yet. Just think, and I will understand," explained Sasha. "My, you have grown into a beauty and so big for a female." Sasha noticed that Pasha's head was bleeding from her adventure in the canyon.

"Lie down, Pasha. Let me clean that wound."

Pasha did as she was asked, allowing her mother to lovingly clean her wound.

Once Sasha's healing licks had managed to stop Pasha's bleeding, she sat back and began to scold her child. "What do you think you were doing tonight?" Before Pasha could answer, her mother continued, "I feel the warrior inside you. You have a natural desire to help everyone and correct all wrongs. I know you are ready, but it is not time yet. You must wait until all of you are ready. One of your brothers… well, let us just say, he is not quite there yet. When you are all ready, everything will be explained, and you will all be asked the question."

What question?, Pasha thought.

"That is not for me to say. Your answers will come by way of this." A glowing orb appeared above Sasha's head. It gave off a beautiful golden light, illuminating the image of a dog deep inside it.

Pasha had instant recognition. She had seen one of these before, a long time ago. "You'll remember, Pasha... soon. However, you must not endanger yourself before the time is right. I am only able to help you pups three times. I have already used one helping your brother and this one on you tonight. That leaves just one remaining, and then you'll all be on your own."

Pasha just sat there, still in shock and not really understanding what was going on.

"Come on, Pasha. It's time for you to go home," Sasha commanded as she turned and walked toward one of two large, marble staircases, which framed a gigantic chair. It reached upwards majestically, nearly touching the carved balcony that linked both sets of stairs. "There are people worried about you, people who love you very much."

As the two reached the top of the stairs and walked along the balcony, Pasha noted it contained five doors with a large mirror set in each.

They stopped at the first door. "Here you go, Pasha. This one is yours. Door open," Sasha commanded in a stern voice. The door obeyed, instantly flying open to reveal nothing more than a black abyss.

"Go on, don't be afraid; it won't hurt you," her mother assured.

Mama, thought Pasha. I do not want to leave.

"You have to go home for now, but soon I will see you again. I love you, my daughter."

Pasha nodded and obeyed, walking into the darkness of the portal. With a blink of her eye, she was standing along the edge of the canyon with the bright moon once again overhead. A man stood just in front of her. His back was to her as he peered down into the canyon below.

Joe had felt a constant vibration, like a shiver along his body, and then it was gone. The canyon floor was empty save for the scrubby bushes and a few scattered boulders. He could see no sign of Pasha. Suddenly, Joe felt a presence beside him. Pasha was standing there wagging her tail and panting. He nearly yelled out in surprise but, instead, just plopped down before her. Pasha came forward and licked his face.

"Huh. Well, hello there, puppy," greeted Joe. "I don't know what just happened, but you are certainly full of mysteries." He patted her gently. "All right, let's get back to everyone. We'll just keep this between you and me."

Pasha barked in agreement as Joe climbed to his feet, and they started back.

"But before we do, help old Joe find his flashlight."

*****

Back at the car, Steve was getting ready to quit for the night and explained to Tiffany that they would search again in the morning. Grandpa Joe would be all right and would call when he found Pasha. Tiffany reluctantly agreed, tears flowing down her cheeks as she climbed back into the car. As Steve started the engine, Tiffany's cell phone rang. "It's Grandpa!" she revealed, looking at the call screen. "Have you found her? Have you found her?" she questioned without so much as a "hello."

"Yes, child," Joe responded. "Stay where you are and we'll be back to you in about half an hour."

A huge sigh of relief overwhelmed Tiffany, and she broke down in a flood of tears. "He's found her and she's all right!"

"Then why are you crying?" asked Steve.

"That's because she's so happy!" Fay remarked, stroking the still sleeping Little Pewter, who was unaware of the drama that had unfolded. "You men just don't understand us women, do you?"

Tiffany sat back in her seat with her eyes fixed on the darkness of the desert, waiting for her Pasha to return.

"At last!" she cried out, as a distant flashlight emerged from the darkness. Jumping out of the car, she ran toward the light, calling to Pasha with every stride. On reaching Joe and the dog, she knelt down and flung her arms around Pasha's neck. Sobbing uncontrollably, she kissed her and told her how much she loved her; Pasha reciprocated by licking her face furiously.

"Thank you so much, Dad," said Fay as she gave him a big hug.

"Thanks, Joe," Steve added.

"You betcha. Now, young lady, Pasha has been through a rough night. You take her home, tend to her wounds, and get some rest."

He gave Pasha a quick scratch behind the ears and winked at her. The dog responded with a bark. Pasha watched the man walk back to his truck, the human words "Thank you" running in her mind. She finally knew what that meant. Tiffany put her back into the car, and the family set off once again for home.

*****

Pasha awoke the next morning to the tickling of her nose. Without opening her eyes, she let out the biggest sneeze. When she finally roused, she discovered that the tickling culprit was Little Pewter. The kitten had been brushing up against Pasha with the fluffiest tail she had ever seen.

How can something so small have such a big tail?, Pasha thought.

Tiffany came bounding into the room. "Morning, Pash! Morning, Li'l Pewter!" she exclaimed, typical of her habit of shortening names. "Look, Mom," she continued, "Pasha's grooming Li'l Pewter! She thinks it's her baby."

Chloe, who had spent the night, immediately barged into the room and announced, "You know, it's common for a female dog to adopt a baby of another species. Girl dogs tend to have strong motherly instincts even at a young age."

"OK, Einstein!" Tiffany chided. It did not take Pasha long to completely soak Pewter's whole body. They slept next to each other the rest of the day.

Chapter Six

Six months passed and Pasha had begun to believe she had imagined her mother saving her. She returned to her normal life, eating, running around town with Tiffany, and trying to keep Pewter out of trouble. The little cat was a mess, getting into everything, and Pasha realized the cat now thought that it was actually a dog.

As far as Pasha was concerned, she had adopted him as her own. She taught him various doggy things, like rolling on his back and begging for food at the family table. Li'l Pewter, as everyone now called him, followed Pasha everywhere. When Pasha barked, Li'l Pewter tried with all his might to bark as well, but all that came out was a faint meow. His tail also seemed to get fluffier every day.

Tiffany's relationship with Chloe had blossomed into a real best friendship. They spent time together most days doing the things teenage girls love to do: shopping, having their nails done, and talking about boys. Pasha tagged along where she could. She listened intently to the girls' conversations, but understood very little about the preoccupations of humans. To Pasha, they remained strange creatures and, while she found them much too loud, she still loved having them around.

The fateful moment Pasha had waited so patiently for finally arrived one warm spring night. With Steve and Fay out for the evening, Tiffany and Chloe were sitting in the family room reading magazines while Pasha and Pewter played on the carpet in front of them.

Pasha walked away from Pewter to get a drink of water. She went through the pet door into the back yard and that is when it happened. A golden glow washed across the yard just as Pasha had her face buried deep in the water dish. She looked up into the bright, shining orb floating just above her head to see the image of a dog floating inside. The orb was so beautiful and Pasha could not resist trying to give it a little nudge with the tip of her nose.

She was just about to touch it when a furry blur went flying through the air. Li'l Pewter was hanging from the orb right in front of Pasha's face. Both the orb and Pewter fell to the ground like a stone, causing the cat to go tumbling. The cat was up in an instant and hissing at the orb. Pasha began barking at Pewter, trying to get him to go away. Seeing Pasha's anger, Pewter went streaking back through the dog door with Pasha chasing fast on the heel.

Inside, the girls had just a moment to take notice of the two pets in a frantic chase, before both their attentions were distracted by a sharp thud against the patio doors. Both nearly jumped off the couch in fright.

"What was that?" gasped Tiffany.

"I'm not sure, but we should check and see."

"Well, I'm not going out there! It may be a mountain lion!" Tiffany shouted in a frightened voice.

"Don't be such a baby, Tiff," Chloe teased, playing the hero. She walked slowly toward the closed patio doors. "I can't see anything; the yard is empty." Tiffany moved slowly up behind Chloe and peered over her shoulder. Chloe took one look at her and opened the patio door.

"What are you doing? Close that!" shouted Tiffany.

"I think it was this," explained Chloe, stepping out and picking up the tiny gold ball. Sensing someone near her orb, Pasha quickly returned to the yard. To her horror, she found the girls examining it.

"It's so beautiful," Chloe stated hypnotically. "The dog inside is really beautiful; it looks like it's pure gold. Someone must have thrown it over the wall."

"Let me hold it," asked an extremely relieved Tiffany. "Wow, this is so cool. I'm going to keep it."

The ball hopped out of Tiffany's hand and started moving slowly backward away from the glass doors. An inquisitive Pasha poked her head through the legs of the shocked humans. The girls stared, disbelieving, as the ball finally stopped at the edge of the patio. They turned silently and looked into each other's eyes, confused and fearful of what had just happened. Pasha knew this orb was very important to her and wanted the humans to leave it and her alone.

The orb suddenly exploded into a brilliant golden light and rose off the patio. The girls screamed again and ran, hands waving about in the air as they made their way toward the safety of the bathroom. Once inside, they fumbled to lock the door with uncontrollably shaking hands.

"W-w-what is that thing?" Tiffany asked.

"I don't know," replied Chloe in a trembling voice. "All I do know is that Pasha and Pewter are out there. Do you think we should go and get them?"

"We can open the door a little and call them," Tiffany offered in a now slightly calmer voice.

Chloe hesitantly unlocked it, slowly pushing down the handle. Not knowing what might be behind the door, she began to open it cautiously. With the door opened just enough to poke their heads out, both girls looked around.

With their heads poked out and nothing unusual happening, they decided to venture further, leaving the bathroom and heading down the hall toward the family room. Both tiptoed slowly, Chloe in front with Tiffany's arms wrapped clingingly around her friend's waist.

On reaching the opening to the family room, both girls once again bent down and poked their heads around the opening. All they could see was Pasha and Pewter sitting next to each other, both looking out of the patio doors. The back yard was lit up in a brilliant yellow.

Tiffany called Pasha, "Here, girl, come here." Pasha turned and looked; instead of obeying, she ignored her master, turning back toward the orb. Pasha knew there was no danger from the golden ball. She could feel it calling upon her to come closer, to touch it.

From behind, the girls crept toward Pasha and Pewter.

"You grab Pewter, I'll get Pasha by the collar," whispered Tiffany. "Then run for the bathroom. Okay?"

"Yeah," agreed Chloe. "Let's make it fast, though."

"That's the idea. On three. One... two... Now," shouted Tiffany and lunged at Pasha. Chloe scooped up Pewter and turned to run for the bathroom. The cat started hissing and spitting at the intrusion. Tiffany's finger only grazed Pasha's collar before the dog bolted out of the open door.

Fearlessly, Pasha ran at full speed and, with a mighty leap, pinned the ball between her paws and the concrete patio. However, even her extremely powerful paws were not strong enough to keep the ball down. It once again bounced up and hovered in mid-air, before continually spinning around her, inching closer with each lap until the defensive Pasha finally lay down and closed her eyes submissively. Tiffany froze as she watched the scene. Pasha just lay on her side while the orb began to flash rapidly. There was one more burst of golden light, bright enough to temporarily blind Tiffany, and everything went back to darkness.

*****

Pasha opened her eyes to find herself back in the great hall. It looked different; it was much brighter and cleaner with large paintings hanging in the alcoves between massive white columns. The paintings all featured dogs of various types, each possessing a glorious stature and magical aura. Hanging from the ceiling were three very large, golden chandeliers, glowing with the flames of hundreds of candles. The floors were tiled in a mosaic of brightly colored panels, except for a large black square directly in front of a great, mahogany chair.

As her eyes scanned the hall, Pasha noticed four bowls at the base of the chair, each filled to the top with fresh water. Surely, those four bowls cannot all be for me, she thought, but on looking around, she could see no one else there. As much as she wanted to be uneasy, Pasha found herself feeling very much at home—that is, until a shrill voice broke the silence: "Ooi, where did you come from?"

Pasha's head whipped in all directions, trying to locate the source of the disturbance. "Up 'ere, Bozo," the voice taunted from overhead. Pasha looked upward, but all she could see was the balcony joining the two staircases, until she caught a glimpse of a moving shadow.

Opening her mouth to bark, Pasha was shocked to hear her own human voice instead. "Where are you? I can't see you... whoa, I can speak!"

Pasha lurched backward and tensed her muscles as though ready to spring on whomever had just spoken to her. Instead, she stood up slowly and watched a figure descend the stairs to stand in front of her.

It was another dog... Looking it up and down, Pasha noted its shimmering ebony coat, then its white tail. Pasha had a flicker of memory.

"A white tail? I remember a white tail," stated Pasha.

"Yeah, yeah, sure you do. I'm ya bruver," confirmed the other dog.

"Yes, my brother!"

"Me name's 'arold, or if you want to be posh, it would be—" the white-tailed dog pulled in a deep breath and forced out, "H-H-Harold. Wot do they call you?"

"I'm Pasha. Why do you talk funny?" Pasha countered.

"I talk Kenisssh Taan; ain't nuffink wrong with the way I talk. Some people call it cockney." Pasha just blinked. Harold shook his head and tried to put on his poshest voice. "I was raised in England—London, actually."

"How did you get here?" Pasha asked, curious if the same thing had happened to her brother as to her.

"Well, that's a strange one. There I was just sitting in the sun when up jumps a glowin', golden ball fingy and starts whizzing round me 'ead. Was I shocked? Well, I can tell you, I was so shocked I nearly gave me bone away! Next fing I know, I'm 'ere. Wot about you?"

"Much the same as you, really," Pasha replied. "Only, I've been here before."

"You been 'ere before?" Harold's jaw dropped.

"Yes. It's a long story."

"Doesn't seem to be any fink pressin' us for time. Get on with it, come on, I ain't got all day."

Pasha took a deep breath and told Harold of the Lost Mountain, the spirit Indian tribe, and the buffalo. She then continued, explaining the mysterious monster of the large fist and the dust that held the White Buffalo. "After that, our mother scooped me up and brought me here. She gave me a good scolding and then sent me home through one of those doors on the balcony."

"Oooooi, now I 'ave an 'eadache. Thanks, Pash. Anyways, you're not the only dog 'ere who took a magical, mumsey trip to this place. I 'ave also been 'ere before!" Harold shouted then, blurting out a complete lie. "Mum saved me from poppin' me clogs; there I was on the edge of a cliff walking wi' me young master. Peter, 'is name is. It was a lovely sunny day. I like a bit o' the ol' sun, you know. Then, all of a sudden, the rock gives way under me feet. I go a tumblin' over the side! So, there I was, getting ready to bite the big 'un, and just before I decorated the rocks with me claret, vroom! I'm scooped up! Nex' fing I know I'm 'ere. Long story short: she told me she loved me, to be careful, and shoved me through one o' them doors up there. Back 'ome I went."

Harold looked aimlessly around the Great Hall, looking for a new topic before Pasha asked any awkward questions about his lie. He finally noticed the dog bowls in front of the chair. "Why are there four bowls, Pash?"

"According to Mom, our other two brothers will be joining us."

"Where are they, then? I don't like to be kept waitin', know wot I mean, Pashy?" Harold bitterly stomped his paw.

"Patience, young puppies, patience."

"Was that you, Pashy? I didn't even see ya mouf move! 'Ow'dya do dat?"

"It was a male voice, Harold."

"Oh, yeah, good point. Now, I'm spooked. There's no one else 'ere," Harold whispered.

60

"Yes, there is," affirmed a tall, slim man in a long, golden gown. He was suddenly standing beside the great chair right behind Harold. The dog spun quickly, tripping over his fumbling paws, and crashed in a heap at the feet of the man, who seemed to take no notice at all.

"I am the Keeper. I control the balance of good and evil, and you, my beautiful puppies, are the tools I will use to maintain that balance. It is now time for you to learn."

"Keeper of wot?" asked Harold, regaining his feet.

The man glared at the dog's response. "Just, the Keeper. I will ask you not to interrupt, young one. All of your questions will have answers in time. Patience is required. Now, there are a few details about this castle which need explaining. I have found you an excellent guide. I believe you know her quite well."

Pasha and Harold looked at each other, wondering who this mystery guide could be.

"Where are my beautiful puppies?" Pasha and Harold looked up toward the sound of the voice. Standing in front of an open door on top of the balcony was their mother, Sasha. Pasha and Harold raced up the stairs to greet her, licking her face furiously. The Keeper smiled at the reunion and vanished.

"Stop that; you're soaking me," she said, chuckling. "Follow, my children. It is time for your education to begin. I will show you around the castle today, and then every day for the next week you will be trained to use your powers."

Pasha perked up. She remembered her mother saving her at the Lost Mountain. Would she be able to make lightning strike? Could she use it to save the White Buffalo and the tribe?

Sasha continued, "At the end of your training, you will be asked the question. Your answer will be the most important decision you will ever make. It will have consequences for both of you, your owners, and the rest of the human race."

"So, no pressure then?" Harold added. Pasha gave him a hushing nudge.

As Sasha moved away from the open door, it swung itself shut. It was of the same ornate wood as the great chair below. The dark colors of the door were a contrast to the white marble of the rest of the hall. Turning back to look, she explained, "This door is the gateway to correct wrongs. From time to time, it will summon you to this place, through this door, which will transport you to a place where others need your help. The mirror in the center of the door will show a vision of you, and what you are doing, wherever you are on your mission."

Harold butted in. "It looks like any old ordinary door wiff a mirror in da middle, know wot I mean!"

"That's because there is no one on a mission at the moment."

"Do people and dogs go on missions, Mother?" Pasha gave a glance to the paintings again. No image of a human could be seen, only dogs.

"Now that's a good question, Pasha. Only the chosen go through that door, although there were once two humans that ventured through with their dogs. Unfortunately, they certainly regretted it."

"Why, Mumsey?"

"I cannot tell you that, Harold. Let's just say that the saga has been ongoing for many years and there have been a lot of casualties."

Pasha wanted to know more. "What do—?"

"Hush, child. All in good time," Sasha interrupted. Pasha stopped in mid-sentence. "Oh," Sasha added, "there is also one other creature that uses that door. His name is Ozzy; you will meet him only when he has a mind to show himself... and, Harold, my son, please don't give him any of your lip." Sasha moved along the balcony to the next of the four remaining doors.

"'Ey, that's me," Harold shouted, looking into the door's framed mirror. Pasha peered into the glass. The image was of Harold, sound asleep on a hardwood floor. A boy walked into frame, chubby, his hair disheveled. He wore such a sad look on his pale face. "That's me master, Peter."

"He looks so sad," commented Pasha.

"Doesn't 'e though?" Harold solemnly agreed. "'E is the poster boy for down in the dumps. I try to cheer him up when I can." Harold turned to Sasha. "Wait, 'ow can I be 'ere an' there?"

"OK, I will explain. When summoned here, as you were today, it is your inner self that comes, not your physical self. Your body stays just where you were, in a sleeping trance."

"What happens if somebody tries to wake me up?" asked Pasha, thinking about Tiffany and Chloe back in Arizona as her last memory, before showing up here.

"That's OK, child. Time here has no real meaning; one year in this place is but a few minutes back there, so no one would ever really know you were gone. Peter just walked by your side, Harold, thinking you were asleep. When we are finished here, you will wake right up as if you had been dozing for only a few moments. Peter will realize nothing odd."

"I'm extremely good-lookin' while I sleep," Harold added, his eyes fixed on the mirror.

"Yes, you are," Sasha agreed proudly.

"Is my door the same one I went through before?" asked Pasha.

"Yes, it's the one at the end of the hall, Sweetie."

"Well, who are these two middle doors for?"

"These doors are for your brothers. They are still not quite ready to come here yet."

Pasha ran off to look at her mirror. "Look, Harold, it's me!" Harold had no interest in seeing his sister in her mirror as he was far too busy still admiring himself.

"Wot 'appens if I open me door, Mum?" he asked, curiously reaching for the handle.

"No, Harold!" Sasha scolded. "You will return, but it's not time to go back yet. There's so much more to see and do today."

"OK, Mumsey, next question," said Harold. "Who is this Ozzy bloke then, and when do we get to meet 'im?"

"He will introduce himself in good time. However, I repeat: do not upset him at any cost, for there will be a time when he will help you beyond anything you can imagine. That is all I can say,"

Sasha warned in a hard tone, turning abruptly to end the discussion. Harold and Pasha quietly followed her down the far staircase. It was not long before Harold broke the silence again.

"Where 'as dat nutty geezer in da dressing gown gone?"

"Harold, you shouldn't talk of the Keeper that way."

"Who is he, Mommy?" inquired Pasha.

"The Keeper is... well, he is everything when it comes to this place," explained Sasha. "He controls everything and sees everything. The Keeper is our ultimate master, and he determines where our help is needed."

"He keeps the everything in balance?" asked Pasha.

"That is the best way to put it, Pasha." The trio reached the bottom of the staircase.

"Wot, so now I 'ave two masters? It's 'ard enough doing wot one wants, know wot I mean?" Harold complained as he jumped onto the Keeper's large chair.

"Get off of there!" Sasha shrieked, lunging toward the chair and baring her teeth. Harold shrank back into the corner of the large chair, but before he could slink off, his hairs stood on end as a thick, Australian voice resonated throughout the hall.

"That white-tailed dog,
Is such a disgrace.
Make him fall,
Flat on his face."

Harold's eyes widened as he began to rise from his place on the Keeper's throne. His paws dug into the air but did not find the comfort of the ground. Instead, he whimpered as he floated further and further away from the safety of the chair. Once clear of everyone else, he found himself quickly falling toward the hard marble floor, where he landed in a heap.

"Ouch, dat 'urt!" he complained, jumping to his feet and shaking his head.

"Maybe that will teach you to respect the Keeper."

A koala was standing beside the Keeper's chair with what looked to Harold like a toy magic wand. Harold stopped his complaining and stared for a moment in disbelief. He then suddenly exploded into laughter, falling on the floor in hysterics. "It's a teddy bear, jus' like da one me master takes to bed with 'im every night!"

"I'm Ozzy, mate," the little bear announced. "And you, Mr. White Tail, have not made a very good start with me, have you? Would you like to give it another blast?" Ozzy replied as he twirled the wand between both paws.

"An' why should I do dat?" Harold asked, rolling his eyes. "After all, you're jus' a little teddy bear with a toy magic stick."

Ozzy lowered his head and started to whisper:

"Teach the white-tailed dog,
That's not good at starts,
For two whole days,
I'll command smelly farts."

Harold immediately let out a fart that echoed through the Great Hall. "Uh oh," was all he could manage before cutting loose another loud one. Pasha covered her nose with her paw. Harold turned and sniffed his backside, quickly pulling his head away, tears now rolling down his cheeks. If a dog's face could turn red, this was as close as it got.

"Right, little puff ball. Wot ever ya name is, you don't wanna be messing with me. I can be really bad, know wot I mean!"

Ozzy pointed his wand once again at Harold and shouted, "Again!"

Harold's eyes got larger and larger as he lowered his body down toward the floor. With his belly just touching the ground, he started to let out the loudest, longest fart anyone had ever heard. The chandeliers started shaking, as did all of the windows in the Great Hall. Harold could only groan with the effort.

"OK, OK!" the dog pleaded. "I give up! You are the nic-
est——" Ozzie grinned and pointed the wand again. A fart followed
it. As Harold finished, "—bear in the world!"

"That's not enough, White Tail. You must promise to respect the Keeper at all times." Ozzie pointed once again.

"I promise! Wot ever you say!"

"All right, Ozzy, enough," commanded Sasha, as she tried
to muffle her sense of smell. "I think my son understands."

The chandeliers were now shaking so violently, plaster had
started to fall onto the hall floor. "Stop," commanded Ozzy.
Harold collapsed into a heap.

"Righty ho, Sash. Let us try again. My name's Ozzy, and
what are your names?"

"Me name's 'arold, and you, sir, are the best koala bear in
the world. It's nice to meet you, Sir Ozzy."

"By dabe's Basha," Pasha said stuffily, her paw still covering
her nose.

"Come again, matey?" Ozzy asked, laughing.

"My name's Pasha," she said, trying again, but could not
help cringing as she took in another breath of air.

"Nice to meet you, Pasha," Ozzy replied, grinning. "No
need to call me sir, Harold. Just Ozzy will do. Where are the other
two, Sasha? I thought there were four of them."

"I hope they will be along in due time," Sasha explained.
"For different reasons, they are not quite ready."

"All righty then, now you know how it works," said Ozzy.
"I realize this is a bit overwhelming. Therefore, tomorrow we will
begin with the powers. Now, go home and rest, puppies. You are
in for a tiring day!" the little koala informed them as he chuckled to
himself.

"Come, my children," Sasha said as she beckoned her children back up the stairs to their respective doors and ushered them
through. Harold gave her a loving lick before jumping back
through his door. Pasha was not leaving without asking one last
question. "Momma, will you be here with us tomorrow?"

"I am afraid I cannot. You must endure the training without help. I think it would be hard for me not to interfere." Sasha gave her daughter a wink and touched Pasha's soft, black nose with her own. "Just know that I love you. Also... please try and keep your brother out of trouble."

"I will, Momma," promised Pasha. "How hard can that be?" She stepped through the door.

Pasha opened her eyes to see Tiffany looking down at her.

"Pasha. You're okay!" Tiffany hugged the dog tightly. Pasha gave her a reassuring bark. "Come inside, Pash. In case that thing comes back." Tiffany and Chloe turned and ran back into the house. Pewter came scampering out of the back room and nearly tackled Pasha as well.

"Uh, Tiff... What just happened?"

"I don't know, and right now, I don't care. Pasha is okay. Whatever that thing was, it is gone."

Pasha had to scrape Pewter off her side as she rose to her feet to reveal the little golden ball lying on the ground. It was dark and made no sign of movement. Pasha casually picked it up in her mouth, dropped it off in her kennel, and went back inside the house as if nothing had happened.

*****

Harold awoke on the hard wood floor of the house. His master, Peter, was making a ruckus in the adjoining kitchen. He soon came out shoving the last bits of a biscuit into his mouth.

"Harold," he called with a spray of crumbs, "you're awake!" The boy gave a rare smile and began to pet the dog ferociously. "Come on, boy. Let's go out to the garden."

'Ere we go again, thought Harold, following Peter outside. The usual routine followed. First, he had to jump up and lick his master on the face, then wag his tail as Peter picked up a tennis ball. With a little yawn, Harold would fetch the ball and place it back at Peter's feet.

He wished that, for just one day, his master would do something different, something a little dangerous, not just the same old thing day in and day out.

Chapter Seven

T he early morning silence gave way to children's laughter as they waited for the school bus. The hot Arizona sun was already nibbling away at the edges of the clouds as they moved gracefully across the deep, blue sky.

Pasha was lying in the yard, her golden ball in front of her outstretched paws, eagerly waiting for the day's events to start. The orb remained dark, but it was hers now. It was the gateway to other worlds, adventures, and she could actually touch it. In the glassy orb, she could see the possibilities. She could help the tribe of the Lost Mountain and any others in need. This was her destiny.

Tiffany opened the glass sliding door; about to wish her pet good morning, when she noticed the golden ball. She froze for an instant, fighting the urge to yell at Pasha to get away from it. Instead, she chose another option. Hurriedly, she retreated into the house, locking the door behind her. She had not forgotten the previous day's events.

Pasha waited patiently with her eyes fixed on the ball, wishing it would move. Hours of intense concentration passed, and finally her eyes began to close. Soon, she drifted off to sleep. She had slept all day and, still, nothing. At nearly midnight, the ball suddenly flashed with a brilliant light, bounced up, and started to spin around her still sleeping body.

*****

At the castle, Harold was sitting and waiting outside of Pasha's door. As it opened, he remarked, "Typical woman. 'ad to do ya 'air, did ya?"

"What would you know of a typical woman, Harold? Don't you live in a house full of men?" Pasha countered as she ran past him and down the stairs.

By the time Harold had caught up with her, Pasha was sitting in front of the Keeper's empty chair. Things were a bit different today. On each side of the chair were two large suits of armor. They stood about six feet high, each holding a large lance and shield. Harold plopped down next to her and, always the impatient one, complained, "Wot? Is everyone gonna keep me waitin' today? Wait, those are new."

"Do I have to teach you another lesson?" Ozzy asked, appearing from behind the chair. "A better idea, perhaps I should have my friends here do it." He glanced back at both the suits of armor.

"No, sir, oh Great One. Yesterday was enough for me. I just wanna learn." Harold beamed a smile at Ozzy.

"If you remember the spell," Ozzy warned, "it lasts for two days." Harold's smile dropped out of sight. "Right then, cobbers. Let us get down to it. Today will be a long day, to say the least." Ozzy jumped up onto the Keeper's chair to start the day's activities.

'Ow come you can get up there? That's not fair!, ran through Harold's mind, but aloud he meekly assured, "I'm ready to learn, sir."

Pasha, still silent, raised one paw.

"Please, sir. Can I talk?"

"Yes, Pasha, what do you want?"

Pasha asked Ozzy if she could have some water. "Yes, Pasha, of the two bowls in front of the chair, the large one is yours." Ozzy pointed his wand at the floor in front of the chair. Two bowls grew from the marble floor with one continuing to twice the size of the other. They both began to fill with water.

Harold's face dropped and he was just about to complain about the size of his bowl when Ozzy raised his wand, warning, "Don't!"

Harold shut his mouth quickly and shrugged. "I wasn't gonna say a word, sir, oh Great One."

"Let's get to it," urged Ozzy as Pasha finished drinking. "You are here to help balance good and evil in your human world. To assist you with this, the Keeper has given each of you certain powers. This has been your destiny since before you were born. No questions!" Ozzy pointed the wand again at Harold who looked innocently at the floor. He continued, "Your parents served our cause extremely well for a number of years, but now it is your turn to take over. Your powers, Harold, are shown by your white markings: your tail and tongue."

"I didn't know you had a white mark on your tongue," remarked Pasha. "I have a small black mark on mine."

"Well, it's not some fink I'm very proud of. It's bad enuff 'aving a pure white tail."

"Well, your white marks are signs of your power. When commanded, your tail will act like elastic and your tongue like a rope."

Harold looked smugly at Pasha and commented that he had more powers than she did, as she had no white markings at all.

"Well, that's not exactly true," Ozzy interrupted. "Pasha has no white markings because she has no restrictions to her power. The small black marking on her tongue is a sign that her power is only limited to her own mind. If she really believes she has a power, then she does. That's why she will be the leader of the pack."

"Oh, that's just great! Yesterday morning I only 'ad dozy Peter as me master, then the Keeper was added as number two, then you at number three, now Pasha is the fourth. Are you sure there ain't anyone else who wants to 'ave a go? Might as well invite the 'ole wide world to be me master, know what I mean!"

"Well, that's just the way it is. Both your powers and human speech will only work when you are here or on a mission, and then only if you have your golden balls with you." Pasha and Harold both looked around for the little orbs. "Don't worry; they're safe and waiting for you. You have finally reached an age where you can responsibly look after them, as they will look after you. Now follow me."

Pasha and Harold followed Ozzy as he jumped from the chair, and waddled behind it, stopping in front of a large door, which rose from the floor. It faded from marble white to dark brown wood. Frameless, it hovered just above the floor. Harold walked around the door, but saw nothing but the other side of it.

"'Ow is that just 'anging in the air?" he asked.

"There are a lot of things you won't understand here. Just accept what you see and all will be well," explained Ozzy as he gripped the handle and opened the door. "Follow me."

The two dogs did as they were told, walking through the door and out the other side.

"Well, that did nuffink for me," Harold moaned, before looking at Pasha in amazement. Around her neck was a beautiful gold necklace that held her golden sphere close to her chest. Harold looked down to see exactly the same thing around his neck, and commented, "Now, that's what I call bling." Pasha and Ozzy just stared blankly at Harold. "What? 'erd it on the telly, know wot I mean."

Ozzy's face turned deadly serious as he explained, "Now remember. If you lose these at any time, you will also lose all of your powers and will not be able to return to the castle or your human masters. From this day forward, as you enter the castle through your door, your ball will automatically be attached to the necklace around your neck; when you leave, only your ball will appear next to you in your human world."

Pasha and Harold walked around the Great Hall, proudly displaying their new necklaces.

"I'm 'ank Marvin! What about you, Pash?"

"What does that even mean?" asked Pasha.

"Oh, get with it, Pash. 'ank Marvin, Starvin'; it's cockney for 'ungry."

Pasha chuckled before replying, "I am a bit hungry too."

"A bit hungry, eh? That's very posh. You sound just like me master on a good day. If you're not careful, you'll end up as boring as 'im."

"I take it you need some tucker, mates."

"I'm not sure I like the sound of this tucker fing. What about putting another shrimp on the barbie, Oz?"

Ozzy just shook his head at Harold's quip, but could not hide an amused smirk. The koala pointed his wand at the two empty bowls and commanded:

> "Two puppies with balls,
> Both new to this club,
> Their bellies not full,
> Fill their bowls full of grub."

Harold ran to his bowl and beheld a magnificent sight: it was overflowing with prime tender beefsteak. "Well done, Oz! This beats the cheapo canned food I get at 'ome."

"Glad to be of service. Now eat up; we have a lot of work still to do."

Pasha and Harold gobbled their meals in record time, both licking their bowls clean.

"Right, mateys. It's now time to get down to the serious stuff." Ozzy raised his wand high into the air and waved it around as he chanted:

> "With nets and bars
> And targets galore,
> With tiles a-soft
> All over the floor,
> A lot of effort
> Is now in need,
> 'Cause both the puppies,
> Have had their feed."

With a flash and a bang, the whole hall lit up and filled with smoke, making visibility virtually impossible. When the smoke cleared, the hall was full of new additions. Wide bars were hanging in the air, and every wall was covered with round shooting targets.

"This equipment will help you get used to your powers," Ozzy explained. "You'll practice daily for the rest of the week. First will be Harold. I want you to swing up to the top of the hall using your tail and your tongue."

"Huh? Are you crazy?"

"You can do it, Harold," Ozzy explained. "All you need is to believe that you can. Your powers are instinctive. Inside, you already know what to do. Your tongue and tail can grip onto things and act as an elastic band, but you must first activate it with this chant:

> "White is my tail,
> Not rigid like a stick.
> I command with the power
> Of Tail-lastic!"

Harold spun his head around to check out his tail, but it looked no different than usual.

"Harold, you have to do the chant yourself, goofball," Pasha informed, giggling.

"OK, 'ere I go," Harold said as he took his stance once more.

> "White is my tail,
> Not rigid like a stick.
> I command with the power
> Of Tail-plastic!"

He turned to check his tail, but his mouth dropped in shock. His tail was covered in a sheet of white plastic that made it stick out rigidly like a flagpole.

"What's going on, Ozz?" Harold asked in a terrified voice.

"I said Tail-lastic, not Tail-plastic! Now try it again!" Fearful his tail would remain rigid, Harold quickly took the stance again and chanted:

74

"White is my tail,
Not rigid like a stick.
I command with the power
Of Tail-lastic!"

Harold closed his eyes and gingerly turned before opening them slowly. His tail looked normal again.

"Did it work?" he asked.

"Well, now, matey, there's only one way to find that out. Get up on the bars."

Harold stood still for a moment, getting his nerve up. "OK... 'ere I go!" He took a leap high into the air and immediately crashed back to the floor in a heap.

"Well, some of us are slower than others," Ozzy whispered with a smirk.

"Come on, Harold," encouraged Pasha. "You can do it."

Harold looked once more to the ceiling, closed his eyes, and leaped again. At the height of the jump, his tongue shot from his mouth and coiled around the lowest bar. That was as far as he got. Harold just hung there, squirming like a fish on a hook.

"Not a good start. It is much quieter now, though." Ozzy winked at Pasha. "All right, my girl, you try."

"But..."

"Yes, well, you have a bit more direct method for getting to the top. I want you to run, extend your paws in front of you, and... well... fly."

"Just like that? Fly?" asked Pasha. She was getting nervous.

"Exactly——oh, watch out." Ozzy pulled Pasha out of the way as Harold crashed once again to the floor. His tongue reeled back into his head like a measuring tape.

"Now go, Pasha."

Pasha walked slowly toward the end of the hall, composing herself, and determined not to fail as Harold had. Running the last few yards to the end, she turned and dived forward at full speed. She did not fall, but flew slowly just above the floor, under the bars, all the way to the end of the hall. However, not knowing how to stop and land, she crashed into the wall at the end of the hall. Her head going straight through the center of a target, the only thing visible was her rear end.

"Well done, Pashy! You scored a bull's-eye!" Harold teased, while laughing on the floor.

"At least she wasn't a total failure like you. Try again, Harold," Ozzy shouted harshly.

"I'll try somefink new," Harold announced as he raced down to the end of the hall just below Pasha's squiggling rear end. He concentrated for a moment and whipped his tail. It extended upward, curled around his sister, and pulled her free. With great concentration, he then gently set her down beside him. "You did well, old girl," he told a bewildered-looking Pasha.

"So did you, Harold," said the enthused koala as he walked toward them. "Teamwork will be crucial on your missions. Now, knowing what you can do, swing up and touch the ceiling."

Harold ran down the hall toward the lowest bar and leaped again. This time his tail extended, wrapping around the bar. He swung in a complete circle, letting go with his tail and shooting out his tongue to the next highest bar. Pasha and Ozzy laughed with delight at his acrobatics. In a few moments, he reached the bar nearest the ceiling and began to swing around in a circle. He kicked his feet off the ceiling every time he came around.

"'Ow, ake at ou uzzy ear!" he said, though he could not be understood with his tongue going to other uses.

"I don't think he's going to stop," an alarmed Pasha said as Harold continued to swing around the bar, winding closer and closer like a spool of thread. The dog finally came to a rest hanging once again by his tongue, now coiled hopelessly in a knot.

"Well, it was fun while it lasted," declared Ozzy, chuckling as he waved his wand high. The bar disappeared, leaving Harold and his now long and floppy tongue heading for what could have been a fatal crash. Pasha gasped, but Ozzy was ready, bringing Harold to a soft landing upon the floor. Slowly, he collected his tongue. Once it was all back in his mouth, Harold could continue with his first love, talking.

"Phew! That was a close one! I was nearly brown bread there."

Ozzy and Pasha just looked at each other, not knowing that brown bread was cockney for dead.

"Well, don't be such a cocky matey, then. You did well apart from that. Now, rest, and we'll try again in a minute."

The two dogs spent their rest time checking out each other's necklaces. "Try and nick me ball, Pash."

"No, we were told to leave them alone."

"OK, goody-two-shoes. I'll take it out me-self." Harold tried to loosen the ball, but, though it did not look fixed in any way to the necklace, it was stuck firm.

"Leave your ball alone, Harold. It's time to get back to it," Ozzy demanded.

Pasha wasted no time and dived forward, flying slowly just above the ground. Ozzy, not wanting any more accidents, shouted, "Think 'stop' and you will." She concentrated on stopping and, just as Ozzy had said, she found herself hovering just above the ground.

"Now think about turning around." Pasha did as she was told and started to turn around, but she was so impressed with herself, she forgot to think of stopping. She continued turning, faster and faster. Predictably, Harold collapsed on the floor laughing at his sister, who by now was spinning so fast, she had become a black blur.

"Sort it out, Ozz. I don't wanna lose me sister, know wot I mean."

"Ah, is that a glimpse of compassion I detect, Harold?" Ozzy raised his wand, pointed at the spinning Pasha, and chanted:

"Oh, black spinning dog,
Spin no more.
Place her back down,
Upon the floor."

Pasha slowly stopped spinning and landed gently on the floor.

Harold rushed over to her, asking, "You okay, Pashy?" while licking her head.

"I think I am," Pasha replied as she jumped to her feet, but fell back down just as quickly.

"You drunk?" asked Harold.

"No, she's just dizzy. Lie on the floor for a while and you will be all right. You can each have one more go, but then you have to return home until tomorrow."

While Pasha recovered, Harold took the initiative and launched himself into the air, swinging between the bars like a monkey, releasing his tongue just in time to catch the next bar with his tail.

"Hey, Pash, this is easy after all!" he shouted as he swung down over Pasha's head. Not wanting to miss out, she jumped up and flew through the air to join him.

As both dogs became more certain, they increased their speed, but Harold, predictably, got a bit over-confident. He swooped down toward one of the knight's armor displays, which stood on each side of the Keeper's chair, getting a little too close and clipping the helmet. The knight's armor started to rock from side to side, finally came crashing down to the floor, and broke into hundreds of pieces.

Harold dropped to the floor, his tail reeling back in. First, he looked down at the scattered armor, and then fearfully at Ozzy. Ozzy just stared back, waiting to see Harold's reaction to what was about to happen.

Harold's eyes bulged as the pieces of armor started to move by themselves. Each piece found its way to its correct place and, before long, the armor was once again complete, though still lying flat on the floor.

Harold planned to try to push the armor back up to its original spot, but before he could put his nose on the tip of the helmet, there was a loud clattering noise. Slowly, the armor lifted itself up and stood in an attack stance, aiming its lance directly at Harold's neck. Harold gulped as he watched the armor start to lunge forward.

"Stop!" shouted Ozzy. "Retire, Sir Knight." The knight withdrew its lance, stood up tall, and shuffled back into its original place. Harold meekly retreated from the stiff knight.

Pasha had witnessed everything from high in the hall and landed next to the visibly shaken Harold.

"Wot was all that about, Oz?" Harold asked.

"That, matey, was Sir Hilderin, one of the original knights who protected this castle from the time it was built over a thousand years ago. The other is Sir Canotin. They still protect the castle and its contents. As long as you only enter from the doors on the balcony, and as long as you respect them, they will not hurt you. However, if you enter through the main castle doors, I will not be able to protect you from them. Anyway, I think that is enough for today, mateys. Tomorrow we will learn about the rest of your powers. Now, go upstairs and through your doors."

For once, Harold was lost for words, his legs still visibly wobbly with fright as he ran up the stairs and through his door. Pasha stayed behind and asked Ozzy if she could practice a little more before she went. "Ah, initiative, that is a good quality for the leader. What would you like to learn?"

"My mother saved me once using lightning bolts. I want to learn how to use them."

"Paw Power! A bit advanced, young Pasha, but very power-ful. Follow me."

Ozzy led her toward the targets at the end of the hall.

"These targets are much better for hitting with lightning than with your head," Ozzy remarked with a chuckle. "I want you to focus on those targets, see the lightning hitting them in your mind, and then call them forth with the magic words, 'Paw Power!' Are you ready?"

"Yes, I am," she answered nervously, as she glared at the target, which was about 30 feet away. The target ceased to be in her mind and turned into a large grasping hand made of dust. Pasha felt a crackle of energy run through her and exclaimed, "Paw Power!"

A large bolt of lightning struck down from the ceiling, hitting the ground midway between Pasha and the target. The lightning blast sent both Ozzy and Pasha flying backwards.

"Okay, enough of that," shouted the dazed koala as he staggered back to his feet. "There will be plenty of time to get that one down, and not hurt me in the process. Perhaps you should return home and rest."

Pasha was suddenly quite dizzy. The effort to call the lightning had zapped most of her energy, and all she wanted to do now was sleep.

"Good idea," was all she managed before trundling back up the staircase to her door.

"Oh, and Pasha," shouted Ozzy from below. She turned back. "You did a great job today. You're a natural, like your mother." Pasha smiled warmly at the koala, turned, and exited through her door.

Arriving back in Arizona, Pasha gave a long sigh. After such a long, hard day's work, it was still night. Wondering whether she would ever get used to the time lapse, she entered her kennel, totally exhausted, only to find Li'l Pewter curled up in the middle of her bed. Pasha nudged the cat over with her nose and settled down.

*****

Morning came all too quickly for Pasha. Tiffany awakened her by banging on the roof of her kennel. "Come on, Pasha! Chloe and I are taking you shopping."

Before Pasha could think of a way to resist, Chloe had put her arm in the kennel and clipped the leash onto her collar. Pasha reluctantly crawled from her cozy bed, accidentally stepping on Pewter with one of her hind legs. Li'l Pewter woke with a shriek and scampered from the kennel to the safety of the house.

Tiffany and Chloe really knew how to shop, and it was early evening before they returned home, each of them carrying so many bags, even poor, tired Pasha had to carry one in her mouth. While making her way to the back door, Pasha thought, at last I can get some more sleep.

Tiffany and Chloe had other ideas. They had bought a jewelry-making kit, and they excitedly dragged Pasha away from the door to Tiffany's bedroom to make some "canine jewelry." It was midnight before Fay shouted up to the girls to stop and go to bed. Those words were like heaven to Pasha's earring-clad ears.

Chloe was to leave for a vacation with her mother the next day, so Pasha knew she and Tiffany would pretend to be sleeping but would talk all night. Pasha was concerned that tomorrow was going to be a tiring day, and the only way she would get any rest was to make her escape now.

Pasha tried to sneak quietly to the door, but the jewelry ruined that plan, clinking all the way with the necklaces and long, stick-on earrings the girls had made for her. As she reached the door, she barked as if commanding that someone let her out; Chloe opened it obligingly. When Pasha reached her bed at last, she decided that if anyone woke her this time, a little nip with her sharp teeth would be completely justified. Li'l Pewter strutted behind her, covered in "feline jewelry." They were both snoring before their heads hit the warm blanket in the kennel.

Chapter Eight

Harold had plenty of sleep in London; his master had been reviewing for a school test all the previous day. He was up at dawn and crawling through the hole he had dug, behind the big blackberry bush at the end of his master's garden. Freedom at last, he thought, starting the two-mile run from his home to Kentish Town where all his friends lived. Although none of them would be out this early in the morning, he planned on marking some trees on the way so no new upstart would try to take his territory.

As Harold marked the last of many trees and gateposts, he felt a strange sense of urgency to get home. It must be time for the castle, he thought. Running home as fast as he could, he scampered back through the hole.

Emerging from behind the bush, he confirmed his suspicions. His orb was rolling frantically all over the garden, as if searching for him. Harold ran toward the ball, meeting it in the middle of the lawn, and lay down, waiting for the ball to do its thing.

As usual, after he entered the castle, Harold sat patiently outside Pasha's door. Being a little tired from his morning's mission, he lay down to have a midday snooze. When Harold woke, he ran down the stairs to see whether Pasha had arrived, but there was no sign of her. Ozzy was asleep, snoring on the Keeper's chair.

Without a second's thought, Harold raced back up the stairs, opened Pasha's door, and dived straight through. Blimey, it's 'ot 'ere, he thought as he checked out Pasha's yard with only one thought on his mind. I bet she's got some tasty bones 'idden 'round 'ere somewhere.

He started to run, sniffing the ground. Not looking where he was going, his nose struck the side of Pasha's kennel. I bet the lazy moo is still in bed, he thought, peering cautiously through the entrance. With his thoughts confirmed, he pulled the still sleeping Pasha out of the kennel, not noticing Li'l Pewter. The kitten awoke at all the commotion and proceeded to follow them.

Pasha's ball was waiting patiently for her, bouncing gently on the ground next to her kennel. It was flashing brightly, a second sun in the bright afternoon. As soon as Harold had pulled Pasha clear of her little house, he lay down next to her. Pasha's orb now sprang into action with both dogs in position. Pewter kept close to the two dogs and remained unseen.

The door was not pleased with the intrusion of the uninvited Pewter. It swung open, and ejected the three onto the balcony. Pasha only awoke properly as her body hit the floor, jumping up in a fright. With her eyes fully opened, she gasped. Pewter was here, in the castle, and walking toward the stairs. Pasha immediately gave chase and Pewter bolted, each accompanied by loud clinking sounds from the jewelry still dangling from them.

"How did you get here?" Pasha asked as she closed in on the stunned cat. Pewter skidded to a halt and turned to face Pasha. He screwed his little mouth from side to side and stared. "Yes, Pewter, I can talk human." Pewter's eyes closed as he fell rigid on his side.

"Oh, great, now he's fainted," complained Harold.

"Leave him alone. This must be a big shock for him."

"A shock for 'im? Are you winding me up? First, you don't show up on time and I 'ave to come and look for you. Then I find you asleep with a cat, which should be your arch enemy! Then, and this is the best bit, you are both done up like a couple of jewelry salesmen! And you fink 'e is shocked?"

"Calm down, Harold!" Pasha gave her brother a little nip. "We'll have to hide him here today and smuggle him back with us later. We can't let Ozzy know there's someone else in the castle."

"Oh, now you're showing your true colors. Not such a goody-two-shoes now, are you?"

"Let's think. Where can we hide him?" Pasha looked down from the balcony. Ozzy snored away from the Keeper's chair. The suits of armor stood their silent vigil. Pasha was not taking the cat near them.

"Well, we can't 'ide 'im anywhere Sir Lancelot and his pal can see 'im. They'll stick 'im with their swordy fings."

"That's what I was thinking," agreed Pasha.

"Tell me, Pash, should we wake 'im up first or do I just carry 'im in me tail?"

"I think we should wake him up first. After all, if he wakes up not knowing he is meant to be hiding, he'll just walk out, and then we'll get it bad from Ozzy."

Pasha walked up to the still unconscious Pewter and whispered, "Li'l Pewter, wake up and don't panic."

That was just too much for Harold, who fell over laughing. "You're kidding me, right? Get out of the way, Pash. I'll wake 'im up."

"OK, but please be gentle with him. Pewter is a bit sensitive. Sometimes he acts like I am his mother."

"Are you for real? You're telling me that the cat finks it's ya baby? Oh wait, let me get this straight! 'E's not really a cat even though he looks just like the one I terrorize every day, and 'e certainly ain't no dog, not with that many whiskers. I've got it! 'E must be a cog!"

"What's that?"

"A cog is a cat that finks 'e's a dog! Ha ha ha!"

"Harold, stop that! He's just Li'l Pewter!"

Harold walked over to Pewter and gave him a big sloppy lick with his tongue. Pewter immediately woke and jumped back, hissing and swiping his claws toward Harold's face.

"Is 'e for real? Whether 'e's a dog, a cat, or a cog, the boy's got guts."

Pewter continued swiping at Harold while Pasha explained things to him. "It's like this, Pewter. We are in... this sounds weird, but we are in a large, magical castle... Here, both Harold and I can speak human. Maybe even you can, but I am not sure about that. Anyway, you must have got tangled up with the magic orb, and... Well, here you are."

85

"You forgot to tell 'im 'bout the powers bit. Your 'mother' and me 'ave powers. I just can't believe I am sitting 'ere explaining me-self to a cog." Pewter, who was then so exhausted he stopped trying to claw Harold, seemed to accept his situation.

"Pewter, you must listen to me now. No one must know you are here, or not only will Harold and I be in big trouble, you may also get hurt. We're going to hide you somewhere and, no matter what, you have to stay put until I come and get you."

"Okay, Mother, I'll do it on one condition: I get to see you fly." Pewter did not seem fazed at all that he could indeed speak human. "Oh, and the dumb one here can give me a demonstration of his, hmmm, talent. So to speak."

"Why I oughta..." Harold towered over Pewter, growling. "You've got a right big old mouf on you."

"Not now, boys," interrupted Pasha. "Pewter, you have to stay up here and keep quiet. I promise to give you a demonstration of our powers as soon as I can, but not right now. Okay?"

"Trust me, Mother, when I say that quiet will be my middle name." Pewter bowed his fuzzy little head politely.

"I've an idea." Harold sneered as his tail flicked around the cat's body and he ran off down the stairs. Pewter could not make a sound with his lungs squeezed tight. "We'll put him behind that big board with the circles on it at the end of the hall."

"Harold, no!" Pasha flew down to cut him off at the bottom of the stairs, when a familiar voice chimed in.

"Oh, great, you're here." Ozzy stretched and rubbed his eyes. "I guess you'll be wantin' some training."

Pasha whirled to face Ozzy while Harold continued off to the end of the hall and behind one of the large targets.

"Mornin', Pash," acknowledged Ozzy. "Where's Brainiac?"

Harold came barking from the end of the hall, emerging from behind a target.

"Sorry, Oz, just needin' nature's call. Know wot I mean!"

"Unfortunately, I do understand; it will take days to get the smell out."

"We're ready to start, Ozzy," chimed in Pasha, pawing at some of the jewelry dangling from her ear.

"What is this, a fancy dress party?" Ozzy remarked. "Take it off this minute. You can't work with that and your ball all tangled up!"

"I'm really sorry, Ozzy. My master stuck it on me and I can't get it off."

"Right then, I'll sort it out. Where is my wand?" Ozzy reached for his wand and pointed it at Pasha, saying:

> "Move the junk jewelry
> That is stuck to her fur,
> Not to a dog
> But the good-looking Bear."

Ozzy looked like a hippie from the flower-power era, or an over-the-top rap star, with the necklaces dragging on the floor as he waddled around. "Righty, mates. Let us get this party on the road. Today you will learn one more of your powers. The first to go will be Pasha—" But then, "What is that noise?" Ozzy asked, having heard a clinking sound coming from the end of the hall.

"I can't 'ear anyfink. You must be imagining it, know wot I mean," Harold assured him.

Ozzy frowned, looking around the hall. Then, shrugging his little shoulders, he continued: "Pasha, come over here. Now you will discover how powerful your powers can be. Move to the center of the hall and raise one of your paws, pointing it toward that target on the end wall."

"Um, Ozzy, maybe I shouldn't try the lightning again?"

"No lightning this time," Ozzy informed her. "Your aim is terrible anyway."

"Am I missing some fink 'ere?" asked Harold.

"I want you to visualize a fireball," Ozzy continued, "and hit the target at the end of the hall."

"Where? What's a target?" asked Pasha, feigning ignorance. Harold gulped loudly.

"That big board with the colored circles, that's a target."

"That's a target?" Pasha asked in a concerned voice.

"That's what I said. Now, do as you are told: point your paw."

Pasha sat in the center of the hall and lifted her paw, waiting for something to happen.

"Now you must repeat after me:

"In a world that is torn,
For good not to sour,
Make evil but a thorn;
I command Paw Power."

Pasha repeated the rhyme and sat still as a statue as she waited. Ozzy explained, "Now you have activated one of your most powerful weapons. You must be careful how you use it, for its power is enormous. Concentrate on a fireball striking the target."

Pasha and Harold looked at each other, knowing Pewter was behind that very spot.

Pasha reluctantly followed Ozzy's command. With her paw outstretched, she closed her eyes and awaited further instructions. "Now shout out, 'Paw Power!'" Pasha did, and flinched as a fiery ball shot out of her paw at great speed. It headed toward the end of the hall. Neither dog could look as the fireball hit the top edge of the target, exploding and destroying a large chunk of it.

Pewter, still draped in jewelry, screeched and ran from behind the smoking target, straight up the middle of the hall. Smoke trailed behind from his smoldering tail.

"Oops," Harold muttered as he turned to Pasha, who took off chasing the smoldering Pewter around the hall, calling for him to stop.

"Now I know it's a fancy dress party," stated Ozzy, chuckling. "One of the other dogs has come as a cat."

Pasha finally caught up with Pewter, dived onto his smoking tail, and patted it against the ground to make sure it would not completely burn off.

"Pewter, please hold still!" Pasha cried out.

"Right-oh, mateys. Who is going to explain this one?"

The secret was out, and Harold could not resist being the one to explain. After all, as far as he was concerned, he was blameless. Without pausing for breath, he gave his version: "I was 'ere on time as usual, and Pashy was sound asleep, so I waited for 'er 'ere. When she came through 'er door, the cog was with 'er. Then Pashy told me to 'ide it until we went 'ome tonight."

"Harold, that's not quite correct, is it?" Pasha asserted.

"Silence! I know exactly what happened. You cannot do anything without me knowing about it. Like the countless trees you marked this morning, Harold, and how you, Pasha, had no control over the jewelry."

"Oh, that's just great. Now we 'ave no privacy at all, know wot I mean."

Pewter, by now fully extinguished, jumped up on the chair and rubbed his head against Ozzy's soft fur.

"Look, he likes you. Don't be too annoyed at him," Pasha pleaded.

"Yes, I really, really like you, Koala Bear," Pewter mewed, "even if you do stink of eucalyptus leaves."

Ozzy stroked Pewter's head. "I'm not annoyed with you, fuzzy, and eucalyptus is a delicacy, for your information. No, it's you two who have done wrong."

"Oh, please, Ozzy, not the farts again! They make me feel really sick." Harold pressed his body as close to the floor as possible, almost bowing apologetically.

"I am going to let you both off this time, and you, Pewter, will stay right here with me while these two go about their drills." Ozzy turned back to the dogs. "Pasha, continue firing on the targets. Harold, I have altered the layout of the bars here in the hall. I will be timing you. I want you to swing up to the ceiling within 5 seconds. Go."

Pasha and Harold both continued to stare at Ozzy as if they did not understand.

"Ladies and gentlemen," shouted Pewter, "I think he means now."

Ozzy raised his wand, making sure to point it at Harold. An electrical spark popped underneath his belly and he jumped straight up in the air, his tongue instinctively whipping out to pull him to safety. Pasha got the message and turned to the targets, which were now brand-new and untouched.

"That's the spirit," said Ozzy.

*****

The training continued for the next few days. Pasha was now able to fly without difficulty and let loose fireballs on target. Harold had become a whiz at swinging with his tail and his tongue, even learning to use them as whips. Pewter was sneakier than ever, devising ways to stick with Pasha and follow her through to the castle no matter what the dog tried.

As dawn broke on the fifth day, Pasha was already awake and ready to go. Ozzy had informed them that soon it would be time for the question, whatever that meant. The bear would never answer follow-up questions. On that morning, she sat outside her kennel with her lifeless golden ball on the floor in front of her. Li'l Pewter was sitting attentively by the side of the kennel, waiting for the chance to jump in as soon as it went active. Pasha saw this and had a plan to keep the cat out. She would start running with the ball as soon as it began to glow. Pewter would never be able to catch up.

When the ball finally started to flash and move, rolling back and forth, and slowly around her, Pasha grabbed it and began to move. Pewter did not hesitate and leaped onto the startled Pasha before she could take a full step. She jumped up and shook her whole body, trying to dislodge the cat, who was hanging on to her collar for dear life. Pasha realized it was too late as they were both already on the balcony. Pasha's door slammed behind her as if disgusted that Pewter had once again invaded the castle.

Pewter was still clinging to Pasha's collar as he apologized. "Sorry, Mom, but I just couldn't resist. You should really try harder."

"Oh, Pewter. Why can't you just stay home?"

"I can stay home, Mom. I just won't."

Pewter turned and purred his way down the stairs toward the big chair. He had only managed to get halfway before Ozzy appeared in front of him.

"Shhh!" whispered Ozzy with his paw against his mouth as he ushered Pewter back up the stairs, explaining that the Keeper was on the chair and Pewter had to return through the door.

"Aw, that's not fair. Have you got any idea how hard it was to get here today?"

"You have to leave now," Ozzy said, stroking Pewter's back. "You can return tomorrow, but only if you go now."

"Who is that up there, Ozzy?" a deep voice asked from the Great Hall.

"It's Pasha; we're coming down now!" Ozzy answered. A shiver ran through his body as he opened Pasha's door and pushed Pewter through.

Ozzy and Pasha made their way down the stairs and sat in front of the Keeper who majestically occupied his throne. "Where is the other one?"

"I'm sorry, Keeper. He must have been delayed."

"Well, go upstairs and look in his mirror. Today is much too important for him to be late!"

Ozzy made his way back up the stairs. Looking into Harold's mirror, he gasped. "He cannot come yet! His master, Peter, has the golden ball in his hand!"

"Then we shall start with Pasha. I have come to assess your progress. First, show me your flying skill," the Keeper ordered with a stern voice. Pasha obliged with a tantalizing display, swooping under and over the metal bars Ozzy had conjured. She finished by hovering before the Keeper as she gently brought herself down in front of the chair.

"That really was excellent, Pasha. Well done, Ozzy."

Ozzy grinned and swayed his head from side to side.

"Now, you will show me Paw Power." Her smiling face dropped as she took her stance.

"Uh... lightning or fireball, sir?" Pasha asked meekly, hoping for the latter.

"Surprise me," responded the Keeper. Pasha concentrated on her specialty: one fireball coming up!

"But first," he continued, "that target is a little too big. Let's try something smaller, and not so boring." The target shrank to half its size and began to move back and forth. Pasha's heart sank.

Ozzy moved out of the Keeper's view, as he knew she might need a little help with this one. With her paw extended, she commanded, "Paw Power!" The powerful ball left her foot. What at first looked like a good shot started to veer away from the target. Ozzy sprang into action:

"Ball of fire,
Don't make me cry.
Make her shot
A certain bull's-eye."

The target at the end of the hall took an obvious jump a few feet to the left. The shot hit the center with such precision that the Keeper jumped to his feet, applauding. "What a good shot! Ozzy, you should be proud. You moved the target with great skill!" he said sarcastically. Ozzy's head sank into his shoulders as he waited for the wrath of the Keeper.

"This is a shambles!" the Keeper shouted, pacing up and down the hall with his hands clasped behind him. "First, one of your dogs doesn't turn up, and then the other one turns up with a cat." Ozzy's eyes bugged out. "Yes, I saw that. Nothing can happen here that does not take place before my very eyes. Although I must compliment Pasha on her flying, her Paw Power was pathetic. It seems to me that you have not been doing anything for the last five days. Remember, Ozzy, I only agreed to allow you to stay here permanently on the condition that these new charges passed their induction... with honors." The Keeper started to leave, glaring at Ozzy and adding, "If you do not turn things around, I will have no choice but to banish you back to the Outback!"

The Keeper disappeared through the door behind his throne. Pasha inquired, "What did he mean, Ozzy?"

"Well, matey, I was never meant to be here permanently. I met your parents many years ago while they were on a mission. I sort of tagged along and helped them from time to time."

"How did you know when they were going to be here if you haven't got a ball?"

"I would hide here in the Great Hall, only coming out when either of your parents were here. I will tell you the whole story, when and if Harold ever comes."

Pasha, now worried that Ozzy may be banished, asked, "Should I go through Harold's door and get him?"

"I'm not sure. Let's go look in his mirror and see what's going on."

Ozzy jumped on Pasha's back and the pair flew up to the balcony and landed in front of Harold's door. "Look, Pasha, his master is just leaving. He will be here soon. Let's get on with some work, since we're so far behind."

Pasha practiced her Paw Power as intently as she had her flight. As the hours passed, Ozzy and Pasha were so engrossed in what they were doing that they never even noticed Harold had not turned up. Pasha was hitting the target every time, now of the smaller and moving variety. Ozzy finally suggested they wrap it up for the day and sent her home to get some rest. When Pasha left, Ozzy went to investigate why Harold had not turned up. He looked at Harold's mirror to find he was lying down in his yard, his master nowhere in sight. Ozzy could see no reason why he had not entered the castle. Confused, Ozzy opened the door and was soon standing next to the sleeping dog.

"Harold, wake up," Ozzy whispered as he shook Harold's back.

Harold opened one eye and sighed as he tried to answer the concerned koala. An ordinary bark was all that came out of his mouth.

"Don't worry, cobber, I can read your mind. Peter has your golden ball, eh? If he still has it tomorrow, I will get it from him for you. You're way behind Pasha now, and if you can't catch up, you'll fail your final test."

Wot test?, Harold thought.

"The day after tomorrow, the Keeper will test your skills. If you fail, you will not be asked the question."

Ozzy could see Harold was not a happy dog as he bid him goodbye. He spent the night worrying, not sure whether the dogs would be ready in time. If not, then the Keeper would surely banish him back to the middle of the Outback.

Chapter Nine

As the next day's dawn approached in London, both Pasha and Harold entered the castle at exactly the same time. Pewter, predictably, was clinging onto Pasha's back. Harold just could not wait to tell his story of why he had been absent the previous day and launched straight into it.

"Hi, Pash and Pewt. You just 'ave no idea the trouble I 'ad trying to get 'ere yesterday," he whined.

"Why was that?" Pasha asked.

"It had better be a believable story," added Pewter.

"Well, it's like this. You know Peter, me master. 'E 'ad some sort of test fingy at school and, although 'e 'ad studied 'alf the night before, 'e failed dismally, coming bottom of the 'ole school. So anyway, if that wasn't bad enough, 'e got bullied for 'is entire trip 'ome. Those big bullies were pushing and taunting 'im. To cut a long story short, 'is dad let 'im 'ave yesterday off and he spent the entire day playing with me golden ball. 'E even took it to bed with 'im last night. Then, being the blinding supa 'ero that I am. I hatched me plan. I sneaked in to 'is room, real stealthy-like, and nicked it back. Mission successfully completed, know wot I mean! So that, me dear Pashy and Cog, is why I couldn't get 'ere yesterday. Did I miss anyfink good?"

"The Keeper came and Ozzy got in big trouble because we are so far behind."

"Well, *you* are so far behind anyway," taunted Pewter with a sarcastic smirk.

"Shush, Pewter," interrupted Pasha. "If we don't catch up, Ozzy may be sent away. We really have to get down to some hard work."

It was not long before Ozzy graced them with his presence. Even though they were all under extreme pressure, he never asked

Pewter to leave. After all, he had invited him to the castle. Ozzy even beckoned Pewter to sit next to him by patting the chair. Pewter proudly jumped up, sat next to him, and rubbed his head against Ozzy's soft fur.

With one paw stroking Pewter's head, Ozzy ordered the two dogs to the center of the hall to prepare to start work. Without hesitation or command, Pasha took her stance, commanded, "Paw Power," and scored a perfect bull's-eye. It destroyed the target, even though it was moving.

"Wow, Pash, that was fantastic! When did they start moving? 'Ow did ya do dat?" asked Harold.

"Never mind how she did it," Ozzy butted in. "I want to see something special today, Harold. Five seconds to the ceiling; go!"

"You can do it, Harold. You just have to want it with all your heart," Pasha whispered as Harold composed himself. He was up and swinging to the ceiling in seconds, barely making the time. Pasha gave him a hoot in congratulations.

"Well done, Harold," Ozzy called out as he clapped his paws furiously.

Harold landed in the same spot from which he had started and awaited Ozzy's next command.

"Now you will learn to use your powers together. Harold, pick up the targets with your tail and throw them in the air. Pasha, you will put a perfect hole through each of them with your Paw Power."

The two dogs were impressive with their precision in working together. Ozzy finally left his chair, clutching Pewter in his paws, and walked halfway down the center of the hall. He conjured a wooden barrel from thin air and placed the cat upon it. "Righty-oh, matey. I want you to stay exactly where you are, and reach out and grab Pewter with your tongue."

Pewter turned his head, and with a horrified look, shouted, "What? Can't he use his tail?"

"I'm probably going to regret this," warned Harold.

Before Pewter could object any further, Harold opened his mouth as wide as it would go. His tongue shot out a good twenty feet, but Harold had misaimed and, instead of scooping Pewter up, his tongue knocked the cat clean off the barrel.

"Oops." Harold dropped his head sheepishly and waited for Pewter to reappear. Pewter poked his head out from behind the barrel, Harold's wet slobber visible all over his face. Ozzy could not hold back his laughter.

"You did that on purpose," hissed Pewter. "You're on my list, White Tail."

"Seriously this time," said Ozzy. "I know you can do it with your tail; now let's get the tongue up to speed with a living target."

"Jump back up, Pewt, and I'll have another try," Harold ordered. Pewter reluctantly obliged, closed his eyes, and waited for Harold's wet tongue to hit. Harold concentrated as hard as he could and once more opened his mouth. His tongue passed just to the side of Pewter's body, wrapped tightly around the cat, and began its return back to Harold's mouth. Harold had not thought about his tongue's return journey, however, and the tongue returned to Harold's wide-open mouth, complete with the cat in tow.

"How do I taste?" asked Pewter.

Harold realized a fine coating of cat hair joined the terrible taste in his mouth. He began to wretch and cough, literally licking the floor to remove Pewter from his mouth. The little cat rolled on the floor, laughing.

"Good job, mate. Both of you," said an extremely pleased Ozzy. "Now you have as much time as you wish to practice here in the hall. I recommend you use it, for tomorrow the Keeper will test you again. He's going to test all of us."

Chapter Ten

As the Keeper turned from behind his chair, his golden embroidered cape swished around him, making him look like an expensive Christmas decoration. He stood in front of his chair, pausing briefly to look down at the two dogs sleeping peacefully at his feet. He could not resist a smile to himself before taking his seat, and then promptly jumped straight back up upon the realization that something was shrieking and clawing at his behind. Both dogs jumped up groggily, awakened by the cries of the now squashed Pewter, who leapt from the seat and ran the full length of the hall.

"What is that cat doing here?" stormed the Keeper.

Pasha and Harold just sat in front of him silently as Ozzy emerged from behind the chair. "What's all the commotion?" he asked, rubbing his tired eyes.

"The cat, it's back! You know what this means, Ozzy," ranted the Keeper in a harsh voice.

"The cat snuck into the hall with Pasha days ago. Should I send him away, sir?"

"I guess you are right. He can stay, but the dogs had better pass with flying colors or he will be banished—along with you!"

Pasha and Harold gulped, knowing that if they failed, they would now lose two friends. Pewter, thinking all was now OK, ran back and jumped straight onto the seated Keeper's lap. He looked down at the cat with disgust before sweeping him off the chair. "You may stay, but do not take liberties. Sit on the floor next to my chair and do not move."

"Sure thing, chief," acknowledged Pewter, who settled in to watch the proceedings.

The Keeper did a double take and glared at the cat's response, but he knew chastising this feline was a lost cause. He turned back to his purpose and clapped twice. "Let the tests begin.

I want a near-perfect demonstration of all your powers. There is no room for error. If you fail today, you will return to your normal lives. Your golden orbs will be confiscated and given to future worthy warriors. Pasha will start; you will give me a demonstration of your flying skills."

Pasha launched forward and upward, twisting as she ascended to the highest point of the ceiling. She arched her back and turned into a steep dive toward the Keeper's chair. As she passed the back of the tall chair, she swooped so close to the Keeper's head that the breeze knocked his tall pointed hat off and onto the floor. Noticeably upset at this, Pasha turned and with expert precision, clasped the hat gently between her paws, slowly hovered upward, and placed it perfectly back on to the Keeper's head.

Although he tried, the Keeper could no longer maintain his stern demeanor and, instead, allowed his face to crack with a faint smile. "That really was very good. Now let's see what Harold can do."

As Pasha landed gently on the floor, Harold leapt to the first bar with tongue and tail. His execution was perfect; reaching the ceiling in 4 seconds, he then began to descend. The Keeper raised one of his large hands and all of the bars disappeared. Harold twisted and began to free fall. Ozzy just looked away sadly, fretting that all was now lost. The dog never hit the ground. His tongue shot out and wrapped around one of the columns of the hall. He swung back to the floor with a perfect landing.

"Excellent, Harold, well done!" Pasha shouted, her tail wagging furiously.

Ozzy turned back to the test, shouting in support, "Bravo, matey! That was quick thinking. Bravo!"

"Yes, it was excellent," admitted the Keeper. "Improvisation will be crucial on your missions. You never know when the bar will be pulled out from under you, so to speak. Now, let us continue. Ozzy, please spell the targets and the two vases with flowers at each end of the hall smaller—at least half their normal size."

"Is that fair, sir?" asked a now really concerned Ozzy.

100

"I don't deal in fair. I deal in the balance of good and evil! Now do as I asked."

"Yes, sir," Ozzy replied meekly:

"Taking both of the vases,
The targets too,
Is the Keeper so wise,
To command them half size?"

Small explosions echoed around the hall, and smoke obscured all the targets and vases. As the haze slowly dispersed, it revealed the now much smaller targets. The two vases—one white, the other black—were then so small they were barely visible from a distance.

"Now let's see what you are really made of," the Keeper roared while he smirked to himself. Harold moved to the center and awaited instructions. "I want you to stay where you are and clasp both vases at once, place them on the floor in front of you, and then return them exactly as they are now."

Harold took a deep breath and began, commanding, "Taillastic and tongue's afar." His tail and tongue shot out, each gently clasping a vase from its narrow stand. He smoothly brought them toward himself and placed them gently on the floor as instructed. After taking another deep breath, he lifted the vases back into the air and sent them on their way back to their original places.

Harold's tongue was a lot quicker than his tail and reached its vase's stand first. With great care, he placed the first vase on its stand and turned all of his concentration toward his tail as it neared its target. Placing that vase proved a lot harder as he tried several times to center it on its stand. Harold, finally happy with the placement, released his gripping tail and watched in horror as the vase rocked from side to side before settling to its rightful place.

He turned to the Keeper, his tail wagging in satisfaction, until instructed to look at the floor. Harold slowly looked down to see a single flower which had dropped from vase to ground without Harold's notice.

"Oh, come on!" protested Ozzy. "That is not a failure."

"Yes, Mr. Keeper, sir," Pewter chimed in. "You said the vases had to go back, not the flowers."

"Hmmm, little cat, so I did. You are very perceptive. You pass, Harold. Now Pasha will continue, with her Paw Power, and remember, if you make a mistake, you will both fail. As a leader, you must learn that your actions affect everyone around you."

Pasha walked slowly to the center of the hall and stopped for a moment's thought. She turned toward the Keeper and asked, "Do I have to stay here?"

"No, you may move anywhere you want, but you must score a bull's-eye on every target and complete the test in less than one minute. Oh, and they, of course, will be moving targets. Clock, please, Ozzy."

Ozzy pointed his wand at the center of the opposite wall. Pewter paid close attention, thinking he could do some wonderful things with that wand if only he could lay his hands on it. Ozzy started his chant:

> "Place a timepiece upon the stone,
> With 60 seconds to lapse.
> Start the clock in a downward trend,
> The moment the Keeper claps."

As a large, lit-up clock appeared on the wall, Pasha readied herself. The Keeper rose to his feet and gave a single loud clap.

Instantly, Pasha launched herself high into the air and turned toward the first target. She aimed both her paws and commanded, "Paw Power!" Bolts of fire hit the first two targets dead center.

"Good shot, Pashy! Come on, girl, you can do it!" Harold encouraged.

Pasha turned her attention on the two targets floating in the air; two more balls of fire also scored direct hits as they darted back and forth.

As the clock ticked into the last five seconds, she accelerated toward the remaining two targets and fired from a greater distance. She knew if those two shots missed, her time would run out and she would fail. With so much hanging on those last two shots, everyone in the hall took a deep gasp of air and watched intently as the bolts of fire raced toward their targets. The clock showed one second remaining as the bolts struck their marks.

In total delight, Pasha hovered in the center of the hall. Pointing her paws in opposite directions, she fired again for a big finale. The two bolts smashed both vases into tiny pieces onto the floor.

"Bravo! Bravo!" the Keeper shouted as he rose to his feet and applauded vigorously. Pasha proudly landed in front of her cheering audience and waited for the Keeper's decision.

"Congratulations to both of you. I must confess, I did not think you could do it. Now, get yourselves some well-earned food. For afterward, you will be asked to make the most important decision of your lives."

Ozzy, knowing that Pewter was interested in his magic, asked, "Pewter, do you want to try your hand at some magic?" Pewter readily agreed and snatched Ozzy's wand from his paw. Pewter sat, composed himself, and then waved the wand around, pointing it at everything he saw, including the empty bowls.

"You 'ave to do the chanting fing," Harold complained as he impatiently waited for his food.

"What is the chant?" Pewter asked Ozzy.

"Point the wand at the bowls and repeat after me:

"Two puppies with bowls,
Their bellies not full,
Give them meat, not a shrub,
Fill their bowls full of grub."

Pewter repeated the chant and was spellbound himself to see the two empty bowls overflow with rich red meat. What he had not seen was Ozzy pointing at the bowls and whispering the chant.

As Pasha and Harold tucked into their feasts, the Keeper and Ozzy were whispering to each other by the side of the chair. Pewter, still clutching Ozzy's wand, saw this as his chance. He hid behind the far side of the chair, which he assumed was out of sight of everyone, and thought hard about what he wanted most in the world.

"I know," he whispered to himself as he started his chant and pointed the wand directly at his stomach:

> "Arizona Sun
> And London Smog,
> Make this cat
> Bark like a dog."

Pewter had no idea that Ozzy was peering through the legs of the chair the whole time. Just as the cat chanted the word, "dog," Ozzy commanded, "frog." Pewter, still unaware of what Ozzy had done, ran around the front and placed the wand on the floor in front of the chair.

Ozzy joined him immediately, unable to resist asking Pewter to meow. Pewter realized his game may have been over, but did not want to upset his friend and tried to meow using his human voice.

"That was pathetic, matey. Now, do it properly or I will send you home."

Pewter took a deep breath and opened his mouth, expecting to hear a deep bark. Instead, all he heard was, "Ribbit, ribbit!" Pewter's eyes sprang wide open. "I sound like a toad!" he screamed at Ozzy.

"No," Ozzy assured him, stifling a laugh, "a toad has a much deeper tone. Are you sure you are not ill? Because it sounds to me like you have a frog in your throat."

"Did you do that to me, Ozzy? Ribbit?" Pewter asked.

Ozzy relented. "Yep, I thought I would teach you a lesson. The magic is not in the wand; it is in me. The wand is just a special effect."

"Will you turn me back then? Ribbit?"

"No, my little friend. You can sound like a frog for the rest of the day."

Pewter kept objecting until Ozzy finally lost his patience and pointed his wand to make things worse:

"Little cat, sounding like a frog,
Keeps moaning and moaning; he just won't stop,
So I say now, and for the rest of the day,
He will not walk, but hop."

Little Pewter tried to run from the spell, but to no avail. He had only made it halfway down the hall when his running turned into hopping. With every hop, he let out a loud, "Ribbit, ribbit!"

*****

When Pasha and Harold had finished their meals, the Keeper clapped his hands and announced, "It's time for your decisions." The hall went silent as the Keeper stood and held both his arms in the air. "Let the scales be shown!"

The wall that had earlier displayed the clock now had a small light shining from it. The light was so bright, everyone squinted their eyes so they could keep watching, as it grew larger and larger until it filled the hall with light. When the light faded, an enormous picture of a pair of scales occupied the whole wall. The two scales each had a label, one "good" and the other, "evil." They were weighted heavily in favor of the evil side.

"What does that mean?" asked Harold.

"That is the balance of good and evil in the human world. It is our job here to make sure evil doesn't overcome mankind."

"How do we do that?" inquired a concerned Pasha.

"I will now tell you what will be expected of you and what rewards you will receive for your endeavors. When the time is right, I will summon you here through the power of your golden orbs, much the same as you have been summoned during your training period. Unlike your training, the missions awaiting you will be fraught with danger. These missions will be to fight evil and maintain the balance on the scales. When you arrive here, you will proceed to the middle door; this door is your entry to an area where evil is dominating. You will not always know where or what that evil is. That is for you to discover. Once you have found the evil culprit, you will bring it here to the Great Hall where the Castle Court will deal with them.

"Your reward for doing this, if you survive, will be a lifespan that will far exceed your master's, as well as the satisfaction of knowing that you have helped mankind. You will also earn Grimits, the castle currency; you may use these Grimits to purchase your choice of many other rewards."

"Wot if we say no?" Harold lowered his brow.

"Then you will leave here today, never to return. You will live a mortal life without any powers."

"Well, fanks a lot, mate, but I fink I'll stick with me boring life and me boring master." Harold tried to shake his ball from his neck. "Where should I put me ball? I fink I'll be toddling off 'ome now." Harold ran up the stairs and tried his doorknob. "Why can't I open me door?"

"I decide when you are allowed to leave here. You may not leave until after I have asked you the question," raged the Keeper.

"Well, let's get on with it then. I already know wot me answer is." Harold paced around impatiently, mumbling to himself.

"Harold, sit down at once!" an unfamiliar voice commanded. Harold looked around, confused. "Up here, Harold," the voice thundered again. Harold looked up to the top of the far wall where he could see the head of a dog.

"Why are you up there?" asked Pasha.

"I have passed away, Pasha. I died over a year ago. My spirit has only been waiting for this day. When you have made your decision, I will move on to my final resting-place. I have something I wish to tell you before you make your decisions. I will start when your mother arrives."

"You... are our father?" Pasha asked.

"Yes, I am, daughter."

"Dad?" asked Harold, temporarily forgetting his quest to leave.

Sasha had quietly entered the castle and was waiting for Spot to finish his exchange before speaking up. "Sorry I'm late. My master had taken me out." She sat down and gave an approving nod to Spot for him to begin.

"It is my job to make sure you know the dangers you may face on your missions. Previously, there have been fatalities, usually through stupid mistakes made by warriors. I call both them and you warriors because that is exactly what you would be. The forces of evil will try anything to steal the golden spheres around your necks. Remember this: those spheres are the only way both your powers and your entrance to the castle are possible. On your travels, you may come across dogs that look like you. They may have the same markings. These are Warriors that have lost or have had their spheres stolen. If evil finds a way to take away your powers, nothing can stop it. The balance will tip and all will fall into chaos. You will find some missions easy, some extremely hard; there has been one mission that has lasted over one hundred Earth years. At some point, you will face this evil and will have to use all your skills to survive the encounter. After your mother speaks to you, we will answer any questions you may have."

Sasha took her cue and explained, "You and your type are crucial to the world's balance, for if evil prevails, man will surely destroy both themselves and this wonderful planet. Your absent brothers will at some point join you. At this time, one of your brothers has lost his golden ball and cannot find it. The other has a master who works on an oil platform at sea and is away from home and his golden ball for another three months. Of the three times I am allowed to help you under the Great Charter, I have already used two. So the next time will be the last time I can assist you in any way."

"You helped me once. Who else did you help?" asked Pasha.

"Well, it wasn't me," Harold butted in.

"You told me Mother saved you when you fell off a cliff," Pasha quipped.

Harold looked to the floor in embarrassment, mumbling, "Just a little white lie."

"Never mind that. It was Wallace, your Scottish brother. He had fallen over the side of the oil platform into the cold sea. He would surely have drowned if I hadn't stepped in."

"Is that it now? Mum, Dad, I love ya and all dat, I really do, but I don't fink I am cut out for saving the world, know wot I mean. You gonna ask me that question so I can go 'ome? Come on, Keeper! Ask me," Harold pleaded.

"Very well, Harold. I will now ask you both. With the authority of the Great Charter, I ask you to make this decision: Would you help the world to maintain its balance? If you answer no, you will return to your human life, relinquishing all powers, privileges, and any memories you have of this place. You must now answer with a simple 'yes' or 'no'."

"Yes," Pasha answered immediately.

"Are you crazy, Pash? They want us to risk our lives for people we don't even know!" Harold cried out in surprise.

"What else are we going to do?" Pasha exclaimed. "We have a chance here to make a difference in the world! This sort of chance doesn't always come along." Pasha paused. "I made a promise to help those in evil's way. There is absolutely no way I would ever turn this opportunity down!"

Harold turned scornfully back toward his door. "Well, fine for you, but if we are all said and done, I'll be on me way now, know wot I mean."

"You haven't answered me yet, Harold," the Keeper boomed, beginning to lose patience.

Sasha jumped in between Harold and the Keeper, looking Harold squarely in the eye. "Before you answer, Harold, listen for a moment. Although I have never had to save you, you shouldn't feel so cocky about that because you have been saved by someone else in this castle."

"Who saved me?" Harold demanded. "I don't believe you." Sarcasm dripped from his every word. "Tell me, Mummy. Who saved me and when? You can't, can you?"

"It was the day your master came to collect you. You had escaped from your home and run away. Your father and his master found you halfway up a mountain; it was snowing badly and you were perched on a thin piece of ice that was the only thing between you and a 150-foot drop onto the ground. An avalanche was heading directly down on you. Your father sacrificed himself in order for you to survive and, hopefully, make a difference in this world. And if that isn't enough, I need you to keep an eye on your sister; you cannot let her face all that danger on her own."

"I don't remember that," Harold muttered, walking around in a few circles before stopping to face the Keeper. "I was a pup; I didn't know any better. Dad, I'm sorry you died, but I just don't know if I can face all this."

"My son," Spot interrupted, "once, I didn't think I could face it either. I too had to choose. It became the hardest decision I ever made. I chose a dangerous life and I am glad I did. I met your mother, together we have saved the world on countless occasions, and we had you. I do not regret giving my life to save yours. You need to stand by your sister now and she will stand by you. Do not be afraid. Besides, it beats a life lying around, chasing cats, or playing endless games of fetch in the yard.

"Well, don't knock it till you tried it, Pop. OK, count me in," he said, if still somewhat reluctant. "But you 'ad better spoil me often with all that beef steak, Ozzy!"

"It's a deal," the koala replied, "and I'll tell you what else I will do. Against all odds, you have both done me proud today. Therefore, as a sort of reward, I will grant each of you one wish. Anything you want, except, of course, for more wishes," Ozzy said with a smile.

"The answers have been given. Take care, warriors, for your trials are about to begin." The Keeper rose from his chair and left through the door behind it.

"So, Harold matey, what is your wish to be?"

"Well, me master is 'aving real trouble with bullies at school. I 'ave tried to talk to 'im but 'e can't understand me barking. Could we bring 'im back 'ere to the castle so I can talk to 'im in 'uman?"

"Mmmm, let's see what I can do. I'll tell you what, go through your door and get him into the yard and I'll do the rest."

Harold ran excitedly up the stairs and straight through his door to get on with his part of the deal. Ozzy turned to Pasha expectantly.

"I want my father back; that's what I want." Pasha's eyes filled with tears.

"That is one thing I cannot do, Sweetie. He is leaving now. You should go say good-bye."

Pasha ran to the end of the hall where their mother was sitting, tears streaming down her face as she and her beloved Spot stared deeply into each other's eyes. Pasha quietly sat next to her mother and joined in the tearful farewell. As Spot's face melted into the brickwork, he spoke in a choked-up voice: "Good luck, my beautiful daughter. Know that my love will always fill your heart and give you courage in times of need."

"Goodbye, Daddy. I love you. Please keep a place for me in Heaven."

As Spot completely disappeared, Sasha licked her daughter's tears from her face and bid her farewell, telling her, "I have to go now. The world is lucky to have such a special dog on its side. You and your brother take care of each other and I hope to see you soon."

Sasha flew up to the chair and disappeared through the door behind it. Pasha solemnly walked back to Ozzy, whose emotions had also gotten the better of him. "Your father really was an exceptional dog," he sniffed. "I will miss him. Now tell me, my tearful friend, what wish would you like?"

"Well, if Harold can bring his master here, I would like you to meet mine. Although she is sometimes very self-centered, I think she has a good heart."

"Consider it done. Bring your master into the yard and I'll get her here."

Chapter Eleven

Harold had no problem getting Peter into position. Tugging on his trouser leg, he dragged him through the door and into the garden. Pasha had a little more trouble with Tiffany; she had been talking to Chloe on the telephone for hours. Pasha sat in front of her and barked endlessly.

"Go away, Pash! I'm on the phone," Tiffany growled, pushing her pet away. Pasha never relented, and eventually Tiffany gave in, telling Chloe she would call her back. She followed Pasha, who backed out of the house and into the yard.

Ozzy was patiently watching the dogs' progress in their mirrors. When both were ready and in position, he started his chant:

"Dogs and masters,
Two and two makes four,
Granting both dogs' wishes,
To bring all through the door."

As both masters entered the castle, they stood silently on the balcony, not moving an inch as their eyes scanned the unfamiliar surroundings. When their eyes finally met, they screamed in unison.

"How did you get here, Peter? For that matter, how did I get here?" Tiffany shouted.

"I have absolutely no idea," Peter replied softly. "And where exactly is 'here,' anyway?"

Harold was the first of the two dogs to speak. "Ooi, ooi savaloy! You made it!" Peter and Tiffany at last had something in common: they both fainted.

Pasha looked at Harold with a confused face before she asked, "Why does everyone faint? And what, may I ask, does 'Ooi, ooi savaloy' mean?"

"Oh, that's just somefink we say daan the taan when we're 'appy. Doesn't really mean anyfink, know wot I mean." Harold sniggered. "What we gonna do with these two, then?"

"Leave them to me," interrupted Ozzy as he stood over the two unconscious humans. Raising his wand, he chanted:

"All the humans who are present,
Sleeping on the floor,
Let them think that they are dreaming
And feel fear no more."

"OK, you can wake them up now, but take things slowly with them. Remember, they have never seen you act as you do here."

Pasha started to lick Tiffany's face, which soon woke her. Sitting up, she rubbed her eyes. "Hi, Pashy. Oh, it wasn't a dream."

Harold, not wanting to seem soft, just barked in Peter's ears.

The two young masters rose to their feet and looked around at the splendor of the castle.

Harold could not resist being the first to speak. "I bet you 'ave lots of questions. Well, let me save you the effort. It's like this, see: me and Pashy are able to speak 'uman, and before you go expecting to 'ave a long, meaningful conversation with us at 'ome, we can only talk 'uman while we are 'ere or on some sort of mission that helps maintain the balance of good and evil, or somefink like that. Now, before you go trying to butt in, there's more. She can fly and do various other tricks. Anyways, I have a magical tail and a tongue that's good for more than yapping to you two. Know wot I mean. Oh, I forgot to introduce you to our little friend 'ere. 'Is name is Ozzy and 'e does this magic fing with 'is wand. Before you ask, Pash and me will give you a little display of our supernatural powers. Just step forward to the edge of the balcony; the show's about to start."

Tiffany and Peter, both with mouths wide open, shuffled forward as asked. Harold was the first to launch into the air, using his whipping tail and tongue. He swung effortlessly between the great columns of the hall. Pasha joined her brother and together they gave their masters a breathtaking display of aerial expertise, Pasha dodging through the extended tongue and tail of her brother.

"Wow!" exclaimed Peter. "That is amazing!"

"That tongue is so gross," blurted Tiffany, with a look of disgust.

"That is not all they can do," explained Ozzy, motioning to Pasha to show her Paw Power.

Pasha looked around the hall for a target. After spotting one at the end of the hall, she aligned one of her front legs and shouted her command: "Paw Power!" A large ball of fire hit the target and shattered it into tiny, flaming pieces.

The explosions awakened Pewter, who had been sound asleep on the Keeper's chair. He stretched his whole body and readied himself to join in the fun. As the dogs flew past the chair, Pewter tried to jump onto Pasha's back. The still sleepy cat's leap was poorly timed. He missed her back but caught the end of her tail. He clung on for dear life as the pair flew around the hall, eventually letting go as he saw his chance to land on the balcony. The very relieved cat fell safely to the floor. Tiffany quickly picked him up and cuddled him. "Are you OK, Pewter?"

"Ribbit, ribbit," Pewter blurted.

Tiffany nearly dropped the little cat in surprise.

"Oh, that cat gets a little too big for 'is britches," informed Ozzy. "He thinks he knows more than the rest of us, so I taught him a little lesson in magic."

Pewter answered with another "ribbit, ribbit." Embarrassed with his vocabulary, he hopped down and away to sulk.

"Would you like to ride on your pets?" Ozzy offered.

"Oh, yes, please, Mr. Koala," Tiffany agreed eagerly.

"Can I as well?" asked an eager Peter.

"Please don't call me Mr. Koala; Ozzy will do fine. You can both have a go. The only thing you must remember is to relax and have total trust in your dogs. That way, you won't fall off," Ozzy instructed, before turning toward the dogs. "Lie down and let your masters sit on your backs." Peter gripped his hands onto Harold's collar.

"Uh, Peter, m' boy," Harold explained. "This is going to get a little dizzying. I have never tried to swing with a rider before."

"I can take it. Let's ride!" Peter's smile beamed ear to ear.

One quick lap around the hall on his back soon wiped the smile right off his face. Peter stumbled off the dog, his head spinning, and sat down on the floor with a crash.

"Guess I'm going to 'ave to work on me technique, know wot I mean."

Now it was Tiffany's turn. She was still a little frightened, and gripped Pasha's collar so tightly her knuckles turned white.

"Ease up on the collar, Tiff, or you'll strangle me," Pasha managed to wheeze out. Once able to breathe again, Pasha did not waste any time in taking to the air.

"I can't believe I am doing this!" Tiffany allowed herself a nervous smile. "Whooooooo!"

As she became more confident, she released her hands from Pasha's collar. Holding on only by pressing her knees against Pasha's sides, Tiffany caught her reflection in one of the mirrors and smugly thought she was looking good. She held her arms out at her reflection and shouted, "Paw Power!"

Everyone was shocked to see two bolts of fire shoot from the ends of her fingertips. They struck the mirror and ricocheted, exploding as they reached a far window. The window shattered into hundreds of small glass fragments.

"Oops. I forgot one little thing," said Ozzy. "I think it would be a lot safer if we stopped the flying now. I had heard that when masters fly on their pets, all of their powers were transferred to them, but this is the first time I have seen it."

"Thanks for letting us know ahead of time," moaned Tiffany sarcastically.

Peter asked, "Can you do some magic, Ozzy?"

"Well, now, Master Peter, what sort of magic would you like to see?"

"I am a trifle hungry, sir," Peter replied as he rubbed his ample stomach.

"You and your dog think just alike. How strange. What about a tea party for all of us?"

"That would be cool," Tiffany agreed.

Ozzy needed no more encouragement to show off his magical skills and moved to the edge of the balcony. Not tall enough to see over the top, he squeezed his head through a gap between the carved spindles, pointed his wand, and began:

"With hungry humans and dogs to feed,
In the Great Hall, the table to be set,
I'm not thinking of just a little bit.
What I want is a full-on banquet."

As everyone leaned over the balcony, watching, a puff of smoke rose from in front of the chair. Tiffany and Peter headed down the stairs as fast as they could. As they reached the halfway point, Harold and Pasha came soaring over their masters' heads. As the guests turned past the chair, their eyes lit up in amazement.

Before them was a large, rectangular table set with two sparkling candelabras. The plates and drinking implements were made from the most beautiful cut glass, which sent twinkles of light from the candles all around the hall. A grand spread of food garnished the table, leaving little room to spare. Ozzy beckoned the children to sit on either side of him. "Tuck in and fill your boots."

"But I haven't got boots on, Ozzy," Peter said in a concerned voice.

Everyone laughed as Ozzy explained, "That's just an Aussie saying; it means sit and eat up as much as you can."

Peter's face went a bright crimson color as he realized he had made a fool of himself yet again. Harold licked his master's hand and asked him, "'Ow is the bullying fing going?"

Peter, getting embarrassingly red, looked at Tiffany. He did not want her to know that he was not strong enough to stand up for himself. He held his hand in front of his mouth and whispered to

Harold, "I'll tell you later." Harold winked at him and buried his head in his bowl of tender beefsteak.

As everyone sat around the table laughing, they were unaware that the Keeper had entered. He stood in front of his chair and ranted, "Humans, humans in my castle! Ozzy, you should have known better! Do you not know what happened the last time?"

Ozzy closed his eyes and nodded as he dropped his head in shame.

"You have ten minutes to get them out of here. It is bad enough that we have a cat, but this is just too much! I will return in ten minutes," the Keeper warned, leaving as silently as he had arrived.

"Come on, you have to go now," Ozzy demanded.

"'ang on a minute, Oz. I 'aven't 'ad time to talk to me master about 'is school. It will only take me a few secs, know wot I mean."

Ozzy relented. "OK, but hurry it up. Take him to the end of the hall for some privacy."

Harold moved next to Peter and allowed him onto his back. The pair swung to where Ozzy had suggested.

"Right, Master, wot's been going on at school? Why ain't you ever 'appy these days?" Harold asked.

"Well, do you remember the other day when I had that test? I am not sure whether you know this, but I came bottom of the whole school. Jimmy Watts found out about my score and told the entire school. He and his friends then made a circle around me in the playground and started pushing me around, calling out, 'The fatty is now the school dunce,' and singing that I have fewer brain cells than the school's pet rabbit."

Harold's eyes widened. "I'll speak to Ozzy later and see wot can be done."

"Thank you, Harold. You really are a true friend."

Pasha had already taken Tiffany through the door, Pewter hopping along behind. A concerned Harold swung Peter up to and through his own door, back into the world that caused his master so much pain.

116

*****

Ozzy waited patiently for the Keeper to return, not knowing if there would be punishment for allowing humans into the hall. He had only wanted to honor the wishes of his new warriors, Pasha and Harold. Finally, the Keeper entered through the door behind his chair. Ozzy apologized and tried to explain himself, but the Keeper just dismissed his excuses.

"It's too late for that now, Ozzy. I was merely hoping to avoid an unpleasant situation. The Great Charter states: 'If anyone is brought to the castle by a warrior, then the guests must be invited to become warriors as well.'"

Ozzy gulped, lowering his head.

"That's right, Ozzy. If those young people say 'yes,' then you could possibly be responsible for them being hurt or even killed. I want you to bring them to the castle tomorrow and try to talk them into refusing the invitation. You have but one day to complete this task. Even if they decide to join us, there is now no time for proper training. Others are already in need of help from our warriors. I want you to give them an easy mission. This mission must be something to test both their skill and their nerve. I will now leave you, but remember, I will be monitoring every move both you and your new charges make."

The Keeper left and Ozzy spent the whole rest of the night pondering how to dissuade Peter and Tiffany from following their beloved canines into the life of a warrior.

Chapter Twelve

As dawn broke, Peter was sitting next to the phone, trying desperately to summon up the courage he needed to call Tiffany. His palms were sweaty as he picked up and set down the plastic receiver countless times, fickly reversing the decision in his mind. Surely, she had not had the same dream, and if he called her, she was sure to think he had gone stark raving bonkers. Peter thought his dilemma through yet again. On the other hand, if she had had a similar dream, then this could be his chance to get much closer to her.

Across the Atlantic, Tiffany was struggling to keep her eyes open. She sat looking at her watch, endlessly converting the time difference between London and Arizona. "It's six o'clock in London now," she mused to herself. "Normal people should be up by then," Tiffany huffed matter-of-factly as she dialed Peter's number.

Peter, startled by the sudden break in the silence, fell off his chair. Scrambling quickly to his feet, he grabbed the handset as fast as he could, hoping not to wake his father.

"Hello," he whispered.

"Peter, is that you? It's Tiffany."

"Yes, it's me."

"I had a dream about you last night. It was awesome! We were in this—"

Peter interrupted, "Castle with our dogs who have magical powers." The phone line was quiet as both children sat in stunned silence.

"Did we dream that or were we really there?" Tiffany asked tentatively.

"I'm not sure. What do we do now?"

"Right! Peter, here is what we are going to do. We both have to stay close to our dogs for the next few hours. Lie down next to Harold and go to sleep. It's our only chance of getting back to the castle." As soon as Peter agreed, Tiffany paused before getting flustered. "OK, off you go then and read your comics."

"Bye, Tiffany." A dial tone was all that replied to Peter's farewell. He hurriedly ran into the garden and crawled into Harold's large kennel. Harold opened one eye as Peter grunted his way through the opening and settled in next to him. Sighing in resignation, Harold scooted over to make enough room, figuring that Peter needed him. It was the least he could do for the boy.

*****

At the castle, Ozzy paced up and down, waiting for everyone to be in position so that he could summon his charges. With both masters now where he wanted them, he activated the golden balls. Pasha and Tiffany entered without any problem. Just before the door shut, Pewter came scampering in as well. Ozzy looked anxiously at Harold's door, which remained closed. Confused, he looked up at the mirror, but all he saw was the golden ball circling around the kennel.

Ozzy turned and nearly bumped into Tiffany, who had moved to stand just behind him. "It is real! Awesome. Where're Peter and Harold?" she asked.

"I'm not sure. His golden ball is not working. I will have to go in and see what is going on."

"You sure you don't want me to handle it?" asked Pewter, followed by a series of deep croaks from his throat.

"No, Pewter, I don't want you to handle it," Ozzy replied. "Go find a swamp to sit in or something."

"No respect. Ribbit!" Tail in the air, Pewter went down to have a nap in the great chair.

"May I watch you in the mirror?" asked Tiffany.

"Yes, just look in it and wish to see. The mirror will obey you, for you are now a chosen one," Ozzy replied as he opened Harold's door.

"Wait! What do you mean, I am now a chosen one?"

"Patience. I will tell all when I return," he shouted as the door closed behind him.

Tiffany focused her eyes on Harold's mirror, but all she could see was her own reflection. "How do I get this thing to work?" she asked, stomping her foot impatiently.

"Ozzy said you had to wish to see them," Pasha reminded her.

"Oh, OK, I'll wish." Tiffany closed her eyes tightly, scrunching her nose. "I really wish the mirror would show me Peter, Harold, and Ozzy."

On opening her eyes, all she could see in the mirror were three framed pictures, one each of Ozzy, Peter, and Harold. "No, that's not right," she snapped, as Pasha burst out laughing.

"Move over and let me try," Tiffany stepped aside as Pasha started her wish: "Mirror on the wall, let me see the other side of the door." The pictures in the mirror faded to reveal Ozzy walking around the kennel. His eyes followed the golden ball as it circled repeatedly. Waiting until the ball passed, he hopped inside the kennel to find Peter and Harold sound asleep on the floor.

"Wake up, you two," Ozzy growled, his hands on his hips. "You have to come to the castle!"

Peter and Harold sat up groggily and yawned. Peter groaned and rubbed his eyes, but when he opened them again, he found himself lying on the floor in front of Tiffany and Pasha. As he rose to his feet, still rubbing his eyes, Ozzy ushered everyone downstairs. "Come on, mateys, I have something very important to tell you."

The koala sat in the big chair, petting Pewter, who still lay asleep. He motioned for her to take a seat on one of the chairs he had placed in front of him. Sensing Ozzy's seriousness, Tiffany frowned and quietly did as told, with Peter quickly sitting on the remaining chair. The two dogs padded slowly to sit in front of their masters.

Ozzy stared silently at his guests for what seemed like ages before Tiffany could not bear it anymore. "Oh, come on, Oz. Get on with it!"

"Just be silent for once, Tiffany. This is very important," snapped Ozzy. She immediately dropped her head at his serious tone.

"As you already know, this is the first time I have trained new warriors. I have learned a lot from this experience, like maybe I should have been stricter with you dogs. However, what I really want to say is that I am very proud of you. I will be indebted to you both for the rest of my days, for without your unfailing commitment, I would not be here now."

"Well, as long as you don't ever forget that," Harold said, chuckling until Pasha growled angrily.

Ozzy continued in a solemn voice: "My next and worst mistake was to invite you, Peter and Tiffany, into the castle."

"Why, Ozzy? I have had a great time here," Peter interrupted.

"He's right; we've had a great time. There's no reason to feel bad about that," agreed Tiffany. Peter's head whipped around to look at her for a moment, unable to contain a small grin.

"OK, mateys, let me explain to you why it was such a bad mistake. I was unaware that if you enter the castle by invite, you are then eligible to become warriors."

"Cool!" Peter shouted loudly, nearly jumping out of his chair.

"Wait a moment, young man. This is something which you must not enter into lightly. Unlike Pasha and her brothers, who were destined to become warriors before their birth, you two have much more to lose. If you choose to accept the offer, without any powers of your own, you will be extremely vulnerable. I have been looking through the Great Charter, and there have only ever been two humans enrolled. One was severely injured and, tragically, the other lost his life."

Ozzy looked pointedly at the two stunned faces in front of him. "Unfortunately, I am forced to extend to you an offer to become warriors. What do you say?"

"So, there are risks involved, but are there any benefits? Would we live longer, like our dogs?"

"No, Peter. Each mission has its own reward, determined by the risks involved. Once you have successfully completed a mission, you will receive an award in the form of currency to spend in the castle. We call our currency Grimits. All the Grimits awarded are split between the warriors who participated. You would then be able to spend your rewards in the castle stores."

Tiffany broke her silence. "If there's shopping, then I'm in."

"What about the risks?" Ozzy pleaded with her, to which she responded confidently, "I risk my life every time I visit the mall on the first day of a good sale. I am an eight-sale veteran now, and tougher than I look."

"That may be, but there will be times when you will regret becoming a warrior—that, I can promise you," Ozzy rumbled, pointing his finger at her. Turning to the other human, he queried, "What about you, Peter? What are your thoughts?"

"To be honest, Ozzy, I really have nothing to lose and everything to gain. If I say no, what do I have to go back to, answer me that? I am constantly bullied; my only friend in this whole world is Harold. On the other hand, if I say yes, I get to live an exciting life. Besides, I'm not letting Tiffany do this without me there to protect her."

Tiffany turned to look him straight in the eyes and gave a slight grin. "That is the sweetest thing anyone has ever said about me. Thanks, Pete." He beamed back at her until the smile fell from her lips. Her jaw dropped slightly as she bristled, straightening her back and sticking out her jaw. Defiantly, she informed Peter, "But that doesn't mean I would be seen out in public with you."

Everyone exchanged awkward glances until Harold again broke the silence. "Cheer up, Oz. Make me some lunch!"

"Do not ever make demands on Ozzy or I will deal with you myself!" shouted the Keeper, appearing from behind the great chair. "Ozzy, have you asked them? What was their answer?"

"I haven't really asked them yet, sir. At least, they haven't said yes or no."

"Why not?" asked the Keeper. "It's a very simple question. Tiffany, Peter, do you wish to become warriors and help us to maintain the balance between good and evil?"

Tiffany did not hesitate for a moment. "Yes, sir!"

Peter was not far behind her in shouting, "Absolutely, Mister Keeper! It would be my honor."

"I'm in as well," said Pewter, waking up with a gaping yawn.

"Shh, frog. You weren't actually invited." Ozzy clamped his paw over Pewter's mouth.

The Keeper dropped his head, shaking it as he exited, muttering, "Humans... that's too bad. That's really too bad."

*****

Once the Keeper had left, Ozzy jumped from the chair, suddenly more invigorated. "OK, mateys! If that is what you have decided, then we had better make sure you are able to protect yourselves. Hop onto Pasha and Harold."

The dogs moved quickly to their masters' sides. Tiffany was first to mount, sitting in the middle of Pasha's back, her arms clasped so tightly around her pet's neck, the dog started to choke.

"Ease up there, Tiff," Ozzy warned.

"What now?" Tiffany loosened her hold.

"Now Pasha's powers are in your hands. Be careful how you use them. If you command her to fly, she will. Once airborne, unless you have a specific route, Pasha will navigate as she sees fit."

"Up," Tiffany commanded Pasha, who lifted them both high toward the castle ceiling. "That's really cool. Now let's go on a tour of the Great Hall."

"What about me, Oz? Can I have a go?" asked Peter.

"You sure you can 'andle it?" asked Harold.

"It's just like swinging on vines; we just need to practice. Let's try again."

Peter put his leg over Harold's back and gently eased his full weight down. It was a shaky ride, but soon the two moved as one, swinging about the hall. They could move nearly as fast as Pasha and Tiffany.

"You don't see that every day," Pewter said and hopped off the great chair.

Ozzy folded his arms over his chest and smiled as he watched the four warriors give an impressive display, ending as they landed in front of Ozzy's chair. "Well done, everyone! It seems you have the flying part sorted out, but you need to know how to control their other powers." He turned to Tiffany and explained, "To use Paw Power, you must point your arm straight out and concentrate on what you want to hit. Then, command, 'Paw Power.' Be very careful and only use it when you absolutely have to. Those balls of fire can be deadly. The window will never be the same," Ozzy chuckled, pointing a finger at the newly repaired window, shattered the day before.

Tiffany, still mounted on Pasha, turned toward one of the targets. Holding her arm outstretched, she commanded in a trembling voice, "Paw Power!"

A bolt of fire left the tips of her fingers and smashed into the dead center of the target. "That had better not have ruined my nails," she mumbled, scrutinizing her manicure. "Phew, that was a close one! Did I hit the target? I just pointed and closed my eyes."

Ozzy laughed boisterously as he confirmed her hit. "Well done, Tiff! Now, you and Peter must never forget that you only control your dogs' powers when seated upon their backs. At all other times, they will have control over them. Righty-oh, Peter, Harold's power works in a different way. Although you control his powers, Harold's powers will always come from his mouth and tail. Does anyone have any questions?"

"I seem to remember something about payment and shopping?" asked Tiffany.

"What does a Grimit look like?" Peter jumped in.

"Yes, that is also very important," Tiffany chimed in. "After all, I have to know what size of purse I need to carry with me."

"Do I get a share?" asked Pewter.

"No, you don't, and a purse is not necessary. You will never carry any Grimits outside of the castle. They would distract you too much on your missions," Ozzy explained. "Let me show you what I mean."

Ozzy disappeared behind the chair, finally emerging with his hands clasped tightly together. "Sit in a circle in front of me; otherwise it may get away."

Tiffany and Peter looked at each other and frowned as Ozzy, still clasping his hands tightly, knelt down to release the contents onto the floor. His hands opened to reveal a gold coin with the face of an old woman engraved into one side. The coin rolled around in a circle, then fell flat.

"That's so beautiful!" breathed Tiffany as she reached out to pick up the coin.

"No, don't touch it!" Ozzy whispered loudly. "It's asleep, and they can get very nasty if they are awakened!"

Harold had to have his say on the matter, muttering, "You are winding me up, mate! It's a coin! This is your effort at a joke, right?"

Before Ozzy could reply, a voice piped up from the middle of the circle: "No joking here, doggy." The coin sprouted two arms and two legs. The eyes on the woman's face opened, and the Grimit sprang up onto its feet. The coin introduced itself: "Good morning, all. I am a Grimit, and as the chosen currency of this castle, I am extremely valuable. You may use me to purchase any items or services available inside the castle walls. You may not, however, take me through your doors; if you do, I will disappear forever, never to be seen again. From the moment you receive one of us Grimits, it will be your responsibility to keep us entertained. As long as we are happy, we will be glad to remain your Grimits. If at any time we become unhappy, our mission will then be to escape and return to the Grimit bank, where we are at our happiest. If you ever feel lonely anywhere inside the castle walls, just take out your

Grimits! We love to chat and play games. Just do not put more than one of us in your pocket at the same time. We would get bashed together, causing us serious headaches!"

Tiffany and Peter were both giggling to themselves, while the dogs sat with their eyes open as wide as they would go.

"This is the strangest thing I have ever seen. Ribbit! Can't you take this curse off me?" Pewter glared at Ozzy.

Ignoring the cat, he explained, "You will get to know more about Grimits as time goes on. This one is mine anyway." Ozzy picked up the struggling coin and put it in the purse hanging around his neck, which he then carefully re-zipped so the Grimit could not escape.

"Where are the shops? I can't see any in here, and if there are no shops, then fighting would be totally out of the question," declared Tiffany.

"You're a real 'ero," muttered Harold.

"Shut it. I am all for the hero stuff, but I also expect to be paid to do it. Right, Peter?"

"Doesn't matter to me; I am ready for a mission," he confidently stated.

"Thanks for backing me up—not!" Tiffany moaned.

Ozzy reached back into his purse and retrieved the Grimit, who was not amused at being disturbed yet again. "All in good time, young man, all in good time. Now, I want to show you another part of the castle, a very important part for those of you with a mind for shopping." Ozzy winked at Tiffany. "Stand on the big black square behind you and do not move, no matter what happens."

"What black squ— oh!" Peter was staring at one of the marble floor tiles. It was now pitch black with a glassy surface like obsidian. Everyone gathered on top of it.

With everyone where they should be, Ozzy held the Grimit between his claws and shouted out as load as he could, "I have Grimits to spend! Come see my Grimits!"

The small bear stood there, stony-faced and waiting. Everyone else looked around, not knowing what to expect. A faint mumbling filled the air.

"Where is that coming from, Peter?" Tiffany leaned over and whispered in his ear.

"I think it's coming from the far wall."

Before she could agree, a small old man appeared, walking right through the wall and mumbling to himself. He wore long, light brown overalls and his head was balding, with what hair he had left wisped over to the other side. Still mumbling, he walked toward them, his head hanging down and gazing at a small book in his hand. As he got nearer, his grumpy mumblings became clearer: "Grimits to spend, ha, as if I didn't have enough to do. You had better be a buyer and not just a looker. Grimits to spend, Grimits to spend."

"Oh, hush up, Orville! I have some new warriors to introduce to you."

Orville stood on the edge of the black square, looked up from his book, and took a quick glace over his small round glasses which were carefully perched on the end of his nose. Having surveyed the new warriors, he looked straight back at his book.

"So, you are the new ones, eh? Humans as well; that could be bad. On second thought, that could be good. No, nothing is ever good around here. I have heard human girls are natural spenders. Spend, spend, and spend."

"Prepare to be proven right," stated Ozzy with a chuckle.

"Well, then I suppose I had better show you where you can spend all those lovely Grimits. The more you spend, the more work for me. I like work; it keeps me busy." Orville jumped into the air. As he landed on the black square he shouted, "Feet to keys!" and twisted his whole body quickly, sending the black square and everyone on it downward like an elevator. The floor descended slowly, and Ozzy reminded them all not to move.

"It's a long way down," mused Peter, peering over the edge.

"Oh, you don't want to be doing that. Better be very careful, child. If you fall over the edge, you will fall forever. Do not want to fall down the never-ending hole. Wouldn't have any Grimits to spend then, would you?" The floor suddenly stopped with a thud.

"Oh, great, now we're stuck in the never-ending elevator in the floor of the castle that really doesn't exist!" grumbled Harold sarcastically.

"Ha, a dog with attitude! He should do well. Bring me loads of inmates. Fear not, we have arrived at our destination. This is the dungeon floor for all your supernatural needs." Orville chuckled in his mumbling way as he pulled a lever which was floating in mid-air. The lever creaked as Orville struggled to move it, and kept up its protest until reaching its final resting place.

"Need to oil that. Been meaning to for the last hundred years," said the little man. The darkness remained as the sides of the lift shaft opened to reveal the castle dungeons.

Harold was the first to leave the safety of the lift. Fearlessly venturing forward, he turned and beckoned the others to follow him. "No, wait here for just a moment. This will be fun," Ozzy whispered grinning.

Not hearing, Harold walked on, looking from side to side as he shouted back, "There's nothing special 'ere, just a bunch o' dark empty dungeons. You lot are just a bunch o' scaredy cats!"

No sooner had Harold spoken than an army of knights in armor fell through the arched ceiling, landing in two straight lines on either side of the dungeons. With modern military precision, they all stamped their armored feet to attention, drew their swords, and pointed them at Harold.

Harold's bravery deserted him. He yelped like a little puppy and ran down the line of knights, jumping back into the lift and hiding behind Peter. Everyone in the lift burst out laughing.

Orville explained as he walked from the lift, "Don't fret; these knights of the keep are here to guard the prisoners, not to hurt the animals. Oops, and people. Must not forget the people now. Can't forget the people, can we?" He walked up the center aisle and commanded, "Lights on; on the lights!"

As a single spotlight shone down from the top of each dungeon, a noise started to fill the air. "Come, Warriors. As soon as you leave the lift, the wall will close and the knights will vanish. They only appear when the lift doors are open."

Ozzy and the warriors followed the advice and, sure enough, as soon as they had stepped foot out of the lift, the wall closed behind them. With the door now closed, the knights pointed their swords toward the ceiling and disappeared as quickly as they had come.

Orville beckoned everyone to the first cell. "Let me introduce you to our first inmate. This is Kittle." Orville waved his hand and the cell lit up.

The cell appeared to have two sections. The front was empty except for a large, silver, jug-like object hanging from the arched ceiling. Floor-to-ceiling bars divided the room, and the space beyond the bars remained dark. The warriors leaned forward and squinted. Though still unable to see, they could hear the sound of something large shuffling around.

Orville continued, "This first section is where, with my permission, you will enter if you wish to purchase anything from this inmate."

Tiffany looked very disappointed as she asked in a disgruntled voice, "Purchase from an inmate? Where is everything? How can we purchase something we can't see?"

Seeing how disappointed the new warrior was, Orville was quick to put her mind at rest. "This is shopping like you have never known before. The goods or services you may purchase are all specialties of the various inmates."

"Excuse me, sir," Peter began as he raised his arm high into the air as if in school. "How do the inmates get here, and how long do they stay locked up?"

"That is a really good question," the old man muttered, "one that should be dealt with before you start meeting the few inmates we have here. I had better deal with that one now. When you or any other warriors bring an accused person or animal, they

130

are presumed innocent until they have been tried and convicted by the Castle Court."

"Where is the court?" asked Pasha.

"I will get to that momentarily. If they are innocent, all memories are erased of anything to do with the episode. They are then returned to the last place they had been before being arrested by the warriors.

"However, if they are found guilty, the judge will impose a fine and custodial sentence that is only determined by how long it takes them to pay their fine. Once they have paid their fine, any powers they have are taken from them. They then exit the castle by the front gates and their memories are wiped, transforming them into normal-looking humans. They live out their natural lives in a small village called Freiheit."

Both youngsters shouted at once, "I've been there!"

"Yes, you have," Orville confirmed. "That is where all the new warrior dogs are born. Now you may ask any questions."

Tiffany was first. Her tone was condescending. "So, if I was a bad guy and I got sentenced, all I would have to do is call my dad and he would pay my fine and I could go home?"

"No. The first thing you should understand is that you are an ordinary human, and as such, would never end up here. Second, the fine imposed is in Grimits. No inmate enters here with any Grimits, so they must earn them by selling their powers to warriors, which in turn helps the warriors fight other evils."

"Seems real complicated to me," Pewter moaned.

Orville did not hesitate. "The system has worked for millennia and shouldn't be questioned by a day-old cat."

"Hey, pal, I am, like, six months old."

"When can we get started, Mr. Orville?" Peter jumped excitedly.

Ozzy grabbed Peter's arm and growled, "Patience, young one! This is no game and Grimits are hard to earn, so spend them wisely. The inmates will try anything to get their hands on your Grimits. They will lie, cheat, and steal, so beware; always remember that there is no such thing as a nice inmate."

Peter sulked back slowly before continuing more meekly, "Okay. So, where is the court, and where do you get the jury?"

"You will find the answer to that question the first time you bring in a suspect. Let me now introduce you to the inmates we have here now. Time is short, and we still have to take you to the village." Orville looked around at the warriors as they tried to squint through the darkness at the back of the cell. "We have four inmates currently here in the dungeons, including a pesky magician, Slyming Rhyming. He is a real piece of work—quite different from any of the others. However, we will get to him later. Back light!"

Everyone except Ozzy gasped in surprise. Revealed in the back section of the dungeon was the most bizarre animal they had ever seen. The creature's head and neck were like over-sized versions of a regular housecat. The neck led into broad, cat-like shoulders, but that was where the feline features ended. At the shoulders, the body separated sharply to look like two cows, standing side by side.

"Meet Kittle."

"Okay, now this is the strangest thing I have ever seen," gasped Pewter.

"Kittle has a gift inside of her; that gift, coupled with her… with her…"——Orville paused, struggling to find the right words—— "unusual physical appearance… left her vulnerable to all things evil in your world. She was imprisoned by those who tried to use her gift to control mankind."

Harold could not contain himself any longer. "Don't tell me; she gives extra thick milk that makes purrrrfectly scrumptious yogurt!" He chuckled, a wide grin splitting his face in two.

"So, you think you are funny?" Ozzy asked, his voice full of scorn. "Well, matey, you are not all that far off. Kittle's milk holds special powers, and if you ask her nicely, she may give you a small sample of what it can do."

"Please, Kittle, may I sample your milk?" Peter asked as he stepped forward politely.

Ozzy entered Kittle's dungeon. Placing four very small glasses on a round table located in the far corner, he tipped the silver jug, allowing only a few drips into each glass. He held the glasses carefully as he exited, gently handing one to each warrior.

"Is there anyfink in those glasses? If you 'adn't noticed, I'm a big, strapping dog, and if you fink a few drips of milk are gonna quench me dry froat, then you 'ad better fink again, my little Australian friend," complained Harold.

"Relax, Harold, this is powerful stuff. You do not want to overdo it straight away. Now, get this down your throat and be quiet," Ozzy snapped. Never one to turn down milk, Pewter impatiently asked, "What about me, Ribbit?"

"Sorry; warriors only."

Harold sniffed at the glass before clearing its contents with one sweep of his tongue. He sat up and waited for something to happen, then started to whistle while he looked around the keep. "Nice milk, Kittle, but that is exactly what it is, just ordinary milk."

Ozzy beckoned Peter to the other side of the keep. "Pick up that large boulder and hold it above your head."

Peter blinked at Ozzy for a moment before shaking his head and bending down. He got a good grip on the big rock and looked over to Ozzy expectantly.

"Well, go on," Ozzy urged while nodding.

Peter grunted loudly as he tried to lift the boulder with all his might. Giving up after a few seconds, he collapsed into a heap on the concrete floor, his face as red as his English post boxes. Everyone burst into laughter. Even grumpy old Orville saw the funny side of this one, giving a little chuckle as he repositioned his glasses.

"Here, matey. Drink up and you will feel better." Ozzy handed Peter his glass and patted his back.

Peter angrily snatched the glass and tipped it upside down. He waited for the few drops of Kittle's milk to flow down the side of the glass and into his waiting mouth. As the last of it disappeared into his mouth, Peter gave the glass back to Ozzy and, in a very disgruntled voice, complained, "I suppose you think that was funny. I get enough of this at school. I thought you were meant to be my friend."

Ozzy whispered quickly, "Hush, matey. Do not go getting all upset. Just try again."

"Try again?" Peter frowned at Ozzy before looking back to the boulder. He took a deep breath and gripped it again, bracing himself for further humiliation.

"Go on, Superman! You can do it... NOT!" Harold blurted, laughing uncontrollably.

With one enormous effort, Peter tugged at the boulder and slowly lifted it from the floor, up past his waist and then his chest, until he was holding it high above his head. "Look, Tiff! I can do it! I can really do it!"

Tiffany did not say anything as she and both of the dogs watched in awe.

"OK, matey, put it down now before you lose your strength. Kittle's milk only lasts for so long. You never know when it will stop working."

Peter started to lower the boulder, only getting it as far as his chest before he felt all of his power drain away. The rock crashed to the floor, shaking the walls and sending pebbles and dust flying into the air.

"Maybe it's time to call it a day before you dismantle the whole castle," grumbled Orville, arms wide apart as he ushered everyone back to the elevator.

"But we ain't met all the inmates yet, and what about this village place?" complained Harold.

"That will all have to wait for another day," muttered Orville. "I'm very busy and Ozzy's little tour has already cost me precious time."

"Exactly what else do you do around here?" asked Ozzy.

"Take out the trash, etc... etc... etc.," replied Orville. "Now you must go, go, go, and go!"

As they all entered the elevator, Ozzy explained Peter's strength. "Peter, you have no strength left now, which is why you dropped the boulder."

"So, I 'ad that super strength as well?" Harold's jaw dropped.

134

"That you did. You could have done something requiring super strength as well."

"When can we meet the other prisoners?" asked Peter.

"Patience, young man, you will meet them soon enough. You should get plenty of sleep, for tomorrow you will embark on your first mission," Ozzy said as they emerged from the floor back into the Great Hall.

"What is it? Can't you just tell us what it is?" pleaded Pasha, her mind firmly focused on the Lost Mountain. Right now, she felt like she could rescue the White Buffalo by herself.

"I shouldn't really tell you until just before you start, but just this once I will give you an idea. Your Irish brother Shamrock thinks he has lost his golden ball. In reality, someone stole the orb. It will be your task to find and return the ball to him. You must also bring any suspects back here to the castle to stand trial.

"On successful completion of this task, you will be rewarded eight Grimits. These you can use when you want just by summoning Orville while standing on the black square."

"Is that eight Grimits each?" Tiffany looked around at the three other warriors. "I don't think I'll be able to get a lot with only two."

The Keeper emerged from behind his chair. "That is eight between everyone who participates. Now, go home and rest, new Warriors, for tomorrow will be tough on you all."

Although still thirsty for more information, nobody had the courage to argue with the Keeper. They all swiftly exited the castle through their given doors.

****

Tiffany's eyes sprang open, horrified at the sound of her mother shouting from inside the house. "I'm here, Mom. I'm in the yard with Pasha!"

After a few moments, Fay walked through the patio doors, insisting, "But I already looked out here and you were nowhere to be seen."

"I was lying with Pasha in her kennel and must have fallen asleep." Tiffany bit her lip and looked toward the kennel.

"Why on earth would you be in there?" asked Fay.

"Uh, I don't know, Mom. I just felt like it."

"Well, you probably smell like a dog now, young lady. Go take a shower."

Pasha emerged from her quarters and licked Tiffany's hand as she walked into the house. Pewter hung back. He had a devious little scheme cooking to get himself a warrior invitation.

Chapter Thirteen

The ringing phone interrupted an engrossed Steve who was watching the late night news on TV. "Will you get that, honey? I'm trying to watch the news."

"It's OK, Mom. I've got it," shouted Tiffany from upstairs.

"You should be in bed, young lady. Where is Pasha?"

"She's up here with me. Anyway, the phone is for me; it's Peter from London."

Fay walked into the family room, wiping her hands on a towel as she commented to Steve, "She is really acting strangely lately. She slept in the kennel with Pasha today. Since when does Peter call her? Tonight she even insisted that Pasha sleep with her in her room. I don't get it."

"That's teenagers for you. We're not supposed to get it." Steve turned up the volume on the television. "Look at this on the news. A whole forest has died in South America for no reason at all. Hundreds of trees have died over the last week."

"Steve, we have more pressing matters here. I am really worried about the way Tiff is acting."

"Don't worry about her; she is just growing up. She's fine, really."

*****

"Are you scared, Peter?"

Puffing up his chest as if she could see him through the phone wires, he said, "No, not at all. I am sure Ozzy would never let anything happen to us. Anyway, how dangerous can it be, going to find a ball?"

"That's if we ever get there. It is 11 p.m. here, so it must be 7 a.m. there. I am sure we have usually been summoned by now. Is Harold with you?"

"Yes, but I had a lot of trouble getting my dad to let me keep him in my room tonight. Is Pewter with you?"

"He's here, but I'm not sure whether we'll be allowed to take him with us."

Pewter, sensing he was the topic of conversation, rubbed his side against Tiffany's arm.

"I have to go, Tiffany," said Peter urgently. "Harold's golden ball is starting to move."

"OK, Peter. I'll see you there."

Tiffany slammed the phone down and focused on Pasha's ball, which was lying motionless on the bed in front of her. Pasha and Pewter joined her on the soft quilt, all three filled with the anticipation of another exciting day. Pewter waited for the ball to start glowing, then put his plan into action. He began to hiss and run around the room like a mad-cat.

"Pewter, what is wrong with you?" Tiffany glanced back at the orb. It was floating above the bed now.

Pewter backed into the corner as if frightened of the orb. Pasha guessed at the cat's motives. Tiffany was clueless and fell right into the trap.

"Pewter, come here. There is nothing to be afraid of; don't you want to come to the castle with us?" The cat did not stop his loud and obnoxious noises. Tiffany tried a different approach. "Pewter! Stop that and come along!"

The cat had his opening and jumped back up onto the bed just as the orb summoned them. The three of them fell unconscious on the bed.

*****

Peter was first to the castle. While waiting for Tiffany, he looked in Pasha's mirror, trying to do something with his flyaway hair. Wetting his fingers in his mouth, he wiped them over the bits of hair that were sticking up.

Such effort, and for what? Someone who does not really care? Is it really worth it?, he thought as he patted down the last piece of out-of-place hair.

As Tiffany emerged from her door with Pewter sitting proudly on Pasha's back, she looked Peter straight in the eyes. His heart melted and his legs turned to jelly, but Tiffany immediately spoiled the moment by walking straight past him.

"Hello, Peter. What have you done to your hair? It looks like you've stuck it down with a whole jar of gel."

"'Ello to you, too, spoiled brat," muttered Harold, bowing, as she walked toward the stairs.

"I heard that, dog. Come on, Peter. Things to do, people to save," Tiffany countered as she walked gracefully down the marble stairs.

Peter, not having the courage to put Tiffany in her place, followed behind. His head held low, Peter thought: I hope it is not going to be like this all day. It will be just like school all over again.

Pewter immediately jumped up onto the Keeper's chair and made himself comfortable, as if it were his own. The rest lined up in front of it, waiting for instructions. Seeing everyone lined up in front of him, Pewter jumped to his feet and began a very bad impression of Ozzy. "Now then, me mateys! Crikey, Peter, me favorite pom, put another prawn on the barbie. Ribbit! Tiff, me darrrrrling, you've turned into a cracking Sheeler. Harold, tie me kangaroo down, sport. Ribbit!"

Pewter did not see Ozzy standing behind him. "Very funny, my feline friend. It is nice to see you. And it appears that I may be stuck with you. All right, which one of you invited the cat?"

"Huh?" moaned Harold and Peter in unison. Pasha sighed deeply. Ozzy was staring at Tiffany.

"What? Pewter was freaking out as if he was scared of the golden ball. I didn't actually invite him."

"Yes," confirmed Ozzy, "you did. Now the fuzz-ball gets a choice."

Ozzy put on his serious face, the one that told everyone else to be quiet and pay attention. "Little Pewter, as you were invited to the castle by an existing warrior, under the rules of the Great Charter, I am duty-bound to invite you to become a warrior, protecting good and persecuting evil for the benefit of mankind. What say you, yes or no?"

Pewter, who had been waiting for this moment, replied, "Well, I have a few words to say to my future fellow warriors before I answer."

"I take it, your answer is yes, then?" asked Ozzy.

"Of course it is. Now, where was I?"

Everyone in the Great Hall cheered at the confused cat. The cheering continued until the Keeper appeared from behind his chair. "That's just great—two dogs that leave everything to the last minute, two humans, and a cat that won't shut up. What an awesome force we are building to fight evil. I am not sure whether any of you will survive a week. Nevertheless, you are the chosen ones and, as such, will today embark on your first mission."

"Keeper, I have a request." Pasha stepped forward. "Can we please take our mission at the Lost Mountain? The tribe there is in need of our help. There is something in the mountain that has taken their buffalo."

"In due time, you will face the evil of the Lost Mountain, Pasha. That day is not today. You are not ready to face that challenge just yet. I ask for your patience.

"Today, you will all be sent through the fifth door. Your task is to retrieve your brother's stolen golden ball and return it to him. The successful completion of this mission will reward you eight Grimits, and, as with every mission, there will be one extra Grimit for every prisoner successfully convicted.

"You will now exit the castle through the fifth door. When on the other side, you will be close to your mission. May your weaknesses be few and your luck last through. Now go, my warriors! Go!"

Without a sound, as if hypnotized, all of the warriors walked up the marble staircase and in single file exited the castle through the fifth door.

*****

Once all were through the door, they found themselves on the edge of a lush green field, just in front of what looked like an enormous forest.

Looking around, Tiffany asked, "Where are we? There are no buildings in sight. Who's going to tell us where to find what's-his-name's stupid ball?"

"'Is name is Shamrock, and if you 'adn't already worked it out, 'e's one of my long lost brothers, so drop the 'stupid' bit," Harold snapped.

"I think we're meant to find it on our own," said Pasha, totally ignoring Harold's comments.

"Maybe we should start by making a base camp... you know... from which to coordinate our search," Peter suggested in the most intelligent voice he could muster.

"Well, it had better be nice and clean. These are new jeans. Do you like them, Pashy?" asked Tiffany, twirling around.

Harold could not resist butting in again. "Why would you ask 'er that? She is a dog, if you 'adn't noticed. Now, ask 'er about wot canned food she likes; then she could give you a truthful answer, know wot I mean."

"Hush, Harold. I can speak for myself, thank you! Yes, master, they are beautiful jeans," Pasha affirmed. "But next time, I would leave them at home." Tiffany looked crestfallen.

"I always said, jeans were never a good idea on a first mission," added Pewter with a toothy grin.

"Over here! I've found a great base camp." Peter had walked away from the fashion argument to the forest's edge.

Tiffany was the first to enter the clearing. Looking around, she commented, "Not much of a base camp, Peter. I was thinking more of a nice little cottage with running water, not a busted-up old shed with holes in the roof." She continued to moan as she forced the broken door open and walked into the shed. "It will do for now. I hope that we can find this ball quickly and get back to the castle. I so want to meet that Rhyming Slyming prisoner."

"Dare I ask why you want to meet the guy?" asked Harold.

"Yeah, a potentially evil character," added a jealous Peter.

"Looking for a matchin' boyfriend?" Harold exploded into laughter, whipping his tail into Peter's open palm like a high-five. Tiffany glared holes right through them.

"I'll tell you what: I'll stay here, look after the base camp, and maybe do my nails. You all go into the forest and find this wretched ball."

"Are you sure, master?" inquired Pasha. "It could be just as dangerous to stay behind."

"Well, now, let's not be 'asty to go persuadin' anyone off their chosen course o' action," said Harold. "If she wants to stay 'ere, then we should all thank our lucky stars... I mean, she should be allowed 'er choice, know wot I mean."

Peter did not need any more encouragement. Leaving the shed, he skipped into the trees, calling to the others, "Come on, we have a ball to find." He did not really know or care what direction he was going, as long as it got him away from Tiffany's constant attitude. The forest became thicker and darker the deeper they penetrated. Still moving with urgency, Peter slipped occasionally on the wet leaves that covered the forest floor.

"Slow down, Pete. I'm 'aving trouble keeping up 'ere. The quicker we find the ball, the quicker we'll 'ave to go back to snooty Tiffany," Harold called from the rear.

Pasha, for once, did not defend her master, knowing she could be nasty at times. I wish they could see her good side. She really can be as nice as pie sometimes, she thought.

Peter, still moving forward, turned his head and laughed at Harold. Suddenly his feet seemed to be taken from under him. Having no time to put his arms out, he landed face down in the rotten wet leaves. "Ouch!" he screamed, as he held his leg.

"Are you okay?" a concerned Pasha shouted as she ran to Peter's aid, licking his hand that hid a bright red line just above his ankle.

"Well, 'ere's the reason for that fall. Check this out: it's a wire stretched between the trees," Harold confidently told them, his head held high as he pawed at it.

"Brilliant deduction, Sherlock," teased Pewter. "Ribbit! Oh, that is getting old."

"Listen, can you hear that? It's a bell," Peter said, still clutching his leg as he struggled to his feet.

Everyone stood silent, listening for the bell. The only thing they could hear was the rustling of the wind.

Harold broke the silence. "You must be 'earing fings, Pete. Are you sure you didn't 'it your bonce when you fell?"

"No, Harold, I never hit my head. The bell rang when you pawed the wire. Try it again."

Harold swiped at the wire, and once again, the bell rang. "See, I was right!" Peter started to follow the wire, shuffling sideways as he ran it through both his hands until he ended by thudding into a massive oak tree. Looking up, he stated the obvious to the dogs: "The wire seems to go up here. I'll have to climb the tree."

"Stand back, everyone. I am the tree climber around here," Pewter stated proudly as he walked up to the base of the tree.

"Wait just a minute there, Pete, *and* you, oh brainy one. 'Ave either o' you ever climbed a tree as big as this before?" Harold inquired.

"No, but I can try," replied Peter as he rested his foot on the stub of a broken branch. Putting all his weight on the stub, he lifted himself up. With a big grin on his face, he looked down and declared, "This is easy!" Focusing his attention back on the job at hand, his confidence did not last long. Looking up the tall tree, his arms clenched tightly to the trunk. "There is nothing else I can put my feet on."

Harold pushed past Pasha and lined his body next to the wide trunk. "Come on, master. Step down onto me back. It's only about twelve inches. You ain't up as 'igh as you fink you are."

Peter, not wanting to give up but knowing it was beyond him, slowly slid his foot down until he felt Harold's back.

"You really 'ave got to go on a diet," Harold complained as his back felt Peter's full weight.

"I don't want to ruin a good idea, but I can fly up there," suggested Pasha. Not waiting for an answer, she started her ascent.

"I knew there was a reason we kept her around," chuckled Pewter.

"Wish we could fink of a good one for you," countered Harold while giving a little snigger.

"Oh, ha ha. Ribbit!" Pewter decided to just lie down against the tree and groom himself.

Pasha rose higher and higher up the tree, dodging twisting branches. The canopy was thick, and soon all view of the forest floor was out of sight. She followed the cord right up to a little brass bell hanging just below a limb.

Elated at her discovery, she shouted down, "I have found the bell! What do I do now?"

Everyone just looked at each other until Peter suggested, "Uh, bring it down!"

"Good call, m' boy," Harold proudly said.

Carefully hovering, Pasha attempted to grasp the bell in her teeth and yank it loose. It was stuck fast. She decided to have one last attempt. She tugged with all her might.

"Now I know I had a little too much happy juice at the Lepraoke bar last night because here I am watching a flyin' dog trying to steal me security system."

Slowly turning her head, Pasha was shocked to see a small man all in green standing on the branch above her head.

"Now, what would a dog like you be doing up a tree thievin' from the likes o' me?"

Pasha grabbed the bell one more time. Her teeth rattled at the effort until the bell came loose. She turned downward and began to descend the tree as fast as she could.

"I love it when they run," shouted the little man in green.

Pasha dodged branches as she sped downwards, trying to yell a warning to her friends below. All she could manage were garbled noises around the bell. She finally just spit the bell out and let it fall.

"Everyone! There's a—" was all she could say before something grabbed her and held her tight.

"Did you guys hear Pasha?" asked Peter. There was a series of thuds mixed with a clonking bell sound coming down out of the treetop. It was getting closer.

"Did she break the bell?" Harold and Peter backed away from the tree. "Hey, ya furry frog, you might want to get away from the..."

Pewter was mid-lick on one of his legs when the bell smacked into the ground right in front of him. The cat jumped three feet into the air, landing to the side of the tree, all of his hair standing on end.

"Where's Pashy?" asked a concerned Harold. No one said a word. A voice from behind interrupted the silence.

"Top o' the morning to ya."

Everyone jumped. They turned to face an old man about two feet six inches tall. He was dressed from his medieval-style hat to his beautifully crafted shoes in a shade of green that made him nearly invisible in the green forest.

"Now listen 'ere, Shorty! This ain't no miniature Robin 'ood film. I want some answers and now! Where did you appear from, and if you are from around 'ere, where is me sis?" Harold demanded.

"Oh, bejeebers, so much front for a dog! Your thievin' friend is right here." The leaves above their heads parted and a tree limb descended, revealing Pasha bound up tight in a fist of branches.

"Please, sir, let her go," pleaded Peter. "We are here on a mission to find a tiny golden ball. It belongs to a dog just like these two. I tripped on the wire and that led us to the bell. We did not mean any harm."

"A golden ball, ya say? Another dog, eh? You be friends of Shamrock then?"

"Shamrock is our brother," Harold explained as he nodded to Pasha as well.

"Well, this is interestin'," said the tiny man as he snapped his fingers and the tree let go of Pasha. She caught herself and hovered down for a soft landing.

"Excuse me, sir," Peter asked in a timid voice. "Are you a leprechaun?"

"So I am, and a fine specimen of one at that, if I say so me-self. My name's Shamus O'Malley, cobbler and general mischief-maker of this here forest. Now, I understand humans are humans, leprechauns without a sense of humor and a trifle bigger, of course, so that takes care of the spotty fat boy. I do not quite understand the cat or the two dogs, though, so I don't. Now, get on with it, boy. What was it ye wanted again?"

"Have you seen a German Shepherd or a golden ball?"

"Like this one," Pasha said as she stepped forward and raised her neck to show the necklace.

"Ah, now, you know it wouldn't be right for a leprechaun to divulge the whereabouts of gold. I could be struck off the Register of Worthy Leprechauns for doing that, so I could. I will make a deal with you, though."

"Anything, sir. We just want the ball and we will be gone from your forest forever."

"Here it is, then. Nothing is negotiable here, so it isn't. It's all or nothing. I know where the ball is, and I will help you find it if you all help me get me wife back."

"Oh, don't tell me: your wife left you for a bigger man!" Harold jumped in, then burst into laughter at the last word.

"If you don't be quiet, mouthy dog, I will leave now and you will never find your brother. This is a big forest, so it is, and there are many hidden places."

As Harold was the only one who thought his little joke fun-ny, he held his mouth closed and tried to stop laughing.

"Mad Mick has stolen me wife and is holding her captive, along with a load of others in the Land of the Lake. Shamrock lives in an old shack on the edge of the forest. We sort of have this understanding since he bit me bum while I was trying to pinch his bone. I leave him alone, and he doesn't sink those big teeth into me bum anymore."

"That must be the shack Tiffany is waiting in. OK, Shamus, you have a deal," Pasha agreed for everyone.

"We can't get to the Land of the Lake until tomorrow," explained the leprechaun, "so tonight you will be me guests, so you shall."

"We have to get Tiffany first, but I'm not sure how to get back there," Peter said, suddenly panicky.

"I'll show you where it is, but I'm not going anywhere near that mad dog's house, so I ain't. Loves ta give chase, so it does. I be liking me bum too much."

Shamus led everyone back through the forest to the edge of the clearing, then stopped in his tracks. "I'll be waiting here." He sat down, rested his back against a tree, tilted his hat over his eyes, and immediately started snoring.

Peter led the others into the clearing, climbing over the tree trunks littering it, before reaching the door of the shack. Being a gentleman, Peter knocked on the door before calling, "Come on, Tiff! We know where the ball is!" Receiving no answer, he slowly pushed the creaky door open, yelling out, "Tiffany? Are you in here?" He looked around the now tidy shack as the others waited patiently outside.

Peter emerged with a worried look on his face. "She's not in there. She cannot be far, though. It looks like she's been cleaning up." He started calling Tiffany's name at the top of his voice and it was not long before the rest of them joined in. Shamus walked into the clearing, rubbing his eyes. "What is all the noise about? There I was, having a lovely dream about me beautiful wife doing a duet with me at the Lepraoke bar. All of a sudden, I'm woken by you lot screaming your heads off. Don't tell me: gone, is she? Disappeared? Nowhere to be seen?"

"That's right," Peter answered. "We can't find her anywhere."

"Well, let me shed a little light on the subject, so I shall. I'd be thinking she's been kiddynapped, same as me beautiful wife was. She'll be in the Land of the Lake by now, captive, supplying fuel for Mad Mick's transportation, so she will."

"Then we must go there immediately and free her!" cried an anxious Pasha.

"Slow down, doggy. We can't go to the Land of the Lake until tomorrow. Today is a bad day to go. The pixies will be collecting food for their babies. They'll be mad if we go today, and you don't want to be upsetting the pixies, so you don't. We will rest tonight at me house and make a start at daybreak. There won't be any great danger to the girl, waitin' a day."

Shamus beckoned everyone to follow him as he disappeared back into the forest. Pasha led the others in hot pursuit of the leprechaun. After about an hour's hard walk, Peter recognized a fallen tree that they had passed a long while back.

"Are we going around in circles, Shamus? I've seen that tree before."

"Oh, you caught me! I was wondering how long it would take ya, so I was. We've passed that tree four full times now! Ha ha ha!"

"Well, enough is enough. Where is your house?" demanded a forceful Peter.

"It's somewhere and nowhere, and anywhere I want it to be. Close your eyes and count to ten." Everyone did as asked, with the exception of Pewter, who had only learned to count to three.

When they opened their eyes, they were standing in front of the fattest tree stump they had ever seen. It was about ten feet tall and just as wide. On top of it was a thatched roof with a little chimney wisping out a faint line of smoke. Shamus welcomed everyone as a part of the tree stump opened like a door. The inside looked cozy. The walls were light in color, and the lines of thick sap running down to the floor made it look like expensive designer wallpaper.

"It looks a lot bigger inside than it does out, but everything is so small," commented Peter as he ducked to miss a thick beam running through the middle of the room.

"It isn't small. It's just vertically challenged, so it is. Just like me."

As Shamus opened a cupboard to offer his friends a drink, out jumped a tiny cat, no more than four inches tall. It ran past everyone and out the door. Looking confused, Peter asked, "What was that green streak that just whizzed past me?"

Shamus explained, "That's me cute little leprecat. I won him in a lepraoke competition singing a duet with me beautiful wife, Shamus-she. Now, it's time for some of the old shut-eye, so it is. Don't you go sleepwalking because it's dangerous around here if you're not as tree-wise as me. Now, sleep where you fall; we'll be making an early start in the morning, so we shall."

Pasha and Harold stared at each other and then looked around the cramped house before saying at the same time, "I think I'll sleep outside."

Chapter Fourteen

Peter woke to a strange animal crying, "Doo-a-doodle-cock! Doo-a-doodle-cock!" He crawled through the door to find Pasha and Harold still asleep. Between them was a misshapen hen. Its head was attached between its legs, and its short tail end was on its shoulders.

Shamus emerged from the house, asking, "So, you've met me backward hen, then?" Peter, still staring at the strange creature, asked, "Yes, but... how does it lay its eggs?"

"They come straight out of her mouth, so they do, and a better egg you'll not find this side of County Kildare." Shamus tapped the still-sleeping Pasha and Harold with one of his pointed shoes. "Wake up, brother and sister of Shamrock. It's time to go, so it is. We have to get to the lake before the sun rises."

"Did you just kick me, Paddy?" moaned Harold, opening one eye. Harold was never at his best first thing in the morning. He much preferred to wake up under his own steam.

Pasha, however, keen to rescue her master, jumped to her feet and was ready to go. Harold dragged himself up, eyes still half-shut as he muttered, "Come on, then. Let's get this over with."

"All we need now is Pewter. Where is he?" asked Peter.

"The last time I saw him, he was curled up on the end of me bed with me leprecat."

Pasha called out for the feline warrior, who obligingly poked his head out through a small window. "Come on, Pewt, we have to go!" Pasha shouted as they all followed Shamus through the early morning mist that clung to the forest floor.

"Be right there, Mother. I am just saying goodbye to my new friend."

A few minutes later, Pewter ran from the house, quickly catching up and jumping onto Pasha's back.

It was only a short while before Shamus stopped and turned to face everyone. "Here we are. Now, you have to be really quiet or you won't get through to the Land of the Lake."

"I can't see any lake. Is this just another one of your tricks, Shamus?" asked Harold, now fully awake.

"Are you blind? Can't you see it? It's in front of your eyes, so it is."

Peter looked at the forest floor in front of him. "All I can see is a puddle. That's not a lake."

"You humans are such unbelievers, so you are. Now, just copy me exactly and you will be travelling first-class, so you will."

Shamus stood on the edge of the small pool of water and jumped as high as his little legs would let him. He landed exactly in the middle of the puddle. Although extremely light, the splash from his landing sent water soaring outward, completely soaking everyone.

"That was not funny," moaned Harold.

"It wasn't meant to be," explained Shamus. "You need to be wetted with lake water before you can move through. Just to prove it, I'll now wet me own self, so I shall."

He knelt down on the edge of the puddle and dunked his head into it, quickly pulling it out and shaking it, complaining, "Brrrr, that be cold, that be. Now we can enter. Just do what I do."

Shamus stepped into the middle of the puddle, which now seemed a little deeper, with the waterline coming up to his knees. Shamus closed his eyes and started singing:

"Pixie pixie puddle poo,
Mix the water and send me through,
Pixie pixie puddle do,
Off to lake land,
With all me friends, too."

Shamus opened his eyes, still standing knee-deep in water, and looked toward the others. Suspicious as ever, Harold shouted at him, "It 'asn't worked, 'as it? This is a load of rubbish. There's no Land of the Lake, is there, L.L.?"

"What's L.L.?" Pasha asked.

"Lying Leprechaun," huffed Harold.

"Here I go!" shouted Shamus as he started sinking into the puddle. It was not long before all anyone could see was his hat floating in the middle of the water.

"It does work! You next, Harold!" cried out an excited Peter as he retrieved Shamus's hat and shook the water out of it.

"Why me? Why not Pasha?" complained Harold.

"Harold, we are all going, so it doesn't really matter who goes next, does it? If it worries you, I will go next. Hold on, Pewter," Pasha warned sternly, looking Harold in the eye.

"Yeah, don't be a scaredy-cat!" Pewter laughed and pointed at Harold.

With Pewter on her back, she walked to the middle of the puddle and started to sing:

"Pixie pixie puddle poo,
Mix the water and send me through,
Pixie pixie puddle do,
Off to lake land,
And all me friends, too."

Harold shouted out to Pasha as she started to disappear, "I wouldn't give up your day job, Pash! There is no way you would win 'Dog Idol!' With Pasha now gone, Harold gulped. He knew it was his turn.

"Go on, Harold, in you go," Peter commanded.

"Why, master, that was so masterly of you. To be honest, I don't fink I can remember dat song. Can I go with you?"

Peter, feeling proud that Harold needed him for the first time, answered, "Oh, Harold, I do believe you're scared. Come on, we can go together."

Peter and Harold walked into the puddle, Peter still clutching Shamus's hat. He sang the song, Harold sitting next to him with his paws covering his ears, as they vanished into the water.

*****

As Peter and Harold emerged from the water, they found Shamus and Pasha next to them, the water up to Shamus's neck.

"Where's Pewter?" asked Peter.

"I can still feel his claws in my back." Shamus moved to the side and plunged his hand into the water. A look of relief came across her face as Shamus's hands emerged clasping a sopping Pewter.

"Thanks for the remembering of my existence," moaned the cat as he spat out a stream of water.

"Let's get out of the lake," Shamus suggested as he waded forward toward the lake's edge. Pewter did not like water at all and was happy to have Shamus hold him above his head. Harold decided it was time to use his power. Concentrating on a tree on the lake's edge, he commanded tongues afar. The little leprechaun looked at him in confusion as Harold's tongue shot across the lake and wrapped itself around the tree. Peter took his chance and quickly climbed onto Harold's back. As the tongue started to pull them, he plucked Shamus out of the water with his tail, causing him to drop Pewter.

Pewter landed on the safety of Pasha's back as she launched herself into the air and flew at great speed, passing over Harold as they traveled to the shoreline. Pasha landed gently at the lake's edge, just beside the tree Harold's tongue was still gripping tightly. Harold was now travelling so fast Shamus had completely dried out, his cheeks flapping in the wind.

"Jump into the water, or you'll crash into the tree!" Pasha shouted.

Peter jumped to the side, the shallow water breaking his fall. Shamus had not heard Pasha's warning and, as Harold released his tongue from the tree, he unknowingly also released his tail. Harold hit the shore with all four paws digging deep into the ground as brakes. Shamus, now released from the dog's tail, continued to fly through the air. The leprechaun quickly disappeared into the distant sky.

Harold looked up sorrowfully at Pasha standing over him. "Sorry, Pash, I didn't mean for that to 'appen. Let's go find 'im now. I'm sure 'e's okay; 'e's such a tough little lepri."

"Come on, let's take this seriously, Harold. I will fly up with Pewter and look from the air. You take Peter and search the forest. Hold on again, Pewter."

"Holding. Ribbit!"

The pair took to the air while Harold and Peter swung under the forest canopy. Pasha spotted a small field ahead, containing a number of haystacks. One of these had grown a pair of kicking, green legs.

Pasha landed next to the haystack just as Harold and Peter came swinging out of the edge of the forest. Peter jumped off and immediately began to climb up the side of the hay mountain. It was hard going for him; with every step he took, more hay fell from under his feet. When he reached the top, Shamus was still kicking furiously, shouting, "Get me out of here!"

Peter took a firm grip on the leprechaun's legs and, with a big tug, pulled him out of the hay. Shamus was a lot lighter than Peter had imagined, and the force he used sent Shamus straight over Peter's head. Both of them rolled down the side of the haystack, ending up on the soft cushion of loose hay that surrounded it. The leprechaun quickly jumped up, his anger plain to see.

"What's going on here? You scared the bejeebers out of me! How can you fly, and what is that thing you have around your neck?"

Pasha explained their warrior powers. Calming down, the leprechaun snatched his hat from Peter and responded, "Well, I must say, that is impressive, so it is. What other powers do you have? Can you teach me some of that there magic?"

"Sorry, Shamus, it is only for warriors, as are our golden balls you keep looking at."

"Well, if you change your mind, you just let me know. Now, let's get off to Mad Mick's place. Can I ride on your back?" Pasha knelt down so the little man could climb on. "Move back a bit, warrior cog. I need a bit more room." Pewter obliged and shuffled backwards toward the dog's tail.

"Are we all ready?" Pasha asked.

"To be sure, to be sure," Shamus shouted out as she lifted from the ground and began moving forward. Holding onto her collar with one hand and waving his other in the air, he shouted, "Yeehaw, a flying leprechaun! You'll be going straight as far as you can see, so you shall. There we will find Mad Mick's forest."

It did not take long for Pasha to reach the very ends of the forest flying at full speed. The warriors landed in a clearing, as Harold and Peter caught up to them. Peter's hair was wind-blown straight back from zooming through the forest. Shamus jumped down, a big grin on his face. "That was the most exciting thing I've ever done! You simply have to teach me to do that! If I could fly, Mad Mick would be mincemeat, so he would."

"We don't know 'ow to teach ya, so you can forget that one straight away. Now, where is this Mad Mick dude?" Harold asked.

"He is just past that line of bushes, but be careful. He has lookouts, and Asmagies."

"Asmagies? Wot is that?" Harold asked as he, Peter, and Pasha crept toward the bushes.

"It's a little creature with pointed things all over its body. It suffers with asthma and allergies, so they call him Asmagies. Get down! They'll see you!" Shamus whispered to Pewter, who was standing up on Pasha's back. The warrior cog tried to jump to the ground but slipped and fell into the bushes, then on through, and rolled down the steep grassy hill that bordered the camp, finishing with a bump in front of a small hut on the camp's outskirts. Two evil-looking bald-headed leprechauns with big earrings hanging from their noses burst out of the hut as a stunned Pewter tried to get to his feet.

"There it is!" one of them shouted as he pointed to Pewter.

The warrior cog faced the leprechauns and teasingly demanded, "Take me to your leader! Ribbit!"

"Right away, Sir Cat. Mad Mick can have ya fer dinner." They picked up Pewter, throwing a length of rope around the cat, and walked back toward the hut. Just before they entered, one of them mentioned the excellent cat stew they would soon enjoy.

Hearing this, Harold moved to jump over the bushes to help the little cog, but Pasha held him back. "Wait, Harold! It will be better if we have a plan. If we get Pewter now, we'll lose the element of surprise and that may put Tiffany in more danger than she already is."

Harold did not like it but agreed, sighing as he gazed at the small hut, its door now closed.

"So what is our plan?" Shamus asked.

"I'm not sure yet. Let's look around the whole camp and see what we are up against," suggested Pasha. It was suddenly starting to dawn on her what being a leader actually meant.

As they moved around the bushes surrounding the camp, it became apparent that this was going to be no easy task. The camp was extremely big, about twenty buildings in all. The camp was also full of all sorts of nasty-looking leprechauns.

As the companions peered through a large bush, Shamus said, "Look down there. Do you see the thing with the needles sticking out of it? That's Asmagies, so it is. If he sticks one of those needles in you, you're a goner for sure."

"That's just an 'edge'og," replied Harold, laughing. "They can't 'urt ya."

"If you say so, but we'll see how brave you are. You will deal with him, so you will."

"What is that big square building with that funnel thing coming out of it?" Pasha asked.

"That is where Mad Mick keeps all his prisoners. They make fuel in there for his transport. It's called the flatu-factory. In all my years, and they be many, I've never heard of anyone getting out of there."

A deep popping sound approached from the distance. "What's that noise?" Pasha asked.

"That'll be Mad Mick, so it will."

As the noise got louder, a horrible smell filled the air. "Arhhhhh! That is foul! What is that smell?" Harold asked, gagging.

"That will be coming from Mad Mick's cycle," Shamus replied, pointing down to a leprechaun entering the camp on a chopper-style cycle. It had no pedals and a box on the back mudguard with a tube sticking out of it. The rider wore a blue Mohawk and rings in every part of his face not covered by the gas mask he wore.

"That is one strange cycle," said Harold.

"That's no normal cycle; that's a fart-cycle! Can you see that human? That's Lance, Mick's second-in-command. He runs the factory for him," Shamus explained.

"So, now all we need is a plan," said Pasha.

*****

At the castle, the Keeper and Ozzy were keeping a close eye on their new warriors on the Wall of Visions.

"They are really in a mess now. Do you think we should intervene? I could go and help them," offered Ozzy as he paced anxiously.

"That would be very helpful to them, but I am afraid you would not be able to get there. They are in the pixies' world now. Their fate is totally in their own inexperienced hands."

Chapter Fifteen

With their plan worked out, it was time to put it into effect. Shamus led the way back into the forest. Everyone agreed that Pewter had to be rescued first, most certainly before dinnertime.

With everyone now in place, Pasha took the lead, running through the bushes and down the hill until she was standing outside the hut containing the captive Pewter. She barked furiously until the two bald leprechauns emerged from the hut.

Pasha was not ready for what she saw when the door opened. Not only did the biggest of the leprechauns have what looked like a gun in his hands, but Pasha could also see past them and caught sight of Pewter sitting in a cooking pot over an open fire.

Forgetting the plan entirely, Pasha aimed at the two leprechauns and shouted, "Paw Power!" She raised one paw and shot a ball of fire directly at the two leprechauns. Seeing it coming for them, they both hit the ground. The fireball soared over their heads and hit the side of the hut, which burst into flames.

With the hut fully ablaze, Pasha disregarded the two leprechauns, who were now getting back to their feet, and flew right past them into the burning structure.

Harold muttered to himself, "That wasn't part of the plan. Oh, well, 'ere goes nuffink." He jumped down to face the two leprechauns, keeping one eye on them and the other on the burning hut.

As the big leprechaun raised his gun, Harold's tongue shot from his mouth, wrapped around both of the leprechauns, and pulled them together so tightly that they looked like conjoined twins. Harold looked up at the hut now engulfed in flames. He paused until he heard shouts and cries from somewhere in the trees: "Get some water, quick!"

Harold pulled his tongue and his two captives close to his mouth and then flung them into the trees. The two leprechauns landed as planned. Peter and Shamus quickly bound and gagged the stunned pair, who had begun to shout out for help from their friends.

Shamus and Peter finally joined a solemn Harold, and the three stared silently at the smoldering hut. Harold hung his head and a solitary tear ran down his cheek until he heard a twig snap and whipped his head around. Shamus and Peter followed suit, coming face-to-face with the type of short, prickly creature that Shamus had pointed out earlier. In fact, it did resemble a hedgehog, as Harold had stated. He had promised to deal with the Asmagies so he stepped forward slightly, sniffing the air.

Before Shamus could warn anyone of the imminent danger, Asmagies sneezed and a shower of his needles shot out of his body like arrows from an army of medieval archers. Harold took the brunt of the poisonous needles, falling to the ground immediately, closely followed by Shamus and Peter. Peter was the last to lose consciousness, hearing the sound of Mad Mick's fart-cycle before finally passing out.

Pulling up to the camp, Mad Mick was flanked by two large leprechauns running on either side of his fart-cycle, which now had a mobile cage attached. Lance followed a short distance behind, panting and wheezing as he tried to keep up.

"Load them into the cage, Lance, and then free those two useless lookouts!" Mad Mick shouted as he pointed to the two captive leprechauns. With Harold, Peter, and Shamus now in handcuffs and loaded into Mick's cage, he started the fart-cycle and headed back toward the flatu-factory.

*****

Not far away, Pasha lay motionless, unaware of the pixie hovering over her head. She still clasped Pewter between her front paws.

"Oh, no, what have you done?" the pixie said aloud, mistaking Pasha for her friend Shamrock, who had once saved her from Mad Mick. She landed on the floor next to Pasha's nose, took a deep breath and, opening her mouth as wide as it would go, placed it over one of Pasha's nostrils and blew as hard as she could.

Pasha lifted her head and opened her mouth, gasping in as much air as she could take. Then, feeling a tickle on her nose, she let out a loud, powerful sneeze, blowing the pixie high into the air. Pasha laid her head back on the leaves until the pixie landed with a bump close beside her, sending a swirl of leaves into the air.

Whimpering, Pasha lifted her battered body upwards until she was standing uneasily on all fours. The pixie jumped back to her feet and dusted off her skirt and jacket. Once again immaculate, she flew up and hovered in front of Pewter's head, asking Pasha, "What is your friend's name?"

Pasha turned and moved gingerly to where Pewter lay, licking his cheek gently. "His name is Pewter, and he is one of my best friends. Can you do anything to help him?"

"There is nothing wrong with him; he is just sleeping," explained the pixie. "See, he is opening his eyes now."

"Hi there. Who are you, hot stuff?" Pewter asked the pixie, who still hovered before him.

"I am Trixie. I am a lady in waiting to Her Majesty, Queen Dixie of the Pixies. What's your story, fluffy one?"

"Well, that is the interesting part. You see, I am a great warrior fighting for good against evil. My squire Pasha and I have come here to retrieve something stolen by that Mad Mick character."

"Squire?" blurted Pasha while tilting her head slightly and frowning. "I'm the squire?"

"Geez, just joking, Ma. What about, 'Warrior Queen' Pasha?"

Trixie looked Pasha in the eye and then scanned down to her front leg. "You are not Shamrock, are you? How did you get into the Land of the Lake? This is our secret world."

"Shamrock is my brother. We have come here to retrieve his magical golden ball. It looks like the one around my neck."

"To be totally honest with you, I haven't seen Shamrock for at least a week. I think we must assume that Mad Mick and his gang have him as well."

Pewter interrupted, "If this is your world, why do you put up with Mad Mick?"

"He has had our queen captive for more than a year now. If we leave him alone, he has promised not to kill her, but our magic doesn't work as long as she is held captive."

Pasha thought for a moment. "If you help us get Shamrock back, in return we will help you free your queen."

The pixie looked hard at the warriors while they waited patiently for her reply. "We have a deal on one condition. You must also help us rid this world of Mad Mick and his gang once and for all."

"That is exactly what I was thinking," confirmed Pasha. "Let's go."

*****

The trio stood on the edge of the leprechaun village, hidden away in the thick underbrush of the forest. The burning hut had long since disintegrated into a pile of cinders. The village was quiet again with no sign of a leprechaun anywhere. Unfortunately, there was also no sign of their friends.

"That used to be our village until Mad Mick and his horde of punk leprechauns took it away from us," Trixie explained bitterly.

"No worries, my dear," Pewter assured the upset pixie. "With my help, we will take it back." The cat gave Trixie a wink.

"Do you think they would have gone on without us?" Pasha asked. "It might be worse than that," Trixie informed her. "Look at the ground; those pointed things lying all around can only mean

162

one thing: Asmagies," Trixie sighed. "If you get stuck with one of the needles, it puts you to sleep. Then, Mad Mick's gang loads you up on a trailer and carts you off to work in the factory."

"Are you telling me they have also been taken prisoner?" Pasha looked expectantly at Trixie, who nodded as she dropped her head. "That only leaves the three of us to get them all out. With all of us it would have been hard, but now it is going to be almost impossible."

"Nonsense," said Pewter confidently. "Let's storm in there, Paw Power blazing, and show these leprechauns who's boss."

"Paw Power?" Trixie scratched her head.

"That is a long story. We could fly in and land on the flat factory roof. There must be a way in from there," Pasha began, growing more confident with every word.

"That's what I like, a good plan to follow. What are we waiting for? Let's go!" Pewter exclaimed. Pasha wasted no time and lifted off, soaring high into the clouds and using them like a blanket to keep the three invisible from the ground as they flew above the lookouts. Once over the factory, Pasha made a vertical descent and landed softly on the factory roof. Pewter jumped from her back as the three split up and started to explore the large roof in different directions.

The roof had a number of skylights scattered in between small chimneys, which oozed thick, black smoke. Visibility was virtually impossible when the smoke came in large billows. The two warriors and Trixie eventually met again on the far side of the roof.

"Well, did you find a door?" inquired Pewter.

"No, it seems the only way in is through these skylight windows," Pasha replied. "You can't see through them, but I did see one that is slightly open."

Pewter and Trixie followed as Pasha led them to the skylight. "Won't it open any farther?" Pewter asked as he tugged at the metal-framed window.

"I don't think so. Can you get through, Pewt?" The feline warrior tried to force his head through the small gap. He had only managed to squeeze it halfway through when Pasha asked impatiently, "What's in there? Can you see anything?"

"No, it's empty, and now my head's stuck!" Pewter shouted back.

"Well, get back out then and I will fly in," Trixie suggested.

As Pewter put all fours against the window frame and pushed with all his might, the door inside opened. The cat froze, not even daring to breathe. He watched as six leprechauns entered the room, carrying Harold. They placed the dog on the floor and exited, their voices melting incoherently together. Pewter continued trying with all of his might to free his head until finally, with one last effort, he came loose and fell flat on his back.

The pixie wasted no time flying through the small gap in the window and down to the still unconscious Harold. Trixie blew into Harold's nostrils, the same as she had done to Pasha's, only this time she had learned her lesson and jumped straight off his nose before he sneezed. Harold opened his eyes slightly and groaned before closing them again.

"Oh, no, you don't, doggy. Wake up," Trixie demanded in her sternest voice while giving him a sharp dig with her wand.

Pewter called through the gap in the skylight, "Harold, wake up!"

Harold jumped to his feet. "Pewter, you're still alive? Where is Pash? Is she okay?"

"Yes, she's here with me. We need you to use your tail to force this skylight open more."

"One tail, comin' up!"

Harold's tail shot straight up and shattered the skylight. He dived out of the way as glass crashed to the floor. The noise was explosive and several of Mick's men came scurrying into the room. They now stood staring up at the hole in the roof.

"Sorry, fellas, can't stay for tea, know wot I mean," Harold quipped.

Harold's tail and tongue shot up to the hole in the roof. He caught the edges and pulled his entire body up and onto the roof.

"That was not the smartest thing to do. Now they know we're here," Pasha sternly told Harold.

Dropping his head, he muttered, "Nice to see you, too, sis."

"Looked pretty cool to me," added Pewter.

"Never mind all that. Harold, do you know where Peter and Shamus are?"

"I was out cold, Pash. All I saw was that pointy little creature and that's it."

Pasha thought quickly. "Now we'll have to change our plan. Trixie, do you know where Mad Mick lives? We don't have much time before he knows we're here."

Harold jumped in: "Who is Trixie?"

"I am Trixie, your friendly pixie, but if you don't do as you are told in the future, I will not be as friendly."

"Well, I am 'arold, Super Warrior, and if you fink I'm frightened of an overgrown wasp dressed up as a 'uman, you 'ave got another fink coming."

"I will deal with you later. Now I am more concerned about freeing my queen and, yes, Pasha, I do know where Mad Mick lives. He has taken up residence in my queen's palace. Perhaps that is where he is keeping your friends. I'll take you there."

"This is what we'll do then," Pasha said, taking charge. "We will kidnap him and hold him hostage until his gang releases both our warriors and your queen."

"You're getting good at this 'ole plan-makin' fing. Let's do it," agreed Harold.

*****

Pasha's plan hit its first obstacle right away. They had all gathered in front of a large stone palace. It was an imposing structure with seemingly countless windows and several towers. That many rooms meant it could take hours to find Mad Mick, and the leprechauns were not going to make it easy. They may not have much time.

"How do we know what room he is in?" asked Pasha. "There are so many."

"Yes, there are many, but remember, this is a palace for pixies and, like me, the queen is very small. Although the windows make all the rooms look big, there are actually only two rooms high enough for Mick to be in: the dining hall and the family room. They were constructed normal size for our non-pixie visitors. Those two rooms take up the whole ground floor, and he must be in one of them. He never goes anywhere without his fart-cycle, and that's in front of the door."

"Yeah, I smelled that," confirmed Pewter.

"Ya know, Pewt, you haven't croaked..."

"Don't jinx it, you big dumb do— Ribbit! Aw, man, why did you have to say that? Ribbit."

"Trixie, can you go and spy through the windows of those two rooms and report back here?" asked Pasha politely. Without reply, the pixie flew as fast as she could toward the palace.

With only warriors present, it was time for some serious discipline. Pasha, turning toward Harold, ranted, "This is not a game, Harold. Not only are our masters at risk, but we have the chance here to make a difference for Trixie's people. Trixie helped me after I rescued Pewter. She helped you too. Now we have a chance to pay her back and it is not a time for joking around. That goes for you as well, Pewter. You will follow my lead and not do anything without asking."

Harold took a deep breath, sighed, and dropped his head again. Turning slowly, he walked a few steps away, only reversing direction when he heard the buzz of the pixie's returning wings.

"I have both good news and bad. What do you want first?"

"Hit us with the bad first. Let's get that one out of the way," suggested Pewter.

"Well, the dining hall is full of his gang. They are having some sort of party with music so loud they have to shout at each other to hear."

"That really is bad news. Wot is the good news?" Harold inquired meekly.

"Mad Mick is on his own, watching his favorite film on TV."

"Well, I didn't hear any bad news there," Pasha stated, grinning confidently. "If all his gang are in one room, then that will make it easier for us. All we have to do is kidnap Mick, and all the others will do as he says. We had better move fast, though, in case he decides to join the party."

Without prompt, Pewter jumped up on Pasha's back as she lifted off the ground to lead the assault. Trixie flew next to her ear, directing the warrior leader toward the correct window. With nothing to grip onto, Harold decided it was time to try something new with his powers. He turned and extended his tail high into the air toward the palace. As the tail hit the ground, he sprang himself upward and, with the precision of an Olympic athlete, he pole-vaulted right over the other warriors.

As the first warrior to arrive, he crept up to the window. As the other warriors closed in, Pasha pointed her paw forward and two bolts of fire exploded against the glass, shattering it into little pieces. Pasha flew over her brother and through the smoldering hole where the window had been. She found herself hovering above a coffee table, looking around the large room richly decorated with fine paintings and sculptures. Most of these had been spray-painted or defaced in some way by the occupying leprechauns. She could not see anyone. Harold jumped in, followed by Trixie.

"Nothing. Let's get out of here," Pasha sighed as she turned, ready to leave.

"'Ang on a min; let's all leave together," Harold said deliberately, putting a front paw to his mouth in a bid for quiet and pointing with the other to an empty couch.

They all remained silent for a couple of seconds. A line of blue hair rose slowly over the top of the couch. "Tail afar!" Harold commanded. His tail extended across the room and over the couch, re-emerging wrapped around a terrified leprechaun. "I do believe I 'ave caught a punk!"

"Well done, Harold!" Pewter shouted as he clapped his paws together frantically.

"Keep him tightly in your tail and follow me," Pasha commanded as she flew against the middle of the adjoining doors that led into the dining room. The doors flew wide open, slamming into the walls on either side as she burst in. Her entrance went unnoticed as the loud, rowdy party raged on.

Pasha decided it was time to end the festivities. "Paw Power!" she shouted and flung a fireball right across the hall, exploding the music system into pieces. Shocked and disoriented, the slew of leprechauns fell silent and stared at the four warriors.

"May I, oh please, Mommy?" pleaded Pewter.

"Be my guest," Pasha said, winking, and gestured to the masses. Clearing his throat, Pewter proudly stepped forward.

"My name is Pewter, Warrior Supreme, and I am commanding that you release all prisoners immediately."

A murmur swept across the dining hall as the stunned guests milled around and debated what to do. Before long, Lance was ushered forward by the insistent hands of his comrades. Hat in hand, he looked at the warriors with pleading eyes. "We have no authority to release any prisoners. There is only one person who can authorize that, and that is our leader, Mick."

"Oh, you mean this Mick?" Harold confidently replied as he shifted to reveal the gang leader wrapped tightly in his tail.

"Don't do anything he says! Get them!" shouted Mick, wheezing as he struggled to get breath into his lungs.

Lance placed a box on the floor, opened the lid, and took out a prickly little creature, which he set beside it. Eyes widened all around as Lance crouched down and yelled, "Asmagies, sneeze!"

The hedgehog-like creature lifted his long, twitchy nose into the air and took a deep breath.

"Hit the floor!" shouted Trixie.

Pasha, Pewter, and Harold were unhesitant, instantly lying as flat as they could, closing their eyes tightly in anticipation of the Asmagies' needle attack. The hedgehog sneezed so hard that it lifted itself clean off the floor, with every one of its hundreds of needles leaving its body like a barrage of missiles.

Pasha, still flat on the floor, peeked through squinted eyes as the room rumbled and then grew silent. Opening her eyes wider, Pasha rose to her feet to survey the room of fallen, sleeping leprechauns.

Only one—Lance—was still standing. He held his head with both hands, muttering, "What have I done?" while pulling at his long, copper hair. The rest of the warriors slowly stood and looked around before their gazes converged on the shaking little man. Lance fell to his knees. "Please forgive me, Mick. I don't know what to do."

"Your destiny is no longer in Mick's hands. We want our friends set free," Pasha snapped, swooping downward to look him in the eye. "I suggest you tell us where they are." Pasha reinforced her threats by firing a single bolt over his shoulder, which exploded just beyond the now terrified Lance.

"There, down at the factory. The mouthy girl and the spotty boy are being put to good use."

"How can that be? We were just there!" ranted Pewter.

"Well, Lancie, march ya-self daan there and show us exactly where they are." Harold's tongue flicked out and popped Lance in the head.

"Okay, okay. I will do it. Please keep that thing in your mouth!"

"What about the rest of them? How can we keep them locked up?" Pasha asked Trixie.

"They can stay in here," Trixie mused. "If we set the alarm by the doors, bars will shoot up in front of every window. Then, all we have to do is lock the doors behind us."

"Let's do it then," Pasha said, raising one paw. "We're wasting time. Let's go."

With the doors bolted shut, Trixie punched in the code for the alarm but was promptly disappointed when it beeped angrily back at her.

"What?" she exclaimed, frowning at the keypad as she hammered the number in again.

"Beep!" said the alarm.

Every time she tried a new number, the alarm display beeped and flashed mockingly.

"Do you 'ave a phone 'ere?" asked Harold. "If you 'ave, it's probably the last four digits o' your phone number."

Trixie tried again to no avail and dejectedly hung her head. "I'm sorry, everyone. I just can't remem—" Trixie's head suddenly popped up. Quickly, she mashed her fingers over the keypad. The welcoming sound of an affirmative chime rang out.

Wasting no time, the warriors cheered and ran out to the lawn to see bars rising up from the concrete sills to cover every window.

With the dining room now secure, Lance led the warriors toward the flatu-factory, with Pasha nudging him in his back every time he hesitated. Lance was under no illusions as to who was now running the show.

Chapter Sixteen

The village had become a ghost town. The only moving things were the brown leaves of autumn, floating on a light breeze that whisked around the buildings. The flatu-factory stuck out against the pixie decor of the village as a boxy, industrial eyesore.

On reaching the main factory doors, Pasha asked Lance whether there were any guards inside. Looking directly down to Pasha's paw pointed right at him, Lance confirmed that there were about four guards spread throughout the factory and suggested that they enter the front and back at the same time.

"You wouldn't be leadin' us into a trap now, would ya?" asked Harold.

Pasha looked deep into Lance's eyes and, seeing the sheer terror, decided he must be telling the truth. Pasha told Harold to go around the back of the factory and give her a sign when he was ready to go in.

Harold asked, "What shall I do with this one?" as he lifted his tail to reveal an extremely dusty Mick who had been dragged along the ground from the dining hall to the factory.

"You'll have to take him with you. We have no rope to tie him up and he may be as valuable in here as he was in the dining hall. They know we are here now, so be ready, Harold... and good luck."

"Fanks, sis. As fer me signal, listen for the sound of an owl."

"Huh?"

"I assure you, me impression of an owl is tip-top, the best, A-1, so you 'ad better be ready!" With that, Harold was gone with a bedraggled Mick still in tow.

As the rest waited for Harold to get into position, Pasha noticed Lance getting very nervous, perspiring heavily. He must have been lying to us, but it is too late to abort our plan now. I had better expect the unexpected, Pasha thought as she composed herself to burst in the door on Harold's signal.

The silence was at last broken: "Woo-woo, woo-droo, wood–drow!"

"Is he kidding? That is the worst impersonation of an owl I have ever heard!" said Pewter, laughing.

Pasha did not break her concentration, determined to remain one-step ahead of her enemies. It was just as well because, when she burst open the front door and pushed Lance through, a net dropped from above right on top of him.

Pasha stood outside as Lance struggled to free himself. Two large leprechauns blocked her entrance to the factory. Instinctively, Pasha raised both paws.

"Paw Power!" Two balls of fire shot from Pasha's paws and exploded directly in front of the door, knocking both guards to the floor. Pasha and Pewter stepped over the still-captive Lance and walked straight past the suffering guards.

Harold had the same sort of trouble, with two guards waiting for him by the back door. The net fell on him and his prisoner and, although caught in the trap, Harold acted swiftly, firing though a hole in the net across to the other side of the hall and at the same time continually slapping the two guards across their faces with his wet, moist tongue.

"No more, no more," they both pleaded as Harold struggled out of the net with Mick still dragging along the floor behind him.

By the time Pasha, Pewter, and Trixie had found him, the roles had been reversed, with both guards now tangled up in the net as Harold sat calmly awaiting his comrades.

"You took ya time, Pashy. 'Ave a bit o' trouble, did ya?" Harold said grinning.

Trixie guided the dogs to the main room in the factory, carefully opening the door and allowing Pasha to enter first. Looking around, she could see a row of empty stools pushed up against what

looked like a conveyer belt filled with plates of food, slowly travelling the full length of the room and disappearing through a hole in
the far wall.

"Where is everyone?" Harold murmured to himself.

"I'm not sure. Maybe they're in one of the small rooms,"
Trixie answered.

Trixie was not as much help as she had hoped to be; the factory had changed a lot over the months of Mad Mick's occupation.
"We will have to check every room," she said.

Pewter decided his natural instincts would save the day. He
believed he could smell his master out, and instantly began trying to
do so. Pasha was happy to let him sniff at the bottom of each door
because opening them with her mouth was a tricky operation.

After trying several rooms, the trio came across an unusual
door. This one was not like the others; it had a rubber seal placed
all around it, making it impossible for Pewter to smell anything.
Pasha tried to open it with her mouth a number of times without
success. Finally, exasperated at her failed attempts, she sent a bolt
that disintegrated the handle and lock.

As the door swung open, a strong vacuum suddenly sucked
Pewter into the room. The cat floated around the room before
disappearing through a steel funnel hanging from the ceiling. Trixie
flew with all her might, trying to escape the pull of the machine, but
for every inch she moved away, she got sucked two inches closer.
As her strength finally gave out, she shouted to Pasha, "Save my
queen!" Twisting and turning, Trixie disappeared into the funnel to
who-knew-where.

Pasha, with all four paws pushing against the doorframe,
willed herself to fly upward. Moving each leg a few inches at a time,
it took all of her strength to clear the frame and fly to the ceiling.
With no pulling force restricting her movements now, she flew to
one side and landed safely next to Harold.

"Wot now?" Harold asked loudly over the roaring hum
emitted from the room. Pasha's eyes were wide as she inched back
toward the door. She tried to see what it was that had sucked up
her two friends, but with the force pulling at her head, she knew

moving any nearer would put her in danger. Looking up to the ceiling, she saw what appeared to be a giant funnel with some sort of turning platform underneath, like a carousel without the horses. As she turned back to speak to Harold, she caught a glimpse of something blonde on the other side of the rotating platform.

Squinting through the suctioned air, she waited until the slowly moving platform turned to reveal Tiffany and Peter, their feet strapped to the platform's base. Tiffany's hair stood up on end from the constant sucking of the vacuum. She spotted Pasha and clamored for her help.

Excitedly, Pasha grinned and took two steps forward before realizing her mistake as she slid into the middle of the room and upward toward the vacuum inlet. Although it had sucked up both Pewter and Trixie without any trouble, a one-hundred-pound dog was a different story. The inlet was not wide enough for her to fit through, and her rear end stuck firmly over the hole.

With Pasha wedged tightly into the vacuum, the pull on Tiffany and Peter was severely restricted. Tiffany's hair gently fell back to her head as the force dwindled to what seemed like just a breeze. Peter adjusted his glasses and bent over to try to free his feet from the still rotating platform. Harold reached the opening and peeked around the corner to see Tiffany and Peter spinning around and Pasha partially stuck up the vacuum shoot, her legs flailing and her eyes bulging.

"Are we comfortable, sis? Look at what we 'ave 'ere! Two 'elpless, trussed up 'umans! Who is the main man now, then?" Harold asked as he strutted around the room.

"Harold!" Pasha squealed painfully. "Get Mick to tell you how to turn this thing off! I think all my fur has been sucked off my behind!"

Harold arched his tail and brought Mick to him, nose to nose. "Well then? Out with it! 'Ow do I turn it off?"

Mick nodded his head toward a small booth in the far corner of the room. "The control panel——I don't know which button, but I am sure it's in there."

Harold moseyed complacently to the booth, clearly enjoying every minute of his heroism. Upon entering the booth, he studied the rows upon rows of colorful buttons and levers. A few pushes and pulls later, Pasha fell to the floor in a heap and Tiffany and Peter's leg restraints clicked open. With wobbly feet, they stepped down from the now still platform as Pasha spun in circles, checking for damage to her back end.

Now back on her feet, Pasha once again took control of the situation. "Now we need to find Pewter, Trixie, and Shamus."

"I can 'elp you there, sis. Blue Hair will take us to them, won't ya?" Harold shook his tail relentlessly, zipping Mick through the air.

"Yes, yes, yes! I will, I promise. Pleeeeassse stopppppp."

"Put him down. It'll be faster if he takes us there," Pasha suggested. Harold reluctantly released his grip on Mick. The now free leprechaun ran to the doorway and through it, his feet moving so fast they looked like something out of a cartoon. It was only on the next corridor that Mick stopped. With the others now catching up, Mick took a key from around his neck and opened the door, liberating Shamrock, Shamus, and a small, well-dressed pixie, who flew out of the door and hovered head-high beside Pasha.

"I take it you are Dixie?" asked a submissive Pasha.

"That is correct. I am Dixie, Queen of the Pixies and the Land of the Lake. You are the warrior called Pasha, I take it. My new leprechaun friend here has told me all about you."

Pasha walked into the room and sat in front of Shamrock, who was sitting there stunned as he watched this dog in front of him speaking human. Pasha leaned forward and licked his face.

"You must be my brother. We have come a long way to meet you and to find and return your golden ball. Do you understand what I am saying to you?" she asked, kindly. Shamrock nodded his head and gave her cheek a reciprocal lick.

"'Ello, bruv. Me name's 'arold and I will be your rescuer today."

175

"We need to find Pewter and Trixie. They were sucked up the vacuum in that room and I have no idea where they ended up," Pasha said, turning to Harold.

Mick began laughing so hard, he fell on the floor and rolled around. "Good luck gettin' 'em back. They are in cans, processed like a good fart!"

"What is he talking about?" Pasha asked, looking to each occupant expectantly.

"I know," Tiffany croaked. "He makes the prisoners eat enormous amounts of this disgusting stuff they call 'fart food,' and then they place you on the rotating platform and the vacuum sucks up all of the wind you pass."

"Take me to my friends," Pasha demanded, frowning at Mick. He dragged himself back to his feet and ran past everyone, homing in like a well-programmed GPS system. Mick had opened the door before Pasha and Harold arrived. Walking straight in, Pasha was not ready for what she saw: rows and rows of five-gallon glass jars stacked on shelving from floor to ceiling. She shouted out for Pewter, but got no response. She then slowly turned to Mick, needing no words; her growling was all it took for him to start searching each aisle.

Reaching the far end of the third row, Mick shouted the words Pasha was waiting for. "Here he is, down here!"

Pasha flew straight down the middle of the aisle and landed so close to Mick that her growling voice made him shudder. "He had better be OK."

Pasha looked around but could not see Pewter.

"He's down there on the bottom shelf." She looked down, while Harold peered over her head. They spotted Pewter, curled up in the bottom of the glass, his eyes tightly closed.

"Is he sleeping?" asked Harold.

"He could be unconscious. It will be pretty toxic in there," Mick informed them as he stepped backwards.

Pasha grabbed the jar, held it between her paws, and tried desperately to unscrew the lid with her teeth. As she struggled,

Pewter opened his eyes and sat up. "Get me out of here!" he shouted, covering his nose.

Pasha snuffed at the sealed lid. The only other opening was a small valve on top, far too small for Pewter to squeeze through.

"Get down, Pewter!" Pasha growled. She picked up the jar and smashed the top against one of the wooden shelves, releasing Pewter, but also bathing the entire room in a nauseating, thick odor. As everyone scrambled around, attempting to evade the stench, Pasha heard a tapping sound. Looking up, she saw Trixie jumping up and down, trying to get someone's attention. Pasha chewed on the valve of her glass. Once it came off, Trixie easily fit through the hole and flew to freedom.

"Now that everyone's 'ere," Harold pronounced, looking pointedly at Mick, "you 'ave some explaining to do. From wot I can see, this 'ole place is used to make fuel for your fart-cycle. If I am right, can you tell me 'ow to do it? I would look so cool driving one of those down the taan!" Harold grinned, nudging Mick and nearly knocking him over.

Mick, steadying himself, flopped down so that he was sitting on the floor. "It all started when I saw this film about a gang of mad bikers. I knew then that I was destined to be a gang leader, but without mode of transport, it would never be. So, when I met Lance in the forest, he agreed to help me. We came to the Land of the Lake, kidnapped the queen, and stole her wand. As long as she did not have her wand, she was defenseless and, with their queen held hostage, the rest of the pixies retreated into exile, leaving us to take over their village.

"Owning the town meant other leprechauns joined me until I had a small army. The only thing I did not have was my transport, so Lance converted a chopper bicycle, making it powered by compressed farts.

"With my transport now in place, I needed a constant supply of farts, so I started taking prisoners, using them as fart machines, and that's about that. I must say, it was working out perfectly until you lot interfered."

Pasha marched toward Mick, pushed her wet nose against his face, and demanded to know where he had taken her brother's golden ball.

"I can't tell ya that. I honestly would if I could, but it is just not possible for a leprechaun to give away the location of his gold."

"He is telling the truth, so he is," Shamus butted in.

"Well, then let's at least lock the guards up with the other prisoners until we figure out what to do next," Pasha said with a sigh.

*****

With all of the prisoners locked in the dining hall, everyone sat on the lush green grass outside the factory. "Does anyone have any ideas about where the gold could be?" asked Pasha.

"If the legend is correct, then it will be in a pot at the end of a rainbow," Peter offered.

"Technically, that is correct, so it is," confirmed Shamus, "but Mick is not the brightest of leprechauns. It could be any-where."

"Well, at least it's a clue. All we 'ave to do is sit 'ere and wait for a rainbow," Harold scoffed.

"I'm afraid you will have a long wait," Dixie sighed as she flew into the middle of the circle. "We do not have rainbows here. The Land of the Lake was made so the leprechauns would stay away."

"Well, that didn't quite work, did it?" Harold smugly added.

"I bet I know where it is!" Tiffany exclaimed, as she jumped to her feet and ran past the factory. "Come on, guys! When they captured me, they brought me to see Mick in this place down here, a drinking place called the Rainbow Grill." Turning a corner, she stopped and pointed up to a sign. Sure enough, it was exactly as she had stated. Mick had converted an old building into a restaurant.

Pasha tugged on Peter's trousers, pulling him inside, then toward the back of the bar. "It has to be here, Peter! We are now at the end of the rainbow."

"That's right, Pashy. You look to the left and I will go right." The pair split up as everyone started searching.

"It can't be this simple," Harold shook his head and joined in the hunt.

"Oww!" Peter screamed. As he had stepped on the end of a floorboard, the other end had sprung up and hit him clean in his face. "That hurt," he whined as he jumped away and held his eye. Harold slid his paw under the board before it fell back into place. He lifted it slowly and peered inside. Everyone came running over to see what he had found.

"I thought so," Shamus stated as he burst into laughter while gazing down at the pile of gold. "I just knew it wouldn't be in a pot! That would be much too clever for my tick brother."

All eyes turned toward Shamus, staring in disbelief at what they had just heard. He held his hands up and nodded. "I'm ashamed to admit it, but it is true, so it is. Why is it that I am good and he is so evil? I disowned him many years ago when he brought shame on the leprechaun nation and was exiled."

"Never mind all that. Help me find Shamrock's ball. Take the rest of the floor up if you have to," Pasha instructed. It was not long before a shout came from the other side of the restaurant.

"Here it is! It was in the corner with this little stick," Peter shouted as he held up a tiny glittering wand.

Trixie whizzed past his hand and snatched it from him. "That is my queen's, thank you very much!" Flying over to Dixie, she knelt on one knee and with the wand resting on her open hands, said humbly, "Your wand, your Majesty."

Dixie accepted the wand, which made her look even more majestic. Shamrock licked Peter and held his ball in his mouth as he left the restaurant.

"Mission accomplished, I do believe," announced Peter as he raised his hands in the air.

"Not quite, Peter," Pasha interrupted. "We still have the problem of the prisoners. What are we going to do with them? Ozzy would kill us if we took them all back. Should we only take the ringleaders back for trial?   After all, the others were only following orders."

Shamus interrupted, frightened that they would forget their deal. "I hate to impose, so I do, but what about my Shamus-She? We did have a deal and I have been so patient, so I have."

"I am so sorry.   I really did forget all about her," Pasha gasped. "We'll go and look for her right now."

"There's no need to look for me; I've been spying on you lot for ages from the trees," said a voice from behind them. Everyone turned to see a pretty, small leprechaun in a tattered dress walking from the forest.

"My Shamus-She!" Shamus shouted as he ran toward her with his arms open wide.

"Don't ya start, Shamus O'Malley! I have been watching ya since you arrived with those big Black Panther things and not once have ya spoken about me. What have ya got to say for ya-self?"

"I had a deal with them, me sweet. I had to get their things sorted before I could look for ya. I luvs ya more 'n more with each and every passing day."

As she put her arms around him, she looked over his shoulder directly at Pasha, and asked, "Is he not the most lovable thing ya have ever clapped ya eyes on? So he is!"

With Shamus and his wife joining the others in the circle, Dixie once again flew to the center.

"I have an idea. You take the worst of the leprechauns with you, and on behalf of the Pixie Nation, I make this offer:

"We will allow the rest of the leprechauns to live here in our world under the rule of an appointed leader, on the condition that they live in peace and harmony and work for the good of everyone in the Land of the Lake."

"That sounds very fair. Whom will you appoint as their leader?" Pasha asked.

Flying over to Shamus, resting her wand on his shoulder, she announced, "Shamus O'Malley will henceforth be known as King of the Leprechauns, and as such, I award you this Pixie wand to enforce your laws. Now, rise to your feet, Shamus O'Malley, and choose your queen."

Shamus, overcome with excitement, swaggered around the circle. "Now, whom shall I be picking for me queen on dis beautiful sunny afternoon?" His eyes glinted with mischief as he held his hand toward Pasha and opened his mouth as if to speak.

"I choose..." he began.

"I be warning ya, O'Malley," Shamus-She interrupted.

He spun around and finished his exclamation: "...Ya as me new queen!" He grasped his wife's hand and pulled her to her feet. "Ya truly are di luv of me life, Shamus-She."

The group cheered and applauded until Pasha interrupted the celebrations. "We have to sort out the prisoners and get them back to the castle. It's getting late, and we want to be out of here before dark."

On reaching the palace, Pasha held everyone back as Dixie proudly walked up her steps for the first time in years.

"This is very emotional," blurted Trixie, sobbing and wiping her eyes.

Once inside, Harold unlocked the dining hall. Mad Mick stood protectively in front of his gang.

"You can save only three of your gang. Who shall it be?" Pasha looked pointedly at Mick, watching him carefully as he chose.

"I'll be saving Lance and the two big ones over there." Mick had chosen carefully; Lance was without doubt the brains, while the other two he had picked were so big they could have probably passed as small humans.

Pasha nodded her head in agreement and told Lance that he could also bring Asmagies with him. Lance smiled, putting the still-bald Asmagies in his little box. With prisoners marched outside and guarded by Harold, Pasha handed the proceedings over to Shamus.

"You now have a choice," she heard him announce as she exited the palace.

Approaching the prisoners, Pasha frowned at the realization that transporting them could be a problem. "How are we going to get them home, Harold?" she asked with a sigh, circling the group like a vulture.

"I can help you there," stated Dixie as she held her wand high. "Pixilisation!"

The four prisoners split into hundreds and hundred of flat squares that floated slowly to the floor where Trixie swept them up and put them in the box with Asmagies.

"Wow," Harold gasped, "that is some serious magic you have there."

"And really specific," added Tiffany.

"We had better get going," said Pasha, tearfully. Peter, Tiffany, and Pewter climbed onto her back with Shamrock clinging onto Harold. The dogs flew off toward the lake and their doorway home.

Chapter Seventeen

Although crowded with beings, a strange silence filled the Great Hall.

"The Court of the Castle of Justice is now in session. The prisoners will each step forward and state their full names."

The prisoners stood in silence, bemused by the magical powers that surrounded them. The Keeper did not have to command them again as a knight marched forward from the back wall and prodded the first one in the back with his lance.

"Me name's Michael O'Malley, otherwise known as Mad Mick." The rest of the prisoners followed suit before the Keeper turned to Peter.

"What are the charges against these beings?"

Peter cleared his throat. "They are charged with," he paused to think, "crimes against pixies, sir."

"Crimes against pixies? What sort of crime is that?"

Peter stuttered to himself and grew flushed as his mind raced for an appropriate charge. "Peter," Tiffany whispered, "say, 'kidnapping and high treason.'"

"I charge these beings and the hedgehog with kidnapping and high treason," he croaked.

"And what evidence do you have of these crimes?"

Looking to Tiffany for help, Peter's stature shrank again when she shrugged and frowned. After a few moments of silence, he turned to the judge. "I have one of the victims here. The prosecution calls Tiffany to the stand."

"Very well, call Warrior Tiffany to the stand."

Tiffany, extremely excited to be taking part at last, marched with a confident swagger to the witness stand. She raised her hand

and swore to tell the truth before sitting and waiting for the questions to begin.

"Could you please tell this court exactly what happened in the Land of the Lake?" Peter began.

"I thought you would never ask! There I was, cleaning that disgustingly dirty shack, when I heard barking coming from outside. Thinking it was my Pasha, I ran outside. Anyway, it turned out to be a Pasha look-alike, her brother, Shamrock. Now, Shamrock and I gelled instantly, and we both continued to clean the shack. I was sweeping all the leaves out and he was dusting with his tail. To cut a long story short, we heard a noise outside. Thinking it was Peter, we ran out, and the last thing I remember was this sharp pain in my leg and feeling really tired." Tiffany continued while looking at her nails, "Anyway, I woke in this room where they fed me this disgusting food that makes you pass wind."

"Enough! Were you held against you will?" asked the Keeper.

"Uh.... YEAH!"

Peter then jumped in and took Tiffany's hand. Pulling her past the defendants, he asked, "Do you see in this court the person or persons who imprisoned you?"

"They were all involved, although Mick and Lance were the masterminds, using Asmagies as their weapon," Tiffany announced, pointing an accusing finger at them all, one at a time.

"The prosecution rests its case," declared Peter as he strolled confidently back to his desk.

"Do the defendants have anything to say? No? Excellent! The court will now be cleared of all warriors while I review the evidence and pass any sentences."

Peter looked around uncertainly until Ozzy appeared from behind the Keeper's chair. "Come with me," he said as he beckoned them all to stand on the big black square. "Grimits to spend! Grimits to spend!" he shouted as they all huddled together. "This is one of the fun parts, after all."

"Ozzy, where is Shamrock? We should be sharing this moment with him." Pasha looked at the bear expectantly.

"Well, I should tell you dogs that your brother, Shamrock, has decided not to become a warrior."

"What?" asked Pasha and Harold in unison.

"He said it wasn't the life he wanted. He loves you both and thanks you for rescuing him. His home will always be your home for visits."

"Look on the bright side," scoffed Tiffany. "That's one less warrior to split our Grimits with."

"You just don't get it sometimes, do you, Tiffany?" blurted Peter as he gave Harold a reassuring scratch between his ears.

"Ah, bro, and I was looking forward to bossing 'im around."

Orville was not as slow as before. Upon seeing that court was in session, he ran as fast as he could, not even stopping as he jumped and shouted, "Feet to keys."

"Yes," whispered Peter as he punched the air. "We are going back down to the dungeons!"

"That is correct, my brave warriors. When we get down there, your rewards for a successful mission will be waiting for you."

"How much do I have to spend?" asked Tiffany enthusiastically.

"That we will not know until we have reached the dungeons. By then, the Keeper will have decided on the sentences. Remember, you will get one extra Grimit for every prisoner convicted, and that's on top of your eight for the mission."

As the walls parted, revealing the dungeons brightly lit, the warriors waited patiently outside for Ozzy, who was whispering something to Orville. Finally emerging, the koala made his way to a small metal door set into the wall on the side of the lift. He opened the door and put his paw in; after shuffling around, he pulled it out, grasping a pile of Grimits.

"How many are there?" Tiffany asked, pushing her way past the others to see. Ozzy tossed them to the floor where the Grimits split up into four piles of two each, with another two running around in circles, not knowing where they should be.

"I assume the two that look less than intelligent are my share?" asked Pewter.

"Only two of your prisoners were convicted; the other two must have been sent back to where they came from. You, therefore, have ten Grimits to share between you."

"At least it is an even number," said Peter.

Ozzy advised the warriors to meet all of the prisoners before deciding whether to spend any of their Grimits. Tiffany naturally led the way, passing Kittle's cell first, not saying a word as she did. Peter caught Kittle's eye and told her he would be back before he left. Kittle purred loudly until Peter had left her sight.

As Peter caught up to the others at cell two, Tiffany was shivering. "I don't know what is in here. All I can see is a big lump of ice, and its ffrrrreeeeeezzzing!"

"You hairless types always complaining about the cold," mocked Pewter. "Is there a section for feline needs?"

Ignoring Pewter, Ozzy explained, "This is Vollice, Queen of the Volls, and before you ask, Peter, Volls are Ice People. They live deep in Antarctica and are invisible to humans unless you summon them. Then and only then will she appear."

Peter jumped in front of the others and commanded deeply, "I am Peter, Warrior of the Castle, and I command Vollice, Queen of the Volls, to reveal herself."

"Why, Peter, so dominant; I do like that," Tiffany whispered into his ear.

The high-pitched voice of Vollice rang out as she revealed herself from behind the darkness of the corner: "Which one of you is Warrior Peter?"

"I am, your Highness," said Peter as he knelt down on one knee, looking at the queen. She was dressed in a deep lilac gown, her pure white face and piercing blue eyes accented with a crown beautifully carved from different colors of ice.

"Get up, matey. Remember, she is only a queen to her own people. Here, she is just another prisoner who will sell you her powers for Grimits."

"And do I have some powers for you to purchase! For one Grimit I will give you the power to freeze five living things."

Tiffany, not believing, demanded a demonstration. "Give me a Grimit, and I will give you the power of five. I am two hundred Grimits short of my six-hundred-Grimit fine, so... no Grimits, no power. Now, do you want some?"

Tiffany looked the queen up and down a few times and shook her head as she continued on to the next cell. There, she burst out laughing.

"Peter, look! It's Mad Mick, Lance, and Asmagies! And what have you to sell us? Farts?"

"How much did you get fined?" Peter asked.

"Tree hundred and fifty of those Grimit things," Mick replied, "and I am only allowed to rent you the use of Asmagies for five Grimits a mission. At that rate, I will be here for years!"

Ozzy pushed everyone past Mick's cell. "You can't rent Asmagies yet; he is still regrowing his needles."

The last prisoner was isolated at the far end of the keep. "This one is the most dangerous. He was fined one thousand Grimits for his crimes," explained Ozzy as they approached the dimly lit cell. With everyone looking inside, a tall, slim man with short, dark hair stood with his back to the warriors. "Why don't you introduce yourself, Slyming," Ozzy suggested.

Lifting an arm out to his side, the dim figure turned on a CD player and a hip-hop beat echoed through the keep. All at once, the cell lit up so brightly, light seemed to be coming from everywhere as he twisted around to face his audience.

"Listen to my rhymes, for a lifetime of fun.
If you're accepted in my posse, you'll forever stay young.
Feel the bass beats a-thumpin', from your toes to your head.
Mixing up the rhymes; live forever, never dead.

"My name is Slyming, Rhyming, so you see.
I'm a hip-hop legend, Magician stylize.
So I'll be rhyming, Slyming to the end.
Got to get out of here, but the bars won't bend.

"Gigging at the gardens is where I was at.
When I saw a streak of black, and asked,
What the heck was that?
Two canine warriors, they came to get me.
Swoopin' 'round and 'round, like a frustrated bee.

"My name is Slyming, Rhyming, so you see.
I'm a hip-hop legend, Magician stylize.
So I'll be rhyming, Slyming to the end.
Got to get out of here, but the bars won't bend.

"Trying to hide, behind a speaker I did cower,
As the two dogs shouted, the words, "Paw Power."
Then they brought me up, In front of the judge,
Framed up nicely, Like a piece of fudge.

"My name is Slyming, Rhyming, so you see.
I'm a hip-hop legend, Magician stylize.
So I'll be rhyming, Slyming to the end.
Got to get out of here, but the bars won't bend.

"Fined 1000 Grimits, will I ever get free?
Stuck in this prison, with a capital P.
An endless little story, my crimes a long, long list.
I'm just a living legend, that the world is gonna miss.

"My name is Slyming, Rhyming, so you see.
I'm a hip-hop legend, Magician stylize.
So I'll be rhyming, Slyming to the end.
Got to get out of here, but the bars won't bend."

As the music faded, Slyming bowed to rapturous applause,
with Peter shouting and whistling louder than anyone.
"OK, Peter, he wasn't that good," Tiffany scoffed.
"I don't know, he's got something there," interrupted Pewter.

"I wasn't applauding him; I liked the three Grimits on the shelf singing the chorus," Peter defended, crossing his arms over his chest.

"So, warriors," Slyming began, his voice velvety smooth as each word rolled off his tongue like butter:

"Would you like some magic?
It's fun to use.
Many different packages,
for you to choose.

"Two spells for a Grimit,
Or a lifetime for a ton.
It's the premium buy
with a lifetime of fun."

"How much is a ton?" inquired Peter, cautiously.

"One hundred Grimits," Ozzy answered, sighing.

"Wow, that's a lot. I only have two," said a dismayed Peter. "What can I get for one?"

Slyming checked Peter out carefully before offering him a deal: "As a once-only offer, I will give you ten spells for one Grimit. You will only be able to use them on missions, though. The only package you can use in your normal life is the lifetime package, and nobody has ever been able to afford that."

"I'll take them, please, Mr. Slime."

"That's Slyming, boy; didn't you listen? Give me your Grimit, then."

Peter put his arm through the first set of bars as far as it would go, his Grimit held tightly in his hand. Slyming did the same, but they could not reach each other to do the transaction. Slyming snatched his hand back into the far cell. "Just put it on the floor, boy."

Peter followed Slyming's instructions; the Grimit looked around before stating, "It's OK. It is not the ice queen; it is Slyming. We Grimits don't like the cold, you know."

The Grimit ran under the bottom of the cell door with Slyming catching it on the other side. Opening a chest in the corner of his cell, he threw the Grimit in and slammed it shut.

"Well, give me the magic," Peter demanded.

"Lesson one, young warrior; never give up your Grimits until you receive your goods. Now, get lost," Slyming cackled and shut off his lights.

"Oh, come on, Mister! I worked hard for that Grimit."

"Give him his spells, or give the Grimit back," Ozzy demanded, bashing his paw on the bars of Slyming's cell. "If you refuse, I will inform the Keeper who will double your fine. How long do you think that will take to pay off at your usual price of two Grimits a spell?" Without turning his lights back on, Slyming started to rhyme again.

"Give the sniveling boy
Ten spells, no more;
They will only work,
Through the mission door."

"There you go, Peter. You must rhyme what you want, and the better your rhyme, the more powerful your spell will be," explained Ozzy. "Does anyone else want to spend their Grimits?"

"I think I will buy some of that freezing thing." Tiffany turned on her heel and marched to the queen's cell, demanding that she show herself. Vollice appeared, asking, "What do you want, oh, pretty one?"

"I want five of those freezing things." Tiffany rolled a Grimit toward Vollice, its little legs trying to stop the rolling motion so it could make an escape from its freezing future. As the Grimit stopped, Vollice plunged her long arm under the cell door, and with one fell swoop, grabbed the objecting Grimit. Taking a deep breath, she blew freezing air on the coin, which froze it rigid, its legs and arms still pointing out as she put it in her ice chest.

"I feel real bad for Grimits, all of a sudden," declared Harold.

Stretching her arm through the bars, she pointed her long index finger toward Tiffany and projected an icicle through the outer bars; it stuck onto the tip of Tiffany's nose, but then melted as quickly as it had landed, leaving her with water dripping from the tip of her nose.

Drying herself with her sleeve, Tiffany complained, "That was a dirty trick."

"Relax, Tiff, that is how Vollice does it. You now have your freezing powers," Ozzy assured her.

"Oh. Well, will I be able to use them in my normal life? I know this girl at school who I would just love to shut up at times."

"No, the only powers that can carry over to your human life are Slyming's lifetime spell and Wizard Hunchings' magic."

"Well, why is that?" Tiffany was not going to let it drop.

"Listen carefully," explained Ozzy. "There are secrets about this place and the way things operate that even I don't know or understand. That is just the way it is. Okay?"

"Who's Wizard Hunchings? Is he another prisoner?" Pasha inquired, looking up and down the keep.

"Not a prisoner. Although he lives in the village, he has committed no crime. If you want to know any more, you will have to ask him yourself. In fact, the village is our next stop before you choose your next mission. There will be plenty more to see and experience there," Ozzy said, ushering them toward the elevator.

"What's it called?" Tiffany grunted as Peter Jostled in next to her on the elevator.

"The village?" Ozzy grinned. "It's called Snydol."

*****

The elevator thudded to a stop, and its doors opened to envelop the occupants with a warm blanket of sunlight. Soft music filled the air as the inhabitants of Snydol went about their daily business.

"Wow," Tiffany gasped. "Where does this elevator not go?"

The warriors clamored off the elevator and stood just in front of the still-open doors. Peter looked upward, trying to locate the strange music that filled the entire village. "Look, Tiff!" he shouted. "That music is coming from up there!"

Tiffany looked up and screamed, "Ozzy! That music is coming from those mouths on top of those poles!" She twirled around in circles, squinting in a vain effort to see the end of them.

"There must be hundreds," Pasha whispered to herself.

"Nothing is as it should be in Snydol," Ozzy said, chuckling, as he stood back and waited for the inevitable discovery of their presence. Pasha sniffed around and ventured a few curious steps forward until her hair prickled upward as silence invaded the air. The music had stopped, as had all of the village inhabitants, everyone standing and staring at the mouths, waiting to see what would happen next.

All the mouths moved in perfect unison: "Attention, Snydol! Attention, Snydol! We are pleased to announce the arrival of the new warriors. All inhabitants must now stand clear of the main square!"

Peter scanned the weird inhabitants who were whispering and mumbling to one another, passing around the fact that the new warriors included humans. Tiffany looked past the neat lines of residents at the brightly colored buildings, most of which looked like shops surrounding the main square.

Without a word spoken between them, the warriors caught the sound of a band coming from somewhere behind the clock tower that housed the elevator. As the sound grew louder, the band came into view: a complete brass band of instruments all playing themselves, with little legs marching in time. The instruments stopped in formation in front of the warriors, who were desperately trying and failing to hold in their giggles as they watched the little legs kick and strut about.

"Show some respect, you lot; they have been practicing all week for this," snarled Ozzy.

The band's cheerful welcome slowly trailed off upon the realization that the warriors were laughing at them. Snydol became deathly quiet, with all the inhabitants looking sternly at the now-silent warriors. The instruments solemnly walked, dejected, out of the town square the same way they had proudly come in just a few moments prior; all that was left was an upside-down top hat, his legs marching toward the warriors, stamping both of its little feet on the ground like a well-drilled sergeant major. It tugged at Peter's trousers.

Looking down, Peter inquired, "What does it want, Ozzy?"

"He wants payment for the entertainment."

"Do I have to give him my only Grimit?" Peter asked with a sigh as he retrieved it from his pocket. Ozzy, seeing Peter's reluctance, threw one of his own in the hat, which then bowed over before running off.

"There's nothing like getting off on the right foot," Orville said, sighing, "and that was nothing like getting off on the right foot." He walked back into the elevator and shook his head. "I will wait here. Not going to be seen with that disgraceful lot."

Ozzy nodded to Orville and then dropped his head.

"'Ey, Tiffy, I do believe those moufs are nearly as big as yours," Harold snickered.

"Shut up, Harold! Can't you see we're in trouble?" Tiffany snapped back. The crowd that had turned out to meet the new warriors silently dispersed about the square, back to their normal activities.

"Guess we sort of spoiled somefink," said Harold with a shrug.

"Well, they'll get over it," Pewter added. "We are keeping the balance between good and evil here. They will have to understand that, as super-warriors, we're under a lot of stress."

"Are all of these shops?" Tiffany asked Ozzy excitedly.

"There are no shops in Snydol. Everyone here is their own shop, all selling something of interest."

Disappointed, Tiffany kicked the dirt before slowly ambling away from the group. "Where are you going?" Ozzy called after her.

"To explore," Tiffany huffed over her shoulder, barely hearing Ozzy's instructions to meet them back at the clock tower. Everyone else looked from one to the other and then around the strange town. Harold and Pasha's eyes lit up as the skeleton of a sheep wearing a purple hat walked by. Looking at each other and both licking their lips, they set off after the terrified skeleton, which was now running as fast as its clattering bones would carry it.

Pewter rubbed up against Peter's leg. The boy bent down to pet him, but Pewter suddenly ran off, joining up with a large group of cats entering a strange-looking alleyway. Peter heard, "Hello, ladies," before they all disappeared from view.

Suddenly finding himself alone, Peter walked toward the edge of town. His thoughts then turned to his ten spells; he would need to practice his rhyming, otherwise they would not work. He shuffled along aimlessly until he reached the sandy banks of a small lake. The air was crisp and clean, so different from the London smog. Everything seemed poisoned in London, not just the air. Sometimes he felt his very life a poisoned thing as well.

Peter picked up a flat, smooth pebble from the waterline and rolled it repeatedly between his fingers. "That's a good skipping stone," he mumbled to himself, maneuvering the rock back and forth before taking aim at the water. "Skip, skip, skip... plop!" Peter said with a sigh.

"Problems, young warrior?" a voice rang out from somewhere overhead. Peter looked up to see a small person perched on the thick branch of a nearby willow tree. His thick, tatty robes hung down over his shoes, and his pointed hat had a severe bend at the tip.

"Hello, sir," Peter politely answered. "What are you doing up there?"

"This is where I live, young Peter."

"You live in a tree?" Peter scrunched his face before pausing. "And how did you know my name?"

"I have been waiting for you, Peter."

"What do you mean, sir?"

"Please call me Hunchings, or Wiz, if you prefer. I have been watching you for the last few of your human years. I know that, sadly, your mother passed away and that you are consumed with a sorrow that stems from the endless bullying you receive at school."

"Stop!" shouted Peter, backing away slowly.

"No reason for alarm, my boy; merely wanting to talk."

Peter turned back to the lake. "What if I don't want to talk about it?"

"Have you even tried?" Hunchings was suddenly standing right beside Peter. The boy nearly jumped out of his skin in surprise. "Sorry about that, but teleportation is much easier than just tumbling out of the tree."

"You said you were waiting for me?"

"I have been. But first, you share and then it will be my turn." Hunchings plopped down on a log and patted the space next to him for Peter.

"I have never found it easy to make friends, and if you haven't any friends in school, you get picked on. First, they used to call me 'Peter No Friends,' and it slowly escalated from there. Now I have to hide when certain boys are around because I know if they see me, they will pick on me. They steal my books and throw them around the playground, and if I try to get them back, they poke me until I cry. The only thing that makes me feel a little better is eating, so, as soon as I get home everyday, I eat loads of food, which has actually made things worse as they now call me 'Fatty No Friends.' I beg my father every day not to make me go to school. I just want to stay inside my house with my dog, Harold."

"Such a heavy burden on such young shoulders," Wiz patted his back gently. "What do you want to do about it?"

Peter looked at Wiz. It was a good question. He had fantasies of beating up all of the bullies, but he knew violence was not the answer. He really wanted to achieve something so amazing that everyone would like him and want to be his friend.

"Ah, great achievements, huh?"

"You can read my mind?"

195

"Not always. That last one was so powerful; you were just about broadcasting it. Strong mind, you have there. It is part of the reason I watch you."

Peter's questions multiplied at this statement, but his time in Snydol was ending.

"You have to go now, Peter," said Hunchings. "Your fellow warriors are waiting at the clock tower. But will you come back and see me?"

"I would like to, but I can only come back when I have Grimits to spend," explained Peter.

Wiz waved his wand again and touched Peter's foot. "There now, whenever you want to visit, just put a small amount of water on your shoe and say, 'By the lake.' You will then bypass the castle and find yourself here."

"How did you…"

"No time for questions, my friend. Go now; Ozzy is waiting." Wiz smiled before disappearing before Peter's eyes. Peter jumped to his feet, wearing a grin so big it nearly split his face.

At the clock tower, all the other warriors were fidgeting as they scanned the square for any sign of him.

"There he is," stated a relieved Ozzy, pointing toward a heavily panting Peter, running at full speed in their direction. Totally out of breath, Peter entered the elevator, gasping for air as he apologized for keeping the others waiting.

"That's fine, I don't mind. It really is not a problem… OK, so it is," Orville, mumbled as he closed the elevator doors.

"Where are we going now?" Harold asked as the doors sealed tightly.

"It's time to choose your next mission," Ozzy said earnestly.

"Going up," Orville announced.

*****

The Keeper sat in his chair, addressing the assembled warriors. "You all now realize the value of working together. Keep these lessons close. If you think your Irish mission was dangerous, you are wrong. Training is now over. It is time to pick your first real mission. I will show you visions of evil, evil that, as warriors, you will eventually have to face. You will look at them all. Then and only then, you will carefully choose one," the Keeper said as he clapped his hands, starting the first vision.

As Sasha had been the only warrior since Spot had died and so many missions were incomplete, it took a long time to screen all the visions. Each of the warriors saw various imagery before their eyes: exotic locales and strange creatures that needed either to be rescued or defeated. Pasha's ears pricked high as she saw a vision of the White Buffalo with the towering image of the mountain above them. As the last vision faded, she turned to Harold and the others and suggested, "I saw the vision that we should choose. It is a place called the Lost Mountain. A tribe there needs our help. I tried on my own, but I was not ready. Together we can help them."

Harold jumped in, "Shouldn't we pick the mission worth the most Grimits?"

"I'm with Harold," declared Tiffany. "Let us go for the payday. What is the most valuable mission, Keeper?"

"Do you remember the blank screen in between the others?" the Keeper asked. "Well now, that was Nex Vesica; that mission has been ongoing for over a hundred of your earth years. The successful completion of that mission would reward you 110 Grimits. You are not ready or strong enough to try that one. Now, what mission will it be?"

"I made a promise to that tribe to help them," Pasha continued. "I am asking all of you to help me."

"That mission will reward you twenty Grimits, with the usual bonus for convicted prisoners," the Keeper informed the warriors before seating himself on his chair.

"I'm with you, Mother," said Pewter. "I can't let you get into trouble alone."

Peter added his support. "You have my help as well."

"Well, sis. Twenty Grimits is a respectable number, know wot I mean."

Everyone turned to Tiffany. "What?" she asked. "Well, I am not going to be the one to say no. I'm in."

Pasha gave Tiffany a playful lick on the face and turned to the Keeper.

"We're going to the Lost Mountain," she said confidently.

"Very well," agreed the Keeper. "This mission you can only do when there is a full moon, so you have a week to rest before you will be summoned here to start. Now go home, warriors, and remember, what happens here is secret. Not a word to anyone."

Chapter Eighteen

The next seven days proved the most stressful Tiffany had ever dealt with. Chloe had returned from her trip and the pair spent every waking hour together. On several occasions, she nearly slipped up and told Chloe about her secret life. Once, she even got as far as asking, "If I tell you something, do you swear you won't tell?" With Pasha barking furiously, she quickly dismissed it by saying, "Never mind, I'm just kidding."

Peter spent the time practicing his rhymes, which pleased his father who thought his son had taken up poetry. Harold was the only one who did not keep the secret, sharing it with his friends in Kentish Town, none of whom believed him anyway. Pasha was too busy keeping Tiffany under control to consider sharing her experiences, even if she had known other dogs she could have shared them with.

When the full moon finally arrived in Arizona, Tiffany, Pasha, and Chloe were listening to CDs in Tiffany's bedroom. Pasha was the first to see the ball flash and vibrate, alerting Tiffany, who looked first at the ball and then in horror at Chloe.

"What's wrong? Why are you looking at me that way?" Chloe asked.

"Oh, nothing, really! Well, actually, I am really tired and I know I said you could sleep over, but I would really like to just spend some time with Pasha, if you don't mind."

Chloe, clearly upset at being shunned by her friend, informed Tiffany, "I can't go yet; my mother's not home and I don't have a key to get in. Anyway, it's only 9:00; what do you mean, you're tired?"

Tiffany frantically looked around the room for another distraction, and just finally lost her cool. "Well, you can watch TV

with my parents, then sleep on the couch. Now, leave my room!
Please?"

Without saying a word, Chloe stormed out of the room,
purposefully leaving the door open just a crack. She walked heavily
down the hallway so Tiffany would think she had gone downstairs,
and then crept back to peep through the still slightly opened door.
Although she knew her best friend had been acting strangely, Chloe
was not prepared for what she would soon witness.

Inside the room, Tiffany and Pasha sat on the rug next to
the bed while Tiffany whispered loudly to Pewter. The golden ball
was patiently bouncing in front of them, waiting for the half-asleep
cat to come from the closet where he had been having a very nice
dream about being a dog and conquering the universe, in that order.
With Pewter in place, the ball started to spin around the trio,
flashing brightly.

Chloe mouthed a silent, "What the—?" She remembered
the night when they ran screaming from this same glowing, spinning
ball. Now Tiffany and her pets were just sitting there as if nothing
was wrong. She could not take it anymore and burst back into the
room. She ignored her fear of the glowing orb and knelt down in
front of Tiffany. Looking Tiff straight in the eye, Chloe demanded,
"What is going on here?"

Within a blink of the eye, they were all standing in the castle.
Chloe just stared at the cat as it grinned and rubbed up against her
leg. "Glad you could make it," he greeted. Chloe began a series of
shrill screams that Tiffany quickly muffled with a hand over her
mouth.

"Please, you have to be quiet and stay calm," she pleaded.
"You need to go back before someone finds you here. Are you
calm?"

Chloe nodded.

Tiffany removed her hand from Chloe's face.

"Would you look at this?" Chloe said in an uncertain voice.
"Where are we? The pets can talk!"

"I promise to explain everything later, but you've got to go
back through the door! You are not supposed to be here; I will get

in so much trouble if Ozzy finds out! Go on, I'll explain everything in the morning, but please, please, please don't tell my parents!" Tiffany's eyes filled with tears as she grabbed Chloe's hands, pleading with her to do as she asked. Seeing how concerned her friend was, Chloe turned toward the door next to her, which opened and then closed on its own once she had gone through.

Immediately, Chloe found herself back in Tiffany's bedroom, her eyes wide open, staring at the sleeping figures of Tiffany, Pasha, and Pewter on the rug. She turned, lay down on Tiffany's bed, and closed her eyes. Somehow, Chloe hoped to meet her friend in that strange castle where animals seemed to talk. She was soon asleep.

In the castle, a very relieved Tiffany stood beside her door, waiting for Peter to arrive.

*****

Peter and Harold were sleeping soundly next to each other on Peter's bed as Harold's ball sprang into action, circling around the whole bed, first upward, then downward, struggling to transport the pair.

As the two arrived, it was clear something had gone wrong. A full-size bed was perched in front of the door. It bumped against the doorframe repeatedly as it tried to squeeze completely through, Peter and Harold still lying on it, sound asleep. Tiffany and Pewter burst into laughter. Pasha just shook her head and smiled. She leapt straight across the pair of them, heading for the mission door. She had a promise to keep. Both Peter and Harold jumped from the bed as they awakened in a hurry.

"Why, Peter, what cool PJs you have!"

Peter stared at Tiffany in horror before looking down at his wrinkled, striped pajamas and put his arms over as much of himself as he could.

"That's not right. What happened here?" inquired Ozzy, jumping on the now-empty bed.

"I'm sorry, Oz. I do not know how it happened. We were asleep, and the next thing I knew, Pasha was jumping all over us."

"Never mind, I will sort it out later. The first thing you have to do, Peter, is spell yourself some clothes. Do you think you can do it?"

"Well, I think so…" Peter gulped, hoping his week of practice would finally begin to pay off.

"Sweaty feet,
And a runny nose,
Replace my PJs,
With a set of clothes."

Tiffany looked in disbelief as Peter stood in front of her, looking like he was on his way to a costume party. He was dressed in a Superman outfit complete with a Lycra suit and a cape that was so long it nearly hit the ground.

"That's not exactly what I wanted," croaked Peter.

"You must have had that suit somewhere in your mind."

"Well, I was dreaming about Superman before I woke up."

"Well, there you go, matey. It is not enough to rhyme your spell; you have to think it as well. No worries, you look quite smart, actually. Now, you have to get on with your mission. As this has to be done while there is a full moon, you have no time to waste."

"Peter, you may be dressed like Superman, but let me tell you, I am not your Lois Lane," Tiffany said scornfully as she whisked past Peter and headed toward the mission door. Peter looked downtrodden. She turned and noticed his face. "I'm just kidding. Gosh, you are so sensitive."

"I will give you one piece of advice, mateys. On your Irish mission, you did not use your powers to their full advantage. Try to stay on your dogs as much as you can. Remember, while mounted on them, their powers transfer to you. Now off you go, and may your mistakes be few and your powers win through."

Pewter jumped up onto Pasha's back as the warriors walked through the mission door, Peter's ill-fitting cape following so far behind that it nearly stuck in the door, which slammed closed behind them.

*****

"Brrrr, it's freezing 'ere," Harold said, his teeth chattering. "I fawt it was meant to be 'ot in the desert."

"It does get cold at night, but then heats up during the day. Isn't Kentish Town like that?" asked Pasha.

"Nah, it usually just rains all the time."

Peter looked around. "Where are we?"

"We're at the Lost Mountain," Pasha replied without hesitation. "If we go over that hill, we will see an Indian village. It'll be quicker for me to try and fly all of us."

"Hold up there, 'ero. Fly all of us?"

"Can you do that?" asked Peter.

"I think so. Flying is not like having muscles to lift. It uses my mind. Can anyone think of a faster way to get all of us to the other side of that hill?"

"Shotgun!" yelled Pewter and jumped onto Pasha's neck. Pasha, with Pewter and Tiffany on her back, flew through the air. Harold hung from underneath, his tail wrapped around Pasha's midsection and his tongue coiled around a disgusted-looking Peter. The group cleared the crest of the hill with great effort on Pasha's part; all of her will bent on freeing the buffalo from the evil in the mountain. The village came into view below and Pasha began to descend in a careful spiral.

When Pasha landed next to the fire directly in front of the chief, Tiffany dismounted and stood next to her dog, her hand lovingly resting over Pasha's head and stroking her neck. She looked the chief over, from his large, beautiful headdress right down to his worn, leathery moccasins. Pewter had also jumped off Pasha's back and was now rubbing himself against the chief's leg.

Harold regained his feet and, with some difficulty, he unwound his tongue from Peter.

"Pash, ask 'em if they have some water," he said. "I'm drying out here."

"Hush, Harold," said his master.

"Welcome back, my four-legged friend," the chief addressed Pasha. "I knew you would return. Both you and your companions are welcome in the village of the Katoka tribe."

Peter could not help himself. "Are you a real Indian chief, sir?" he inquired, calling to mind the books he liked to read about the American "Old West."

"Native American chief, stupid," blurted Tiffany, rolling her eyes in annoyance. The chief's wrinkled face cracked into a smile. "I am Chief of the Katoka, oh Great Caped One."

Just then, the rumbling of the buffalo from the canyon interrupted the conversation. The entire tribe put their hands over their ears and began to hum as if to drown out the relentless escalation of the thundering hooves.

With unsteady feet and wide eyes, the warriors all turned to Pasha for guidance and explanation. "Follow me," she commanded loudly, sprinting out of the village and toward the canyon's edge. With the full moon lighting up the whole mountain, the warriors followed Pasha's lead and peered over the edge.

"Wow, look at all those big hairy things," whispered Tiffany.

"The Indians call them buffalo." Peter leaned over and pointed to the front of the stampede. "I see a white one at the front. Is that the one we are here to save?"

"We will save them all. These buffalo have passed away, but their spirits cannot move on. They're trapped," Pasha explained, her eyes fixed on the horizon. "When they are free, the tribe will be free as well."

"Trapped by what?" asked Tiffany.

Pasha did not have to answer as the entire canyon became engulfed by a large dust cloud. At least it looked like dust, but it glinted like metal in the moonlight. A portion of the cloud formed itself into a great hand and grabbed the white buffalo. Behind the hand, the rushing dust cloud trapped the other buffalo and pulled them back toward the Lost Mountain. The entire scene lasted only a few seconds; then all was quiet again.

"Well, it's been fun," quipped Pewter, turning around. "See ya back at the castle. Where is that pesky door?"

"Pewter, please don't go. I need you to stay and help us."

"Ah, Mother, why do you do that? You know I could never say no to you." Pewter sauntered back to the group. "Just the same, when we get to the big, scary hand, I'll be at the back."

"You're starting to sound like Harold," said Peter.

"'Ey!"

"I meant you've gotten better... braver... oh, never mind."

"We have an hour now before they come back," said Pasha, "so we need to think of a plan. First, we need to get down to the bottom. Jump on, Tiff!" Tiffany hesitated and looked back toward the village before cautiously turning back to her dog. "Oh, come on, Tiff! It'll be okay; we're all scared." Pasha walked over and nuzzled her hand.

"Okay," Tiffany agreed with a sigh and slowly settled onto Pasha's back, holding her arms out for Pewter to jump on.

"Not the tongue again!" pleaded Peter. "I will just hang onto you this time, Harold."

In a moment, they were passing over the canyon edge and spiraling downward to land on the soft, dusty ground.

From the bottom of the canyon, the Lost Mountain towered above them. It was an imposing sight, complete with jagged peaks and steep cliffs. Pasha thought of the evil presence somewhere within the mountain. They would have to face it soon enough, and she hoped they were ready.

They reached the base of the mountain just as the rumbling began.

"We've got to get out of the way right now!" Pasha shouted as a hundred spectral buffalo thundered out of the rocks before them. Pasha grabbed Pewter in her mouth and flew straight up. Peter jumped onto Harold's back as the dog lassoed Tiffany with his tail. They just made a rocky out-cropping on the edge of the canyon.

The world vibrated around them, making it nearly impossible to keep a straight thought. Tiffany held her eyes shut tight and her hands over her ears. Peter watched the herd stampede by; then something blotted out the moonlight.

Pasha watched from the air. Her friends were out of the way of the buffalo, but not the rising cloud.

"I can't see the others anymore!" yelled Pewter over the rumbling below.

"I don't know what I can do to help them. They've just got to hold on!"

Harold felt a sudden pull from the blinding dust cloud and it began to drag him back toward the mountain. His claws were useless, scraping against the sandstone helplessly. He could not let go of Tiffany or Peter either.

"Can you grab onto somefink, Peter?" Harold yelled and began coughing. His throat was now full of the choking dust.

Peter managed to scream, "What?" before something tugged him away from Harold. He tumbled end over end, lost in the swirling cloud. Somewhere along the way, his head struck a rock and he was out cold.

Harold, still coughing and retching, could hold on no longer. He pulled Tiffany tight against him to protect her and let the sucking cloud take them both.

Pasha watched the familiar scene. The great fist grasped the white buffalo. From above, she noticed something new. As the spirit buffalo disappeared deep into the wall of rock, the dust split, disappearing into large cracks on each side where the canyon met the base of the mountain.

"Did you see that?" asked Pewter.

"Yes, I did. That is where we are going into the mountain."

The pair landed in the eerie and silent canyon. There was no sign of their friends except for claw marks in the rocks. Pasha approached one of the large holes in the mountain. It was about four feet across. There were old wooden beams supporting the entrance.

"It was a mine," Pasha informed the others.

"I guess you want to go inside?" a terrified Pewter asked, even though he already knew what the answer would be.

"It has our friends, Pewter. Are you ready?

"Not at all, so let's get on with it."

Chapter Nineteen

Peter awoke in the cold and the dark. He was lying in what felt like a pile of dirt. It was everywhere, down his pants and sleeves, and in his hair.

"Harold?" he called. "Tiff?" There was no answer as he coughed out the dusty air.

He then remembered that he still possessed nine rhyming spells and elected to try to get some light going. He took a few moments to compose something appropriate. The last thing he wanted was to conjure up some strange monster or another useless superman suit.

> "This cave is too dark,
> As black as the night.
> What I could do with
> A big shiny light!"

The world blazed into light and Peter immediately shut his eyes. All he could see were spots behind his eyelids. He tried opening his eyes just a crack but it was blindingly bright. He would have to tone it down.

> "With a light so bright,
> Like the one that I made,
> It's hurting my eyes,
> So give me some shades."

A large pair of sunglasses shielded his eyes. It allowed him to open them and get a look around. Peter saw that the first spell had created a massive spotlight, much too big to carry. He was sitting waist-deep in a mound of glimmering dust. He picked up a handful and let it fall through his fingers. It reflected a beautiful, metallic yellow. It looked just like... gold!

He pulled himself out of the heaping pile of gold dust and examined his surroundings. It was a large room, carved right out of the sandstone. Heavy wooden beams ran across the ceiling, supported by upright sections. He realized that it was not a room at all and that he was in the middle of a gold mine. There was a sudden series of coughs coming from a tunnel directly to his left. The spotlight did not penetrate deeply enough, but Peter could see something moving inside.

"Hello? Harold, are you in there?"

"Nope, I'm in 'ere!"

Peter screamed and whirled about. Harold's head was coming out of the pile of gold dust. A tiny cone of it sat squarely on top of his head like a party hat.

"Harold!" Peter shouted and threw his arms tightly around his pet's neck.

"Watch me orb, kid. Ease back on the 'ug." Harold dug himself out and shook the gold from his coat. There was a sneeze from the first tunnel and Tiffany emerged, staggering and brushing gold out of her clothes.

"Hey, guys. That wasn't much fun at all, was it?"

Peter walked up to her and gave her a great big hug. She was surprised at first, but relaxed and embraced him as well. "Thanks, Peter."

"I'm just glad you are okay," he said.

"I can't see a thing in 'ere," moaned Harold. "Can we turn down the sun over there?"

"Oh, sorry. I tried a light spell. We are going to need something smaller, maybe some torches. Okay, here goes:

> "Light up this cave
> Bright like the day,
> To help the warriors
> Find their way."

The spotlight went out immediately while three much softer lights turned on from the floor of the mine. The light came from three flashlights. Peter picked up a couple, handing one to Tiffany.

"Even one fer me; how considerate." Harold picked up the last flashlight with his tail, holding it above his head to light the way.

*****

Pasha, with Pewter on her back, was progressing through the darkened mine very slowly. Between the two, they could vaguely make out shapes in the dark and navigate the tunnels. She had twice let loose a couple of fireballs to light up the way. Otherwise, they had seen no sign of their friends, or anything else for that matter. The mine was empty and dead.

"I take it you have a plan, Mother?" asked Pewter.

"If it moves and it is not Tiffany, Peter, or Harold, then I am shooting it with fireballs. Remember, while you are touching me, you have Paw Power as well."

"Oh, right, I forgot. Time to earn those Grimits, I suppose."

"Just be careful, Pewter, and make sure you know what you are shooting at."

*****

As the other three warriors ventured deeper into the mine, the floor became much more rugged and uneven with large boulders scattered around. Although nobody would admit it, everyone was a little scared—not as much of the dimly lit passages as of the unknown future. Peter thought of the four spells he had already used. With six left, he could not afford to make mistakes. The greater evil of the mountain was still somewhere ahead.

"What's that black stuff running across the floor up there?" Harold asked. Peter held his torch as high above his head as he could so they could see farther up the passage.

"I'm not sure, but look; it's everywhere." Footsteps echoed through the cavern as the warriors approached the streams of black goo that appeared to be bubbling and flowing toward them. Peter shined his torch down toward his feet, noticing that the silent stream was creeping uncomfortably close.

"AHHH, they're bugs!" Tiffany screeched, jumping and skipping in place. The others followed suit until Peter squished one under his Superman boot. Picking up the foot, he squealed as loudly as Tiffany had, "They aren't bugs; they're scorpions! They are going to sting us! Get me out of here!"

In no mood to debate, the warriors turned to run as fast as they could, but what faced them in the other direction was even more frightening. Ready to pounce was surely the biggest mountain lion that had ever graced the earth. The huge animal growled, showing a full set of razor-sharp teeth. With no other way out, the warriors huddled together, fearfully looking between the crouching lion and the sea of stingers. His teeth chattering, Peter cried out,

"With living things all around,
Just get us off the floor!
If this spell does not work,
We'll surely be no more!"

The three of them lifted off the ground by about three feet, just high enough to strike Tiffany's head on the roof of the mine.

"Ouch!" she yelled.

"Sorry."

"What sort of spell was that? You really do 'ave to do better!"

Harold moaned as he pressed himself further into the cowering troop. "This lion thingy is about to 'ave us for dinner."

"Paw Power!" Two fireballs came blazing along the mine passage, striking the mountain lion in the back. It sent the great cat rolling to the ground where the scorpions immediately swarmed it. The lion roared as it was stung repeatedly.

Instinctively, Harold's tail whipped out, grabbed the cat from the middle of the scorpions, and tossed it to safety. The mountain lion, disoriented and in pain, roared again and retreated down a separate passageway.

Pasha now came bounding out of another tunnel; the scorpions went right for her and Pewter. She fired off a few more fireballs but could not keep the entire swarm back.

"Pewter! Help me!"

The little cat joined in, and fireballs zinged across the interior of the cave.

"Watch your aim, fuzz-ball," Harold yelled.

"Peter, the fireballs are not working," squealed Tiffany. "There are too many scorpions. Use another spell!"

If the fire was not enough, then Peter thought something else might just work:

> "Where fireballs fail,
> Landing with a thud,
> Clean the mine,
> With a tidal flood!"

A whooshing sound filled the mine. It was coming down the tunnel behind Pasha, who was too busy holding back the scorpions to notice. Pewter, however, did hear it and stopped his fireball barrage just long enough to start yelling.

A mighty wave of water came pouring out of the tunnel, picking up Pasha, Pewter, and the scorpions and sending them all down the farthest passage, much deeper into the mine.

"Good job, master. Now get us down so we can go collect those two."

*****

"Pasha!" called Tiffany, running up to the soaking wet and unconscious dog.

213

"Come on, sis," urged Harold. "Don't go faking on me now. You're a warrior. You can snap out of this."

"Peter, can you do something?"

"I can try... I don't know."

"Please try," pleaded Tiffany.

"This dog, our friend,
A warrior true,
Heal her wounds,
As good as new."

Pasha jumped right up from the ground. She felt amazingly energized and ready to take on anything. Tiffany kept hugging her while Harold gave her loving licks.

"You're okay!" he shouted. "Thanks, Peter."

"You saved me, Peter?" Pasha asked.

"I just used a spell. The rhyming is getting easier. It was nothing."

"Thank you for using one of your precious spells for me. I won't forget this."

"Luckily," said a voice coming up the tunnel, "he won't have to use another on me. Ta-da, Pewter is okay——miserably wet, but okay." Tiffany pounced on the cat, scooping him up for a hug.

A deep, shuddering laugh broke up the happy reunion. It came from the darkness ahead, and chilled the warriors to the bone.

"I forgot that fing was somewhere up ahead," Harold sighed.

"Come on, guys." Pasha walked a little ahead, staring into the dark. "Let's see who is home."

*****

The warriors emerged from a narrow passageway into a large cavern. They gazed in amazement. Thick jagged veins of gold that looked like golden lightning covered the interior rock face. The gold lit up the cavern with a bright yellow hue. Something moving in the shadows diverted Pasha's attention.

"Show yourself or I will shoot," Pasha stated firmly and readied herself to defend the warriors.

"Your so-called 'Paw Power' is useless against me. Leave now and you might live to fight another day," commanded a fully cloaked figure.

The two warrior dogs leaped in front of their masters. Pewter slid off Pasha's back as she raised her paws, preparing to fire.

"Take one more step and you're toast," warned Harold.

"My name is Wokindo, Guardian of the Gold." Now fully visible, the figure was of medium size and had an old wrinkled face with golden streaks running from both eyes. Lifting his arms until they were level with his shoulders, he silently ascended high above the ground, stopping only when his head nearly touched the roof of the cavern.

Pasha did not wait any longer and fired two fireballs. Wokindo retaliated, firing a stream of golden dust from the tips of his wrinkled fingers. The dust engulfed Pasha's fire, disintegrating both shots.

"Was that your best shot?" asked Wokindo. "Here is mine."

Wokindo raised his hand. Gold dust came together in his palm and formed a large golden sphere. He dropped it to the ground where it began to transform into an armored knight made of pure gold.

As the golden swordsman approached Pasha, Harold whipped out his tail and gripped Wokindo's bare ankle. He tugged with every bit of strength he could muster, but to no avail. Another stream of dust unlocked his grip and traveled from the tip of his tail, back along the full length of his body. The gold dust completely engulfed him and transformed Harold into a solid statue of gleaming gold.

"Run, everybody, run back into the tunnel," Pasha yelled. Tiffany and Peter retreated with Pewter back into the tunnel. Peter knew he should do something, but he was petrified. How would he be able to come up with a stupid rhyme while that monster was attacking him?

Pasha, now more frightened than she had ever been, fought for her life. She fired two shots, scoring direct hits on the swordsman, shattering him into tiny pieces that scattered across the cavern floor.

Wokindo once again laughed deeply and released another stream of dust toward the warrior. Pasha jumped from side to side, trying to shake off the dust trail. Nevertheless, she could not avoid it; before long, it covered her whole body and left her in the same condition as Harold.

With Wokindo's laughter still echoing through the mine, he himself turned to dust and disappeared into a thick vein of gold on the wall.

*****

Silence filled the air. Tiffany and Peter peered into the cavern, shocked to see their pets in the form of rigid golden statues. Tears immediately streamed from their eyes.

"We can't just sit here," sobbed Tiffany. "We should go back."

"What about Wokindo?"

"I don't care. Pasha may be alive." She ran back into the cavern.

"Tiffany!"

"You should go too, Peter," urged Pewter. "I'll watch our backs from right here."

Peter followed Tiffany toward the two golden dogs. She was lovingly petting Pasha's form. Peter put his arms around Harold and could feel his sides moving. It was not solid, just a thin coating that in some way had totally disabled them.

"I can feel his breath!" shouted Peter. "He is still alive! Don't worry, Harold, I will get you out!"

"Pasha's breathing as well!" Tiffany exclaimed. "Quick, Peter, use your spells!"

216

"OK, but I better think about this one because I only have two left." Peter closed his eyes and wandered around the cavern, running over possible rhymes to free the warriors. Finally, taking a deep breath and pointing toward Harold, he chanted.

> "Each dog encased,
> In a golden tomb,
> Free them now,
> In this very room."

With all eyes concentrating on the canine statues, it was not long before they all realized that the spell had not worked.

"What sort of spell was that?" Tiffany spat out in obvious frustration. "I could have done better than that. I thought you had been practicing."

"Okay, okay, I'm trying as hard as I can," Peter shouted and again burst into tears. "This is my last one!"

"Then get it right. Please!"

Amid sobs, he tried another time:

> "Only dogs that battle
> Cased in a thick crust
> Turn the gold
> Back into dust."

All three remaining warriors waited and waited, not wanting to acknowledge that the spells had not worked, and that their pets might not have long to live.

Tiffany sighed. "I don't get it. You can create a giant wave of water in a mine, but we can't save our dogs."

"Wait, Tiff! Water!" Peter shouted excitedly.

"What?"

"This is a cavern. Help me find some water!"

Peter was the first to find the water, falling drip by drip from high in the roof. It had poured for ages, wearing a little hole through a large boulder in the middle of the cavern.

217

"You have to wait in the narrow passageway; you can't see this. I promised Wiz."

"Who is Wiz, and what can't I see?" argued Tiffany.

"There is no time to explain! Just go, now!"

Tiffany, shaking her head, retreated into the tunnel with Pewter. There was a definite vibration from overhead.

"The buffalo are trying one last escape," Pewter sighed.

"I just hope it keeps Wokindo busy."

Finding he was alone in the cavern, Peter positioned his foot on top of the boulder where the next drip would fall. As he saw it approaching his shoe, he closed his eyes and muttered the words, "By the Lake."

*****

Peter knew the magic had worked as he could hear the chattering of birds in the trees. Opening his eyes, he shouted, "Wiz! Help me, Wiz! Where are you?"

Receiving no response to his pleas, Peter sat on a log next to the water, put his head into his hands, and cried as he had never cried before.

"What's up, Master Peter?"

He knew that voice and raised his head quickly. He blurted out the whole story so fast; most of his words ended up all jumbled.

"Hey, child, slow down."

"Sorry, Wiz, but we are in the middle of this mission and we came up against Wokindo."

"Wokindo, huh? You took the Lost Mountain mission; very dangerous, that one. Hmmm."

"I realize that, sir."

"Let me guess: everyone but you has been turned into a golden statue."

"Yes, Wiz—well, the dogs have been. But how did you know?"

"I came across Wokindo once before. Your spells are no good in that part of the mine; for some reason they just will not work."

"I know, I tried them already, and now I have none left. I need you to teach me some magic quickly so I can free my friends."

"That is not possible, child. You agreed to take on the responsibilities of a warrior. The master wizards would not allow you to battle such a force with my help. I am afraid there is nothing that can be done legally."

Peter dropped his head, turned, and, with unrestrained sobs, started to walk slowly away from Wiz.

Seeing such pain in his charge, Wiz relented. "Wait, Master Peter. In all my years, I have found that some things must remain illegal. I will accompany you. I am tired of being constrained by what is legal around here."

Before he even lifted his head, Peter's face transformed from extreme sadness to uncontrollable joy. With Wiz's arm now around his shoulder, they both closed their eyes and wished to go back.

*****

"How did you do that, Peter?" Tiffany clamored. "And who, may I ask, are you? You look like a reject from the Wizard of Oz."

"Take no notice of her, Wiz. She is a trifle spoiled, to say the least."

Wiz did not have time to answer, as Wokindo oozed out from the golden vein into which he had previously vanished. Apparently recognizing Wiz from their past encounter, he wasted no time in firing two streams of golden dust into the air.

Wiz's reflexes were lightning-fast, and he swooped his cape over his head. As the golden dust settled on his cape, it turned into snow, which quickly melted in the heat of the cavern.

Wiz spun around and started chanting:

"With the entire Wizards' power in command
For good to win and evil be dammed,
I summon that power throughout this mine,
That no evil survive in perpetual time."

Wiz spun faster and faster until a small light emerged from the blur. Brighter and brighter, it grew, finally leaving him. Wokindo screamed as the light entered his open mouth and made his whole head glow. It spread throughout his body, destroying him from within. Within a few seconds, a smoldering cloak was the only thing left on the golden dust-covered floor.

Peter, transfixed by what he had just seen, stared at Wokindo's cape, smoldering on the ground. Only the warm moisture that could be none other than Harold's lick diverted his attention. Peter turned and shouted with glee, "Harold, you're back!"

Both human warriors were so wrapped up in the joy of their pets' freedom, they did not even notice that Wiz had left.

"Hey, where did the old guy go?" asked Pewter.

Tiffany shouted in an excited, shrill voice, "I don't care! Let's get out of here!"

Nobody had any arguments with that suggestion. Harold even complimented her on the best idea she had had all day.

*****

The warriors emerged back into the moonlight from the entrance to the mine. A milling herd of buffalo covered the canyon before them. Peter realized he could see right through them.

"They are free!" shouted an excited Tiffany.

"Well now, we did it!" Still, Harold looked confused. "I think we did it. Somebody did somefink, didn't they?"

"We all did it," confirmed Pasha. "Thank you all so much for helping me fulfill my promise."

"We're all warriors, Pash. Your promise is our promise." Peter beamed a huge smile at her.

"Oh, you're welcome. Anytime," added Pewter.

There was a great snorting sound from behind Pasha. Turning, she found herself face-to-face with a gigantic white buffalo. It walked right up to her and nuzzled her, its own form of "thank you."

"You are very welcome."

From the night air, the warriors could hear a soft chant. It was a rhythmic song, composed of many voices. Behind it was the constant beat of a drum.

"Look!" shouted Peter as he pointed to the top of the canyon wall.

Against the moonlight, they could see the chief of the tribe. He was backlit by a large bonfire. The chief raised his arms to the night sky. The White Buffalo turned and made its way back through the herd. A deep rumbling started as it picked up speed, joined by the rest.

"Not again," said Harold. "Should we hide or somefink?"

"No," Pasha assured him. "There's no reason to hide. This will be their final run."

The herd thundered away from them across the canyon. Eventually, they could only be heard in the distance, and slowly even that faded. The night was silent again. There was no sign of the fire or the chief.

"We can go home now."

Chapter Twenty

Tiffany wasted no time at the castle, marching directly up to Ozzy and demanding payment for the completed mission, with the others not far behind. Ozzy looked them over carefully as they all spoke at once, their words crashing together like cymbals.

"How do you know the mission was completed?" he asked matter-of-factly.

"The mission was to free the buffalo, save the tribe, and bring whoever was to blame to justice. Right?" Tiffany's rant was just getting started. "In that case, the mission was completed successfully. Now, give us the Grimits. I am sore, dirty, and the only thing that will help me now is some well-earned shopping!"

"Now then, young warrior, you faced Wokindo alone, and saved the day. Is that correct?" The Keeper's voice startled the chaotic huddle of friends. They had not seen him approach.

The warriors fell silent and just stared at him. Harold decided that he would save the day with his usual tactic, a little white lie.

"Yes, Keeper, sir. We did it. We beat Wokindo and saved the day... by ourselves."

"That's not exactly true, Keeper."

"Peter, keep your chubby mouth shut," blurted Tiffany, trying to back up Harold's lie. Then to the Keeper, "He's confused; he got hit on the head in the mine."

"No, I have to tell the truth. The Wiz——I mean, Hunchings——he helped us. Please do not get him in trouble, Mr. Keeper. I met him in Snydol and he told me how to find him whenever I needed help. I was out of spells and Wokindo had already hurt Pasha and Harold. Please, don't do anything to him!" Peter was crying as he pleaded endlessly with the Keeper. Harold came up and nuzzled Peter to calm him. The boy grabbed his dog and began to cry even louder into Harold's furry coat. "I didn't know what else to do! I did my best!"

The Keeper reached down and picked up the boy.

"Dry your eyes, boy. You are correct. You did what you had to do. You are a warrior, and now you have proven yourself brave and smart. There is no need to cry."

Peter looked at the Keeper in awe. He had expected harsh treatment from the usually gruff man.

"I will have a talk with Hunchings, but I promise that he will receive no punishment. Deal?"

"Deal," agreed an elated Peter, as he wiped his tears away. "Thank you, Keeper."

"I thank all of you. Wokindo is no more. Congratulations on a successful mission." The Keeper turned and disappeared into the door behind his chair.

"Good job, everyone," said Ozzy stepping up. We will work out payment later. I want you all to go home and get some rest. There are more missions ahead of you. Evil never sleeps."

Chapter Twenty-One

Tiffany, Pasha, and Pewter opened their eyes, finding themselves back on the rug in Tiffany's room. She jumped up urgently and fixed her eyes on Chloe, who was asleep on her bed. She shook her friend's shoulder gently, whispering, "Wake up, Chloe, wake up."

As soon as Chloe opened her eyes, Tiffany pounced again. "Did you tell my parents?"

"No, you've only been gone a few minutes."

"Oh, yeah, that would be right."

Chloe sat up and smiled. "What happened to you? Your new jeans are ruined!"

Tiffany looked down at her clothes. "Oh, no! If my mom sees this, she will freak out!"

"All right, look, Tiff. I know you have a bunch of secrets right now, but I think it is about time you tell me what is going on. I'm your best friend; you can tell me anything." Tiffany felt she had no choice but to tell Chloe her story. After she had finished, Chloe sat still on the bed, her mouth hanging wide open. Finally, she broke the silence.

"I want to come on a mission."

Tiffany's eyes widened. "You can't! I mean, I don't think you're allowed."

"Well, if you don't let me, I'll tell your parents and that will be the end of it all."

"You think my parents would actually believe you if you told them?" Tiffany scoffed.

"There's only one way to find out." Chloe slid from the bed and made her way to the door.

"Wait," Tiffany called out reluctantly. "Let's talk about this."

The argument went on for hours until Tiffany started to think it might actually be fun to have Chloe on missions; then she would not have to be stuck with boring crybaby Peter.

"OK, Chloe. I do not know when the next mission will be. You stay over at night and I will invite you along with us. Right now, I am going to shower and sleep for a week."

"Agreed," Chloe squealed, bouncing on the bed.

*****

Peter awoke with one thing on his mind: going to see his friend Wiz. He crept off the bed and quickly dressed, making sure he did not wake the snoring Harold, and proceeded toward the bathroom. He twisted the creaky, steel knob of the faucet and stuck his finger under the gentle stream of water. Closing his eyes, he flicked a drop of water from his finger to his shoe and whispered, "By the lake!" Before he even opened his eyes, Peter could hear the trees rustling in the wind.

"Good day to you, Peter," greeted Wiz, warmly. Peter opened his eyes and grinned at the tiny wizard.

"It worked; it really worked! Thank you so much for helping us!" he shouted, dancing around in a circle.

"Ah, well, don't expect me to help you on all your missions. After all, you are the warrior here, not me."

"I have a request. Will you teach me real magic?"

"Well, now, that is a mighty large request. I could get stripped of my powers by the Master Wizards." Wiz scratched his chin as he slowly circled the tree. "But that hasn't stopped me in the past. Next time you visit me, I will give you an answer. I will have to get authorization before embarking on such a massive task. Shouldn't you be resting?"

"Yes, sir, but I wanted to thank you."

"And so you have. Get back home and we will talk soon."

Peter had no sooner blinked than he found himself back in the bathroom, water still streaming from the tap. He smiled to himself for the first time in months, holding on to the faint hope that the wizard would teach him real magic.

*****

Three nights later, Pasha's golden orb began the summoning ritual. Chloe had been sticking to Tiffany, Pasha, and the orb since their return. She was not going to miss her chance to return to the castle. In minutes, Chloe stood with everyone else on the balcony overlooking the Great Hall.

"This is insane," she declared. "And you guys can talk here?"

"You could say that." Pewter ran down the stairs to take his place in the Keeper's chair.

"Welcome to the castle, Chloe," greeted Pasha.

"Yeah, I 'ope you enjoy the ride."

"Thank you, Pasha, Harold. So, someone point me to this shopping."

"You did it again! What are you doing; building an army?" Ozzy shouted as he and the Keeper ascended the stairs.

"Oh my, you are so cute!" Chloe went to scoop up Ozzy and hug him. The koala bear pointed his wand at her.

"Stay back. You have no idea what you are in for, human. Well, there is no hiding you. You have been invited, and now you must be given the question."

"The question?"

"Young lady, do you wish to join these warriors and protect the balance between good and evil?" the Keeper asked, as he looked solemnly toward the floor. Pewter tried to rub up against his feet, but the hem of his robes kept batting him away.

Chloe was not as quick in deciding as the others had been.

"Wow, that is kind of a heavy thing to put on a girl," she stated. "Do I get some of these Grimits for shopping?"

"You have to earn them," interjected Ozzy.

"I can do that. Yes, Mr. Keeper, I want to become a warrior."

"It's just Keeper, and I welcome you." Not happy with the way things were progressing, he turned and left, beckoning Ozzy to follow him.

A short time later, Ozzy returned to the celebrating group looking frazzled.

"If you have any compassion for me at all, warriors, do me a big favor," he asked.

"Anyfink, Oz," agreed Harold.

"Do not invite anymore people to this castle or we may all end up stuck in the outback. Just a little warning, mateys."

"Grimits to spend, Grimits to spend," shouted Tiffany.

"Now you're talking. I'll help you spend yours," offered Chloe.

"As if I didn't have enough to do today; always busy, me. Feet to keys," Orville muttered, jumping onto the square. With Grimits to spend, the group felt the elevator took forever to reach the dungeons.

"No, Orville, we want to go straight to Snydol," insisted Tiffany.

"Stop, start, stop, start! More time wasted with so much to do. Very well, hold tight." Orville stamped his left foot on the floor, and the elevator shook violently as it hurtled downward. "Next stop, Snydol," shouted Orville as the elevator came to a screeching halt. Before the warriors could right themselves, the doors of the elevator flew open, allowing them to tumble out on top of one another; but before any of them could complain, the doors had closed and the elevator could be heard making its way back up at lightning speed.

As they got to their feet and looked around, the square quickly filled with the inhabitants of Snydol. The warriors gazed at the bustling town square, the mouths filling the air with calming music. Instantly, the music stopped and the mouths exclaimed, "Attention, Snydol! The warriors have arrived!"

Harold turned to Tiffany and said, "Look, Tiff! There's a bigger mouth than yours!"

"You said that already," Tiffany quipped, rolling her eyes.

"Uhhh… yeah." Harold busied himself with the sights of the village, eager to change the subject.

They all looked in amazement at the occupants of the village; they had apparently been waiting eagerly for their arrival, just like before. The warriors took note of the eclectic collection of inhabitants standing at small markets and bazaars; some appeared normal, but others showed odd behavior, looking mystical and out of place in the world. All the warriors continued walking through the town square, hoping to go about their business without standing out too much, but the hope was short-lived.

Merchants, all running up with their products, bombarded the five companions, so much so that they became stuck in the middle of the boisterous crowd. Though the bunch was looking to shop with their Grimits, they did not want to be in such a claustrophobic and noisy situation.

Tiffany put her hands to her mouth, shouting, "We all want to shop for items, but it would be much easier if we came to you! So go back to your market stalls and wait."

The crowd grumbled but obeyed her instructions. The group followed one of the sellers to his stall.

"Tell 'em, Tiff," said Chloe excitedly. "Point me straight at the clothes."

"So, what's this place called? Is it a barber shop?" Pasha asked.

"Yep! I am Cuttercrimper, but this is actually more like a beauty salon. I cut, trim, and style hair and fur. I also file horns, shells, claws, noses, ears, and, of course, nasal hair. Plus, I have paling beds and mystifying skin-shedding baths."

"You can file noses, ears, and nose hair?" Pasha asked incredulously.

"Paling beds?" Peter jumped in.

"Skin-shedding baths? Ewww… gross!" Tiffany cried, rubbing her arms.

"Well, a lot of reptilian people and reptiles like to shed loose skin faster," Cuttercrimper explained.

"Yuck! I don't want to hear any more about skin!" Tiffany shook her head.

"And paling beds are like tanning beds in your world, but it's the opposite. Pale skin is a beautiful feature in Snydol. You would also be surprised how many people here need filing. Witches need their noses filed, elves need ears filed, and the ogres need their nose hair filed as well," he explained.

"Well, Peter would like his hair done," Tiffany scoffed.

"No, I don't," Peter countered, scrunching his face up and turning away.

"But, Peter, your hair is so scruffy!"

"But I wanted to save my Grimits for a spell."

"Well," Cuttercrimper thought aloud, "since it is clearly your first visit to me, you can all get whatever you want done, on the castle!"

"On the castle?" the mouths shouted.

The whole of the town went deadly quiet. Realizing his mistake, Cuttercrimper quickly assured everyone he did not mean the castle would pay. "Free. You know… on the house. I mean, no charge to anyone, most definitely not on the castle."

The townspeople visibly breathed a collective sigh of relief and went on about their business. Seeing the worry on his face, Peter asked, "What was that all about?"

"I can't give away the castle's money. The Grimit Police will arrest me and send me to rehabilitation, and that, I can tell you, is not a pleasant thing."

"Oh, well, thank you, sir! I would love to get my hair cut for free," Peter agreed excitedly.

"You're not touching mine." Chloe took a step back.

"But I don't understand. You are a criminal, so why would you do it for free?" Harold asked. Pasha quickly shoved her tail into his chest.

"No, it's okay, it doesn't offend me. I will tell you my story some other time. Now come here, boy, and sit on this chair."

Peter sat on the chair as commanded, but was surprised when the chair began floating to adjust itself to the proper height. Then, a sheet wrapped around him by itself.

"Don't worry about that. You will get used to it. Now, look at the picture on the wall to decide what cut you would like. There is the Leprecut, the Frankenhair, Dracustyle. We also have the Invisigray, but I don't think you need to be getting rid of any gray hair at your age. I'm only 189 years old and I still haven't got into the grays yet." He ran a finger through his dark, greasy hair.

"Well, what are your most popular styles?" Peter asked, pretending not to act surprised by what Cuttercrimper had just said about his age.

"The most popular cuts and styles are the Mad Mick and the Wizard's cut. The Wizard's cut is straight and tall like a cone and the Mad Mick is a green Mohawk."

"Actually, I would just like my hair to be tidied up a bit, please, Mr. Cuttercrimper."

After everyone, save Chloe, had received their free treatment—including Pewter who had his fur styled like a dragon's points—Peter made his excuses: "I'm going to go explore a bit."

"Whatever. We'll be shopping," Tiffany huffed as she disappeared into the town, giggling with Chloe.

Peter toured the town's markets but stopped at the sight of a beautiful ring he thought Tiffany would like. It was moderate in size, but it was amazing how the ring's stone changed to the colors of a rainbow.

"Can I have that ring, please?" Peter asked, pointing toward three rings. "I want the one that changes colors."

"Well, they all do that. The dragonstone rings are two or three Grimits each, depending on if you'd like the regular or thermal protected one. Since you don't look to be blue-blooded, I would recommend the one that doesn't heat up. Otherwise, it could burn you. Flames appear in the Dragonstone, and depending on your mood, the flames can go from simmering to raging. The chameleon—now, that one changes to green, blue, red, purple, pink, orange, and a few other colors continuously. It is two trumpets," the seller explained, her blue, scaly skin glistening in the sunlight.

"Um… I like the chameleon, but I do not have any trumpets. I'll go get some and I'll be back soon." Peter, still determined to buy the ring for Tiffany, began asking if anyone had any trumpets when a ratty old woman approached.

"I have trumpets," she confirmed, grinning. "As you are new to Snydol, I will do you an extra-special deal. I usually sell them for a lot more, but today I will sell them for one Grimit per trumpet."

"Okay, that sounds like a bargain. I cannot imagine how much others would pay for one trumpet. I'll buy two," Peter agreed, smiling.

Peter was so excited he ran straight back to the store to buy the ring, not knowing that trumpets are actually of lower value than Grimits and he had just been ripped off.

After buying the ring from the young, blue-skinned woman, Peter spotted Tiffany and Chloe. They were sitting on a floating bench, basking in the afternoon sun.

"What happened to you?" Peter asked Tiffany.

"I just got through with visiting all of the shops."

"What did you buy?"

"Show him what you got, Tiff," said Chloe, nudging her in the side.

"Shut up, Chloe," Tiffany hissed. "I got nothing! Nada, nil, zip, zilch! One of the imps pick-pocketed me! I can't believe I'm going to leave with nothing from my first real shopping visit!"

"Don't worry, Tiffany. You'll get something sooner than you think," Peter assured her with a big smile across his face. "But first I have to go and see someone. Wait here." Tiffany huffed, folding her arms across her chest and mumbling agitatedly to herself while Chloe giggled at her.

Peter ran as fast as he could to the lake. Panting heavily, he arrived at the water's edge where Wiz was waiting for him.

"I was wondering," he began slowly, "if you actually wanted to learn real magic. You seem more interested in pleasing a certain demanding female than coming to see me," Wiz said with scorn.

"No, Wiz! I really do want to learn magic! Please, please teach me."

"Well, I have asked the Master Wizards and they have agreed, on one condition."

"What? Anything," Peter pleaded.

"You must donate all of your future Grimits to Snydol's rehabilitation center. It is the town charity center; they try to teach evildoers to repent. But think carefully, young man, for as long as you are being taught by me, you will donate every Grimit you earn."

"I'll do it. When can we start?" asked Peter excitedly.

"Soon. You know how to get here," Wiz chuckled to himself, and then disappeared.

*****

The long journey back to find Tiffany was a blur. Peter kept imagining himself as a trainee wizard and all of the interesting spells he would learn. He raced toward the elevator to find all the warriors waiting for him again. As Tiffany got up, they all headed to the elevator. Peter smelled something burning.

"What is that smell?"

"Oh, Pewter wouldn't stop bothering the Pyronese people, so they set his tail on fire," Tiffany replied, not even acting surprised.

"Is he okay?" Peter asked, cringing as he waited to hear their response.

"Oh, of course," Pasha answered calmly. "He jumped into the nearest fountain, but the fire had already spread to part of his back, so his dragon spike hairstyle is ruined."

They all made their way into the elevator. Pewter was on top of Pasha with his paws wrapped around her neck. His fur was as frizzy as a clown's hair, and his tail was sticking straight up with a missing patch of fur on the end.

"Some people can be so rude," ranted Pewter. "Why does all of the bad stuff happen to me? Ribbit! Not again..."

Peter held out his hand toward Tiffany.

"What are you doing? Get your hand away from me!"

"But I..." Peter stuttered.

"You what? Whatever it is, forget it. I lost all my Grimits. I have to start all over."

Peter withdrew his clenched hand and placed the ring in his pocket. He balled his hands into fists as he waited impatiently for the elevator doors to open.

Pasha moved over beside him as they entered. "Don't worry, Peter. She'll grow up eventually."

*****

The group stood in front of the Keeper, looking through the available missions. Tiffany was still sullen from the Grimit theft, and the mood was spreading to the rest of the warriors. Peter just stared at the floor. He was tired and wanted to go home. He did not want to deal with her spoiled attitude anymore today.

"Choose, warriors. You have to choose the next mission," demanded the Keeper.

"Which one pays the most again?" Tiffany asked.

"That would be Nex Vesica, but I would..." Ozzy was cut short.

"We'll take that one, then," Tiffany huffed.

"Do you know what you are doing, girl?" the Keeper asked as Tiffany turned and ran up the stairs to the doors.

"I'm with Tiff. I say we go for the big-un." Harold followed Tiffany.

"Pasha," asked Ozzy, "is this the mission you choose?"

Pasha was torn. She knew the mission was too dangerous, but she did not want to make Tiffany any more unhappy. The others all looked at her for a decision. Under such pressure, she had no option than to side with her friends.

"Okay. We'll go after Nex Vesica."

"Well, that, I do believe, was a bad choice for ones so inexperienced." The Keeper stood, towering above the remaining warriors. There was a warning in his voice. "The choice is made, and now I fear that you will learn there are always consequences to unwise decisions. You will go in two days. Return home now and prepare yourselves."

Chapter Twenty-Two

The next two days passed quickly, with Tiffany and Chloe vowing to help each other, no matter what the risks.

As the warriors waited patiently for their pre-mission briefing, it was not Ozzy who appeared from behind the chair. Instead, Sasha sat silently in front of the warriors.

Harold leaned over and whispered to Pasha, "Why is Mumsey 'ere? Wot's 'appened to Ozzy?"

"I don't know," Pasha whispered back, frowning.

"What do you think you are doing, picking this mission?" Sasha barked angrily, shattering the silence that had blanketed the hall.

With the warriors all stunned into silence, a white-faced Tiffany was the first to break the quiet. "Is this mission that dangerous?"

"In accordance with the Great Charter, the only thing I can tell you is that this mission has been ongoing for over one hundred of your human years. To survive the Petrified Forest, you must work as one team. Do not believe everything you see. My children, this will be tougher than anything you have faced previously. I urge you, please be careful. Know that I love you both."

Pasha and Harold exchanged anxious glances. As they made their way to the mission door, they were all showing their nerves, bumping into each other as they disappeared on their toughest test yet. Sasha immediately commanded the wall of visions to display the mission. Making herself comfortable in front of the Keeper's chair, she settled down to monitor the goings-on.

*****

Once they were all through the door, the warriors instantly felt the eeriness of the forest.

"Oh, boy, this is spooky," Tiffany blurted as she wrapped her arms around herself.

"It's not that bad," remarked Chloe.

As they looked around, the one thing they all noticed was the odd appearances of the trees. The forest floor was soft under their feet, a thick layer of damp, brown leaves. A dense, green mist rolled toward them, passing and disappearing just as quickly as it had appeared, as though it were being controlled and had somewhere else to go. Pewter burst into a fit of coughing as the mist surrounded him.

"I have a bad feeling about this. Can we go back now?" moaned Tiffany.

Pewter, still feeling the effect of breathing in the strange mist, scampered up the nearest tree, ending up perched on a branch that overhung the rest of the warriors.

"Pewter, what are you doing up there?" Peter asked as he looked skyward.

"I'm not taking any chances. That green stuff may come back at any time!" he answered between coughs.

Tiffany suddenly did not want to do this mission. She kept hearing the Keeper's warning of consequences swirling in her mind, over and over again.

"Does anyone know what our mission is here? The Keeper's visions for this one were just blank. This is ridiculous; I think we should just go back now."

"Oh, come on, Tiff," Chloe coaxed. "This was your choice. Let us see what we are up against first. I say we have a good look around before we make a decision to chicken out."

"Well... I'm all for the chickening out right about now," Peter said with a sigh.

"No," said Pasha sternly. "We keep going for now."

They walked for what seemed like hours before Peter suggested a break. With everyone in agreement, they all sat on pieces of fallen trees. Pewter, not wanting to risk another mist attack, climbed back up onto a branch just above the others' heads.

"What's that noise?" questioned Chloe.

"Yes, I can hear it as well," Peter said. "It sounds like a bird flapping its wings."

With all the warriors standing up and looking around for a hint of where the sound was coming from, a downward gust of wind swept over their heads as a giant eagle-like bird flew above the tree line and then swooped down at the warriors.

"Quick, on the floor!" shouted Peter.

Tiffany dived to the ground, pointed her finger, and shouted, "Freeze!"

The bird was moving too quickly from side to side, easily avoiding the frozen stream.

"Quick, Peter, spell it!" shouted Harold as Pasha commanded, "Paw Power!" It easily dodged her fireballs.

Peter yelled back, "I used them all at the mountain."

The bird hovered over Peter, its squawks sounding almost like laughter. The warriors looked at one another until the bird suddenly dipped down and grabbed Chloe in its talons. Its wings flapped hard as it ascended high into the sky.

"Quick, we have to follow or we'll never see her again!" Tiffany shouted, remembering her pledge of allegiance to her friend. Pasha took to the air with Tiffany on her back.

"You guys go on ahead," urged Pewter. "I'll just be lounging right here."

*****

Now high above the forest, Pasha shouted back to Tiffany, "Can you hit it without hitting Chloe?"

"Even if I could, Chloe would fall!"

Pasha glanced down and saw Harold and Peter swinging through the gnarled trees, keeping pace. She had a new plan.

"It can dodge my fireballs, but it can't dodge everything. Tiffany, hit it with your ice when I say so. Ready?"

"Okay."

"Do it," Pasha instructed as she concentrated on the bird with all of her might. Tiffany yelled, "Freeze!" and struck the bird right in the back. It only irritated the massive creature, causing it to drop Chloe and turn back to face them. Pasha was as ready as she would ever be.

"Paw Power!" The sky streaked with lightning, striking the bird with a direct hit. It squawked in pain and tumbled from the sky.

Below, Harold was ready, swinging high above the treetops and snagging Chloe with his tongue. The giant eagle crashed to the forest floor below as Harold lowered the screaming girl back to the safety of the ground. Peter jumped off Harold and tried to calm her down.

Pasha and Tiffany quickly joined them. With all the warriors back on solid ground, they all agreed that this mission might indeed be a little too much for them.

"Does anyone know the way back?" Pasha asked. Everyone looked blankly at one another. They had all been concentrating on where the eagle was going, not on how to get back.

"Well, it's getting dark now. Maybe we should camp here in this clearing and make a start back in the morning," suggested Peter.

"What about Pewter?" asked Pasha? "We can't leave him alone in this place."

"Hey, guys," Tiffany asked, "anyone noticed that this forest has suddenly gone quiet?" The usual evening forest chatter was ominous in its absence. "Don't you think that's strange?"

The warriors listened intently to the nothing, their ears ringing as their blood pounded harder in their chests.

"You are not as clever as your mother, young warriors."

"Who was that?" Peter shouted as he jumped to his feet.

"Let me introduce myself. I am Nex Vesica, otherwise known as the Death Blade."

"Show yourself," Pasha demanded.

"But I am, young warrior. You see, to your eyes I am invisible. That's why I have defeated so many of your predecessors." The voice cackled eerily, sending chills up the warriors' spines.

Pasha jumped to her feet and started firing aimlessly at anything she thought might be the new enemy. She was confident in her lightning power now, but needed a target first. The fireballs might force Vesica to show itself.

"Everyone, run!" shouted Tiffany. The warriors scattered in all directions to the tune of a shrill command. "Capture them!"

Each warrior fell to the ground as tree roots wrapped around their ankles, then up around their bodies, each left totally helpless.

With all five warriors bound tightly by the roots, Nex Vesica spoke again: "The roots around your bodies will now tighten slowly until you find it hard to breathe. You will then fall into an unconscious state, just before you die."

As the roots tightened, one by one the warriors drifted into unconsciousness. Harold was the last, trying with all he was worth to resist the need for breath. With all of the warriors just moments away from death, a voice came from the distance.

"Wait! It is me you want, not my children."

Unable to resist the opportunity to finally rid himself of his old adversary, Nex Vesica replied, "Agreed. I will spare these pathetic warriors in return for your life, Sasha. You must realize their desire for revenge will just bring them back to me one day in the future."

Sasha landed in the middle of the clearing, allowing a long, twirling branch to entwine her. It then whisked her up into the trees. "Yes, but before that day, I pray that they will be ready and that you will finally be destroyed."

*****

Some hours later, the warriors, including Pewter, awoke in the forest. They were right beside the doorway back to the castle. Slowly, one by one, they filed through the mission door, dejected

241

and silent. Ozzy, as usual, was waiting for them. This time, however, his head was hanging low and his hands folded. "You must all follow me," he growled, making his way down the hall.

The warriors followed him silently, their eyes to the ground. It was not until Ozzy stopped in front of a large wooden table that their fog of self-pity lifted to reveal a mass of confusion, as they gazed on Sasha's lifeless body.

"Why is Mum asleep on the table?" Harold asked as he sniffed at Sasha.

"She's dead," Ozzy croaked, turning away.

"How did she die?" Pasha demanded, stomping in front of Ozzy before he could leave.

"She saved your lives."

"No," whispered Pasha, taking a step back.

"Wot you saying, Oz? She saved us and lost 'er life?" asked Harold, frowning.

"Listen, warriors," Ozzy offered gently. "Sasha had a wonderful life, a life full of adventure and risk. She loved you all dearly and gladly gave her own life to save all of you. Do not feel guilty, for she knows you would have done the same for her." The koala gave them a strained smile. "Now, you must go home. I will return Sasha to her cottage in the forest."

The warriors exited robotically through their respective doors, trying to rationalize the day's events and to accept Sasha's death as a reality.

Once home, Pasha ignored all attempts by her friends to comfort her, instead making her way to her kennel where she lay solemnly, planning how to avenge the death of her mother.

Epilogue

The visions faded and the hall of the castle was silent. Even the Wizard of the North had not touched his food, a monumental feat. The Keeper swept the room with his eyes, taking in the expression of each guest. They stared back, not daring to speak out of turn. Behind the Keeper, the unidentified figure bowed its head.

Finally, the Southern Wizard spoke: "Keeper. What does the vision mean?"

The Keeper cleared his throat before answering. "The vision is about first steps and consequences. Every being that holds the position of Keeper learns well these two things. The most important part of a great journey is the first steps taken, and all those upon the journey must understand the consequences of their choices. If every living thing thought about the consequences of their actions, then this realm and any future Keepers would not be necessary."

"The new Keeper?" asked the Wizard of the East. "Is he or she one of these warriors we have witnessed?"

There was a deep chuckle from the great chair. "Ah. That question is the only thing that has driven every one of you here tonight. I remind you to have patience. There is still much more story to tell."

Understanding Harold

Kennish Taan	English U.S.
'arold	Harold
'ank marvin	Starving/Hungry
'appens	Happens
'appy	Happy
'ard	Hard
'as	Has
'ead	Head
'eadache	Headache
'earing	Hearing
'edge 'og	Hedge-Hog
'ere	Here
'igh	High
'is	His
'it	Hit
'ow	How
'urt	Hurt
'Ow'dya do that	How do you do that
Ain't	Haven't
Anyfink	Anything
'Ave	Have
Bite the vig 'un	Die
Blimey	Shocked
Blinding	Excellent
Bonce	Head
Bozo	Slang for idiot
Brown Bread	Slang for Dead

Kennish Taan	English US
Bruv	Slang for Brother
Bruvver	Slang for Brother
Claret	Blood
Da	The
Daan	Down
Dat	That
Dozy	Stupid
'Ey	Hey
Fawt	Thought
Fer	For
Fing	Thing
Fingy	Thing
Froat	Throat
Jus'	Just
M'	Me
Me	Sometimes used to replace My
Min	Minute
Mouf	Mouth
Mumsey	Mommy
Nah	No
Nex'	Next
Nick	Steal
Nuffink	Nothing
O'	Of
Ol'	Old
Ooi	Used to get attention
Poppin Me Clogs	Slang for Dying

Kennish Taan	English US
Posh	Slang for someone who thinks they are better than others
Sis	Sister
Taan	Town
Wanna	Want to
Wi	With
Wot	What
Ya	Your
Ya-self	yourself
Yeah	Yes

Printed in the United States
219595BV00001B/2/P